BLOOD & ASH

A Snarky Urban Fantasy Detective Series

DEBORAH WILDE

te da media
vancouver

Chapter 1

There was nothing like sitting in a shitty car with a broken heater covertly filming a teenager for cash to make me question my life choices.

My target, Charlotte Rose Scott, had taffy blonde hair, big blue eyes, and a manic enthusiasm that made me want to slip her an Ambien.

Not that I'd waste one on a child.

Her can-do spirit was currently being applied to a bit of breaking and entering. The sixteen-year-old had tried every point of entry on the ground floor of this weathered Craftsman house that was thirty-two blocks and worlds away from her own home. She'd graduated from tugging on the windows' security bars to wobbling her way up a bare trellis to the second-story balcony.

Good to know all those gymnastics and dance classes of hers had a practical application. It was so hard to make it in the arts, but crime was always a growth industry.

I slapped another memory card into my Handycam, absently rubbing my right thigh. I'd been sitting out here in the damp cold for too long, exacerbating the dull ache from the rods holding my femur together, so I grabbed the

Costco-sized bottle of Tylenol that I'd tossed on the passenger seat and dry-swallowed a couple of pills.

She wrenched on the sliding door handle and I winced. Leave a few more fingerprints, why don't you? If it wouldn't completely compromise my case, I'd show her how to break in myself and put us both out of our misery.

I zoomed in, ready to capture C.R. living her best truth. Or better yet, get some answers. Come on, you little adolescent fiend. Why the uncharacteristic foray into robbery? You'd even blown off piano lessons for this and you thrived in your overscheduled teenage existence.

What was I missing?

Denied entry, she shimmied back down the trellis to run at the solid back door. When she bounced off it with a yelp, only one of us was surprised.

Spare me from amateurs.

I dug my buzzing phone out of my hip pocket. My best friend and part-time employee, Priya Khatri, had come through with the land title search on this property. I frowned at the text, trying to place the homeowner's name. Oh, fuck balls. I wasn't being paid to save Charlotte Rose from making a really stupid mistake.

This was not my problem.

Charlotte Rose rubbed her elbow, red from where she'd smacked into the door, and bit her lip, eyes watery.

Grumbling, I turned off the camera and got out of Moriarty, also known as my car, using both hands to swing my poor stiff leg onto the concrete. Tucking my fingers into the armpits of my battered leather jacket, my breath misting the air, I limped over to the tiny backyard of the crime spree in progress.

"Yo, Cat Burglar Barbie," I called out. "The jig is up!"

She froze for a second and then vanished into thin air.

I blinked, gaping at the empty space. "Charlotte Rose

Scott, you get your butt back here this second and explain yourself, because you are not supposed to have magic!"

I'd done my due diligence before taking this case. Verified that she was a Mundane. No powers. Zero. Nada.

Except, apparently, she wasn't. And now, thanks to this unpleasant and unforeseen magical development, I was about to get royally fucked by House Pacifica.

Charlotte Rose flickered back into view, just a fist with her middle finger extended. I mean, impressive control on invisibility magic, but what a little shit.

"Leave her alone!" Another girl about the same age, who spoke with a light musical accent, raced into the backyard. Her worn denim jacket had "Fuck the patriarchy" written in thick silver marker across the back and her dyed black hair showed the ragged edges of someone who'd cut it herself.

Interesting choice for a co-conspirator.

When Victoria Scott had hired me to spy on her kid who'd been "acting cagey" and therefore obviously had some drug habit, she'd casually sported a linen dress that cost more than my much-needed car repairs. We'd spent a grand total of twenty minutes together, all of them in her vanilla-scented Williams Sonoma kitchen with its neatly shelved cookbooks—written by obscure foodies—whose spines weren't even cracked.

I'd bet anything that this wrong-side-of-the-tracks friend was not part of Victoria's bourgie starter-pack vision of the good life.

"Stand down," I told the new girl. "And if you know what's good for you, you'll tell Charlotte Rose to show herself."

The newcomer called up a gust of wind and flung it at me.

I flew backwards, stumbling over a plastic Adirondack chair, and cracked my skull on the corner of the house so hard that I saw stars. My leg buckled briefly as I bounced off the wooden siding and staggered forward, choking on a hot rush of bile. Gritting my teeth, I touched a finger to the back of my head and came away with a wet, red smear.

Awesome. A pissy air elemental. Just what my day needed.

I found the tiny box stashed in my jacket pocket and pushed its single button. It produced a high-frequency sound barely within hearing range that made the newbie double over and caused Charlotte Rose to become visible once more, clapping her hands over her ears and moaning in pain.

I braced a hand against the bricks to combat my own dizziness. This admittedly illegal sonic weapon should not have affected me this way because I'd built up a tolerance.

Why, hel-*lo* concussion. On the upside, however lackluster the case had been to solve intellectually, I *had* solved it so at least I'd get paid. With C.R.'s true nature revealed, billable hours took a back seat to getting this kid home safely before she ended up with a juvie record, so I powered through the nausea and slapped a pair of cuffs on these criminal toddlers before they could regroup.

I dialed a number on my phone.

"It's Ashira Cohen," I said, when Victoria answered. "Tell your daughter she has permission to get in my car."

Victoria stuttered out protests that she had no idea who I was or what I was talking about, but I cut her off with an exasperated huff. Not this again. Everyone thought they were so clever denying they'd hired a P.I. when things got tough. It didn't work that way.

"Enough bullshit. If you want help getting out of the mess you've landed in with your unregistered Nefesh kid, then give the all-clear for me to drive her home."

Victoria answered with a meek "okay." Damn straight, you better comply.

Nowadays, most people preferred to hire private investigators who had magic, wanting the extra abilities that Nefesh brought to the table. I was the only female P.I. in town, very much outside the boys' club of this industry, and a Mundane to boot. I'd worked my ass off to carve out a niche for myself and Victoria wasn't going to jeopardize that.

I passed the phone to Charlotte Rose, who listened to her mother without comment, glaring at me the entire time. I held that gaze and raised her glower with an arched eyebrow. Snotty teens were the worst. I'd know.

C.R. handed me the cell and linked hands with her friend, the two of them edging closer together.

"I have rights," the second girl howled, shaking the cuffs as if trying to blow them off.

"Nope," I said. "You lost them under Statute 7.5, 'demonstrating exceeding stupidity.' And save your energy. Those puppies suppress magic."

"You're not a cop," she countered. "You'd have identified yourself. And if you had magic you'd have used it. That means, you're not Nefesh and you're not allowed to have shit like this. Or use it on me."

It's true, the cuffs were totally a "fell off the back of a van" purchase, but a woman did what she had to. Just because I wasn't allowed to work magic cases, that didn't preclude supposedly Mundane ones from going sideways— like this one had. "Yeah? How would you know?"

"Television," the girl said. "So what are you?"

I flashed her my P.I. license. "A real-life detective who knows what equipment she's allowed to have far better than you."

Charlotte Rose puffed out her chest. "I won't let her hurt you, Meryem."

"Aw. That's… deluded." I herded the girls to Moriarty, trying not to limp too badly. Never show those monsters weakness. Weirdly, I could still smell blood, as if it was gushing out of me like a waterfall. It wasn't even that bad, kind of earthy and rich. I touched the back of my head. There was some matted in my dark waves, but the bleeding itself had stopped.

Meryem refused to get into my fine vehicle, holding her wrist pointedly against her chest once I'd uncuffed her as though I'd caused permanent nerve damage. "You gonna kidnap me?"

What a drama queen. "Much as I hate to deprive myself of your stellar company, no."

"Then I can get myself home."

"Mer—" Charlotte Rose sighed. "Be safe, okay?" She leaned in and gave Meryem a quick kiss.

Meryem blushed, scraping one of her raggedy high tops along the ground.

Even I, with my cold, dead heart, found their coupledom adorable.

"Here." I fished out what was pretty close to my last forty bucks.

"Fuck you. I'm not a charity case," Meryem said.

Maybe not, but she was in a jean jacket and had to be freezing in the miserable March weather. No way she had a good home to go to, if any at all. However, she was also prickly and if I was too nice—generally not an accusation thrown my way—she'd bolt.

"Consider it compensation for pain and suffering." I shoved the bills at her.

They disappeared so fast into her pocket that I made a note to get this girl some help.

"Thanks," she said, her eyes flickering uncertainly up to mine.

"Get lost before I change my mind."

She squeezed C.R.'s hand and bolted.

I fumbled at the door handle because there seemed to be two of them, then sank gratefully into the driver's seat, taking a couple of steadying breaths before I leaned over to unlock the passenger door, knocking the Tylenol bottle onto the floor.

C.R. got into the car, keeping her distance.

Using the rag that I kept to defog the windshield since the heater didn't work, I wiped myself down because my hair was sweatily plastered to my neck. I ignored Charlotte Rose's grimace that came with huffy sound effects.

Once I was dry-ish and reality had stabilized enough to drive safely-ish, I patted Moriarty's dashboard twice and turned the key, whispering, "Who's a good boy?" and praying this wasn't the moment he died on me once and for all. Not like he hadn't faked his death more than once. But he started with only the mildest choke.

Neither C.R. nor I spoke for the first half of the ride.

"You going to out me?" she said.

I braked at a red light and glanced over at her. The world swung sideways and I gripped the steering wheel tight until my equilibrium was restored.

C.R.'s words were sneered but her pupils were slightly dilated.

I slowly faced forward so as not to jiggle my brain. "Contrary to popular belief and genetics, I have a moral compass. It's up to you to tell your mom about Meryem. So, why invisibility magic?"

"Mom used to play this game where she'd pull the blanket up over my eyes and say, 'Where's Charlotte Rose?' Apparently, I went nuts for it."

Uh-huh. Cute answer but there was more to it than that. While Nefesh were born with magic, the precise nature of it developed during childhood and was rooted in psychological primal drives.

The light turned green and I hit the gas, wincing at Moriarty's jerky start. "And the attempted robbery?"

"I wasn't going to steal anything," she said hotly.

I let the silence grow.

7

It took her all of two blocks to break.

"It was my birth mother's place," she said. "I wanted to see…"

"What Darleen's life was like without you?"

Charlotte Rose shrugged, a mess of emotions playing across her face that she tried to hide under a sullen disinterest. Then it hit her. "You knew? Is that why you stopped me?"

I made a smooth left. "Figured you didn't want your big reunion to be from juvie."

She crossed her arms and stared straight ahead.

Thankfully, it was a short drive from there, because by the time we pulled up to her large Tudor home with its pricy S.U.V. parked in the driveway, my skin felt two sizes too small, and the world's worst itch had settled between my shoulder blades, exactly where I couldn't reach.

This time, I met Victoria in her living room, decorated with that faux rustic charm involving unpainted wood, a chunky stone fireplace wafting out the scent of pine, and cutesy large prints with sayings like "Laugh. Live. Breathe." that made me want to "Gag. Run. Drink."

Victoria greeted me in a purple bamboo yoga number that would have been very comfortable to move in, except I doubted she did classes in full makeup, her blonde-streaked hair twisted in a chignon and large diamonds flashing in her ears.

Inner peace through Tiffany's. Namaste, bitches.

"Charlotte Rose," Victoria said. "What's going on?"

"You hired her to spy on me?" C.R.'s glower at her mom should have incinerated her.

"I hired her because I was concerned that my daughter was a drug addict!" Victoria planted her hands on her hips and the two of them broke into a furious squabble.

I whistled loudly, pain flaring inside my skull. Eyes half-squinted shut, I massaged my temples. I could patch myself up with some aspirin and a good night's sleep. Nothing to fear. "Your mom was worried. Suspicious and over-paranoid but worried. Charlotte Rose is not on drugs. Fight it out later."

Victoria sat down on the sofa next to her daughter. "Then why has she been behaving this way?"

She'd hired me to get answers and I had them, but this was a delicate situation. "She was curious about her birth mother. It's natural and isn't any reflection on you."

Victoria plucked at her sleeve.

"Mom?" Charlotte Rose reached out for Victoria and I braced myself for her mother's hurt dismissal, but Victoria surprised me and took her daughter's hand.

"I wish you had come to me first but I understand. When we adopted you, Darleen made it clear that if you wanted to meet her, she was open to it, but we need to do this properly, okay?"

"Okay."

Victoria smiled at me and stood up. "Thank you. If you'd care to send your invoice—"

"Sit. Down."

She dropped like a stone onto the cushions.

I perched on the edge of a scratchy wing chair, hoping my casually braced elbow on the back didn't look like the desperate support to remain upright that it was. "Victoria, I specifically asked you in our intake interview if you could think of any Nefesh connection that would prevent me from taking this assignment. I'm not legally allowed to handle cases involving magic."

The law was asinine, supposedly "designed to protect Mundanes like me." Right. Try more money in House coffers since all Nefesh paid taxes towards House resources and protection. But it was what it was and if House Pacifica found out, I'd be brutally fined, because they took this very seriously. I was already existing by the skin of my teeth. This would ruin me.

"Magic?" Victoria said, and flushed a faint pink.

I stared at her until her shoulders slumped.

"Her birth mother was from a good Mundane family and there was no father listed on her birth certificate," Victoria said. "Nothing in the adoption showed that Charlotte Rose might be Nefesh through the birth father."

"Yeah, I'm aware of that part, since I investigated it thoroughly. However, you knew about Charlotte Rose and you kept it from me." I practically threw my arm out of its socket trying to get at the itch but it remained maddeningly out of reach. "Why me? You could have gone to a Nefesh P.I."

"I didn't want them to suspect. And you were cheaper," she admitted.

Slight as my accomplishments were, and my mother had written a treatise on that, they were mine and I was super proud of them. Maybe I didn't have the interesting cases— yet—but a woman had to start somewhere and I was pulling this off on my terms. I'd get there.

I gave up on the itch and my anger. Victoria was not worth committing grievous bodily harm and losing everything. But man, it was close.

"Here's my advice," I said, catching myself before I did a slow slide off the chair and onto my ass. Okay, maybe my condition was a bit worse than presumed. "Take Charlotte Rose to House Pacifica and point her baby blues at them. Squeeze out a tear or two for good measure while you throw yourself on their mercy. Mom, you didn't know. Kid, you were scared to lose the love of your adoptive parents."

Charlotte Rose bit her lip, exchanging a glance with her mother.

"Hit the mark there, did I?" I said. "Let me guess. Dad

has a few beliefs in common with the Untainted Party?" That explained the invisibility magic.

"How'd you know?" Victoria squeaked.

"I'm well versed on those people. They're a pretty popular political affiliation around here."

"I can't tell him." Charlotte Rose looked genuinely scared.

I softened my tone. "You don't have a choice. If you don't do it by tomorrow, I'll have to because all people with magic must be registered with the House in their region. A fact you damn well know. But since it'll be worse if I'm involved…" Mainly, for me. "It's in your best interests to keep me out of it and pile on the remorse."

"This feels really unsavory," Victoria said. "There has to be another way."

My dad's voice rang out loud and clear in my head. *There are two types of people in this world, Ash, my girl. Those who are marks and those who aren't.*

It had only taken me one harsh lesson to swear I'd never make that mistake again. Victoria had tried to play me. Operative word being "tried."

"There isn't," I said. "Your kid is currently a Rogue. Fix it."

Charlotte Rose surged up like a fury of Greek myth. "I'm not registering with the House. They experiment on people."

Her voice hurt my ears. It was too loud, too grating.

"While I'm happy to think the worst of Levi Montefiore and House Pacifica…" I dabbed at the sweat on my brow. "They aren't running some mad scientist lab. They're legit, annoyingly so, and believe me, it's much worse to be on their bad side than on the same team."

My words sounded funny, all long and drawn out. Fuck. I was going to have to brave a hospital. Warning Victoria again to contact House Pacifica and reminding her that late payment on my bill was subject to interest, I made my excuses and stumbled out to Moriarty, whose headlights seemed to smirk evilly at me.

The drive to the closest Emergency Room was a blur. I pulled up to the entrance, tossed my keys at the attitude-laden valet in the fireman costume who totally wasn't getting a tip, lurched inside, and collapsed, unconscious.

Chapter 2

I woke up in a bed to a doctor taking my pulse.

"Hello. I'm Dr. Samuels." She had coffee breath, one of her glasses lenses was smudged, and a half-opened package of Peanut Butter Cups peeked out of her doctor's coat. Someone was on the late end of her shift.

I tried to sit up, but the world swirled around me in a kaleidoscope of trippy colors. It was a vast improvement on the gray perforated ceiling tiles and light blue curtain that separated my narrow bed from my neighbor's. "Am I concussed?"

"I expect so since you lost consciousness. But I'm more concerned about your elevated heart rate and clammy skin. We need to do some tests." She wrote down some notes on a chart that rested at the foot of the bed and promised to return soon.

As with all things medical, "soon" turned out to be relative.

It took a long time for the tests and the results and since the nurses kept coming around to make sure I stayed awake, I called Priya to keep me company and take my distress over being stuck here down several hundred notches.

She breezed in wearing her customary pink, her fingers adorned with gold rings and her custom-built laptop tucked under her arm, having been at one of the half dozen cafés she preferred to work in when I'd called. "Good job getting concussed, dumbass. And by a child. I despair."

I shot her the finger.

Priya shrugged out of her jacket, flashing a glimpse of the gorgeous pink-and-black lotus flower tattoo on the inside of her right wrist that she'd gotten on her last family trip back to India to visit her grandparents. She tossed me a folded-up blanket. "Here. Erika gave me another one."

"Thank you, Erika. Whoever that is." I pushed my current blanket aside and snuggled into the warmth of its replacement, fresh from the heating closet.

"She's the short, older nurse who's checked on you three times?" Priya shook her head at my not having befriended everyone during my stay. Why this continued to astound her was beyond me.

"Of course. Erika. With the three budgies and the asthmatic husband. Or was that the asthmatic budgie and the three husbands?"

Priya's stern look was blown by her unsuccessful attempt not to smile.

"Enough chitchat," I said. "I need you to work your magic, Adler." I'd nicknamed her that after both Irene Adler, the woman admired by Sherlock Holmes for her wit and cunning in the original stories who was one of the few people to have bested him, and Raven Adler, a brilliant and successful hacker.

"But of course, Holmes." She flipped open her pink computer. Many a dude had underestimated Pri and her mad coder skills at their peril. Sparkly and girly she may have been, but she was also a ruthless genius.

Priya cracked her knuckles and set her fingers to the keyboard.

"Remove all traces of my search on the Scott family from the House Pacifica database." I explained about Charlotte Rose's hidden magic and how I didn't want any links leading back to my involvement with them.

I rubbed my back against the pillow because I was still super itchy between my shoulder blades, but that made my head throb more. The tests had determined there was no bleeding in my skull and a nurse, not Erika, had given me some pain meds but they had yet to kick in.

"Speaking of House Pacifica…" Priya said.

"What now?" I tucked the blanket more tightly around my toes.

"You got an email."

I waved at her to open it, having given up years ago on private passwords where she was concerned. "What missive from His Lordship this time?"

Priya barked a laugh. For a five-foot-ten stunner of Indo-Canadian heritage, with brown skin, a sleek black flapper bob, and green eyes, she laughed like an asthmatic donkey. She clicked on the email and read in a gruff voice.

"Dear Ms. Cohen,

It is truly an honor and a delight that you, a private investigator of some renown, take such an interest in our House database that you created a platinum-level profile to mine our resources. While getting hold of my credit card number to pay for the aforementioned account (Hello, Priya) was a nice touch, that constitutes fraud and theft and you have been shut down.

Out of respect for our longtime acquaintance, and the fact that it's no fun trampling on the little people, I am generously willing to put aside all thoughts of prosecution. Should you wish to actually pay me, and may I clarify I mean in legal tender, not IOUs, eggs, or sexual favors, none of which hold any appeal, House Pacifica will, of course, be happy to review your application for a legitimate account.

Sincerely,

Levi Montefiore
Head, House Pacifica"

"He cc'd me on it." Priya said. "I liked the shout-out."

"That… *Fraud? Sexual favors?*" I jabbed a finger at the laptop as if I could reach through it and stab him. "He should be so lucky!"

"Weeeeelll."

I gaped at my betraying bestie.

She shrugged. "You've been living like a Jewish nun. Which isn't even a thing. Before you start doling out sexual favors to all and sundry—"

"Yeah. Big plans to spread 'em wide like a seaside doxy."

"You might want to get back on the horse and practice a few moves. Kai texted earlier. He and Aiden are wrapping early tonight."

"I'm not sleeping with Aiden."

Priya pursed her bubblegum pink lips. "He's cute and he likes you for some reason, which is amazing since you don't do more than grunt two words at him."

"Why are you even dating Kai? He's the human equivalent of Cheez Whiz."

"He's nice."

No, he was safe and manageable and as their six-month anniversary was fast approaching, they'd soon break up with no hard feelings, like every single one of her relationships in the past couple years. The fact that she didn't even get upset over this should have been a clue that she was dating the wrong guys. Hopefully, eventually she'd be ready to date the right one.

"He's a peach." I twisted around to present my back to her. "Scratch please."

She groaned, but I invoked best friend hospital bed privileges and got my way.

I practically moaned at the relief.

"Give me one reason why you're not into Aiden?" she said.

"He assumes his mouth is for talking. Left. Higher. Higher. Over. More. No, there. Ahhh."

Priya stopped scratching. "You're impossible."

"Perfect. Let's channel that into a response that will make Levi's head explode." I leaned back against the pillows. "Take a message."

Her left eyebrow twitched; her desire to tell me to shove it since she wasn't my secretary warred with her never letting anyone touch her laptop. "Dictate away. Just this once and only because you're so pathetic."

"Pathetic right now."

She stared at me.

"Whatever." I cleared my throat. "'From the desk of Ashira Cohen, Cohen Investigations.'"

Priya dutifully took down my response.

Dear Exalted Leader,

(not mine thankfully)

Allow me to refresh your memory about the cocktail night fundraiser at Science World shortly after New Year's that I was unfortunate enough to see you at. It's hardly my fault that you have both an ugly competitive side and a shit throw and failed to beat me at the water ball toss. Owing me exactly $1537, you handed me your credit card and loftily told me to "go nuts and drink my boozy heart out."

You always did have such a way with words, Mr. Monte-fiore. If you would care to check your credit card statement and your memory, you would recall that I never purchased said drinks. Instead, I told you that I wanted access to the House database and while you smirked like the condescending ass that you are, you did not specifically say no.

Thus, I transferred the balance of $1537 owed to me into setting up top-tier access to House Pacifica records, the total of which was $1200 for the year.

Please reinstate my account and remit the difference of $337 immediately to my office address. Interest will accrue on any outstanding amounts over thirty days.

Sincerely,

Ashira Cohen

"Is it too much to add 'P.S. Bite me'?" I said.

"Take the high road," Priya advised and hit send.

"That's what playing by the rules gets me. Accusations of fraud and never letting me live down that egg thing from Camp Ruach." I drank some lukewarm water that a nurse, Erika actually, had left for me. It was extremely unsatisfying so I gave up and used the straw to scratch my back. "About the search records?"

"Already deleted," Priya said.

"You are a prize among women."

The curtain around my bed was pulled back and Dr. Samuels stepped in. She consulted her chart, nodding hello at Priya. "It's only a mild concussion and your other symptoms seem to be abating. How's the head?"

I shrugged. "Better than it was. Though I'm still really itchy."

She smiled at my straw back-scratcher. "I can prescribe you some cortisone cream. You were lucky. Had the angle of the blow been even slightly different, your condition would have been far more serious. I guess your God was looking out for you."

"Huh?" I was the world's most secular Jew. I mean, I ate BLTs on challah. Which, really, was the best bread to eat them on because the bit of sweetness from the challah went perfectly with the bite of the almost burned bacon. I stopped salivating and focused on her answer.

"The tattoo," the doctor said. "Unusual, but you see all kinds of religious expression in my line of work."

I lost my grip on the straw and it fell to the floor. "Hang on. What tattoo?"

"Your Star of David?" At my blank look, the doctor tapped a spot on the bottom right of her skull. Exactly where I'd been coshed. "Under your hair. We shaved a small patch to better examine the lump while you were unconscious."

Reality cracked, dark tendrils of WTF rushing in to fill the gaps. I'd gotten bruises before without knowing how, but a tattoo? I'd never been blackout drunk, which limited the possibilities to either when I was a baby or when I was in the hospital at age thirteen.

The doctor stared at me like she was going to call a drug and alcohol rehab center if I couldn't remember tattooing my head and even Priya looked alarmed.

I forced a laugh. "Oh, that one. The one that I got probably a year ago."

Dr. Samuels frowned. "It's a shame that the blow left a scar through it."

"Real shame. However, I'm sure God will understand." It seemed appropriate to punctuate that statement with something religious so I waved my hand in benediction. "Borei p'ri hagafen."

I'd recited part of the Sabbath blessing for the wine, but it was the only suitably religious sounding line I could remember.

"Borei p'ri hagafen," Dr. Samuels responded.

Priya let out a strangled cough, her shoulders shaking.

Now that we'd blessed each other with grapes…

"Can I go?"

Dr. Samuels scribbled something on a prescription pad. "Here's a list of symptoms to watch out for. It's highly unlikely any of these are going to present, but if they do call 911. Otherwise, take Tylenol for any headaches in the next little while."

Then, assured that Priya would drive me home, she discharged me.

19

The curtain had barely fallen into place behind her before Priya moved onto my bed and shoved my long, dark brown hair out of the way. She whistled. "Odd choice for a tattoo. Why'd you get it?"

"I didn't," I hissed.

"Well, that's weird and alarming. Hmm. If I had to pick a tattoo for you, this wouldn't be my first choice."

"You think? How big is it?"

"About an inch high. Black lines, no color."

I twisted around to look at her, narrowing my eyes. "Out of curiosity, what kind of tattoo did you see me with, were I to have one?"

"Tramp stamp, baby. Something glittery and pretty for Big Daddy to look at when he's spanking you." She enthusiastically mimed the actions, dissolving into guffaws.

So inappropriate, but I cracked a smile at her ridiculousness anyway and she winked at me.

I probed the tattoo gingerly with a finger. "Travel, a rich and fulfilling professional career, discovering I have a patriarchal religious symbol branding me. Nope. Not one of my life goals. Though points for the *Handmaid's Tale* vibe."

Priya slid her laptop into its protective sleeve. "Who could have pulled this off?"

"I dunno. My parents? But why? It's not like they were religious. Or totally batshit crazy because what the hell?"

"Your grandparents were super Orthodox."

"Yeah, and Talia was scarred from it. She wouldn't have put a Magen David on me."

"What about your dad? To shine good favor from the Almighty on his cons?"

"That seems farfetched, even for him." I folded up the two hospital blankets that I'd used. "I really hope it wasn't Dr. Zhang. Tattooing an unconscious kid seems like a serious contravention of the Hippocratic Oath."

"Maybe it was some kind of marker and you narrowly

missed having your organs harvested for a black market ring," Priya said.

"Yup. We Jews have prime resale value on kidneys and livers." Motioning for Priya to turn around, I dumped the ugly, breezy hospital gown, threw on my faded jeans and purple sweater, grabbed my leather jacket, and headed out to Moriarty.

There was an aluminum foil-wrapped tray on the passenger seat and my car smelled like cinnamon buns, which was a vast improvement on the stale "new car smell" air freshener dangling from my rearview mirror.

"This is creepy," I said. "Tattoos, mysterious pastry, what's next?"

"Pity buns from Mummy. She drove me here." Priya pulled out her personal set of my car keys and got into the driver's seat.

I adored Priya's mother Geeta, who was an amazing cook and often sent pity food home for me. "In that case, I'm not sharing."

"You will." She turned the key without even doing the superstitious double pat and whisper and Moriarty hummed to life. The slutty bastard. "Or good luck guessing all your new passwords."

I unwrapped the foil, broke off a piece of cinnamon bun and held it out to her.

Priya popped it into her mouth then pulled out into traffic on West Broadway.

How had my day gone so wrong that being lied to by a client who might cost me my business was not the low point?

"You going to keep it?" Priya said.

"No, I'm going to find it a good home with two parents who'll love it and give it the life I couldn't."

She slammed on the brakes to avoid an idiot jaywalker, flinging her arm protectively across me.

My head bounced off the seat. "Ouch."

"Sorry."

"Obviously, I'm removing this damn tattoo at the first possible opportunity." Growing up with a dad who twisted the truth to his own ends and couldn't even go to the grocery store without getting something out of someone, even a smile, left me with zero tolerance for people trying to pull a fast one. Especially on me. So someone inking me without my knowledge or consent? Fuck that.

Knowledge was power and right now, I had a decided lack of both. I rested my head gingerly against the head rest. The back of my skull pounded like a bitch but there was no vertigo.

Rain pattered against the windshield and the wipers were a rhythmic hum, but Moriarty's cold interior kept me from falling into a sleepy daze. At least the tray was nice and warm on my lap.

Priya fiddled with the radio dial, turning up the volume as she launched into "Shoop" by Salt-N-Pepa. She nudged me with her elbow until I joined in, the two of us rapping our little hearts out, busting out the moves we'd made up to go with it. It was our happy song and I was helpless to resist.

Singing away, we hit our Commercial Drive neighborhood. While still branded as Little Italy with its banners hanging from the streetlights and crosswalks decorated in red, white, and green, its population was actually far more diverse. After Canada opened its doors to a fresh wave of Nefesh refugees several years back, the area had become quite the magic hub. A lot of the newcomers were from the Middle East and Africa and preferred the mild weather out here to the rest of the country.

Priya braked at a red light, rapping along with Big Twan, while I stared out the window at the massive cherry tree in the yard at Green Thumb Nursery that was doing its hourly magic cycle through the four seasons in defiance of the actual weather. In contrast to all the other trees with bare branches lining the sidewalks, this cherry tree was transitioning from spring to summer, ablaze in sumptuous pink petals that were already falling gently to the ground to make way for green leaves.

Outside the store, one of the employees in a jacket with the Green Thumb logo silkscreened on the front wrestled a large ceramic planter into the back seat of a car. Its owner, a bald woman with multiple piercings, adjusted the front seat.

I'd seen the employee around before. He'd shaved the stupid hipster beard he usually wore but the real change to his appearance was the smudgy shadow flowing sluggishly out of him and into the woman that had depth and an oily viscous texture, pulsing with malevolence.

I started.

Beside me, Priya rapped away like nothing was wrong.

The woman broke into a coughing fit, some essential part of her seeming to fade, all while the employee cheerfully assisted her with her purchase.

I grabbed the handle, intending to roll down the window and yell some kind of warning, when the shadow paused its movement.

Neither completely free of the man nor fully possessing the woman, the weird ghostly creature swiveled as if seeking something out, then stretched a tentacle in my direction.

My skin prickled, iciness permeating my core, and I fought the urge to wrap my arms protectively around myself to keep my heat and my soul from being sucked out. Instead, I practically choked the handle to keep that window sealed tight.

Five seconds until the light turned green and we could get out of here.

I yawned, staring out the front window with feigned disinterest and keeping every ounce of tension out of my body.

The smudgy tentacle drew closer.

The rest of that shadow was now only attached to the Green Thumb employee by the thinnest of tethers, having gone mostly inside the bald woman. Black lines slithered along her hands and across her face, yet none of the pedestrians walking by noticed.

Oblivious, Priya sang the final chorus.

Two seconds.

Come on, green light!

The tentacle plastered against my side of the car, pushing on the glass.

My stomach roiled and I stuffed my shaking hands under my ass.

A tiny tendril of darkness seeped into the car…

And snapped backwards into the woman, whose features were momentarily obscured by the shadow, a dark wraith standing in the rain.

The smudge broke free of the man entirely. He clutched his heart, convulsed, and fell to the ground, his expression a vacant stare.

The shadow had possessed him, used him up, and discarded him.

The shadow had killed him.

It was now housed completely within the bald woman, though there was no sign of it on her person or in her behavior. Like any concerned citizen, she had already dialed 911, yelling about a heart attack, but it was too late.

Priya turned to look—

The light turned green.

"Go!" I yelled.

Priya hit the gas and we moved on.

"What happened? Was that guy all right?" she said.

I couldn't catch my breath. Just seeing that thing, I'd lost a tiny piece of myself.

"Hey. You're pale and sweating again," Priya said.

I wiped my brow with my sleeve. "Residual shit from the blow."

Because that couldn't have been real. But my shoulders didn't crawl down from around my ears until we were within a couple blocks of home and the front window of Muffin Top came into view.

Priya and I automatically checked out the new display. They'd recreated the Mad Hatter's Tea Party with vintage wooden painted dolls lining the table. Teapots magically hovered in mid-air in front of the guests, pouring piping hot tea into delicate china cups, while brightly iced cupcakes marched up and down the center of the table, and jam tarts in the shape of hearts swooped around the dolls. A giant Cheshire Cat smile faded in and out above it all.

There was a lineup out the door for the treats these earth elementals produced.

"Ooh, Beatriz's jam tarts. She wasn't sure she'd have time to make them because Miguel was running a fever the past few days." Priya pulled into park in front of the low building that housed a funky art gallery, a Greek restaurant, and our apartment on the second floor. "Want me to come up?"

I checked the time on my phone. "Nah. You're barely going to make it to your meeting as is. Take the car. And feel free to tell them that phoning you at 3AM because they had yet another brilliant change is not acceptable."

For the past six months, Priya had been coding some major database thing for a local high-end restaurant group. It made her eyes glaze over only slightly less than mine but it paid the bills.

"I can't burn that bridge," she said.

"Who said anything about going scorched earth? I'm talking about setting some boundaries."

"It's fine. The project is almost over." She'd said that two months ago. Priya wasn't even supposed to be working for them this week, given the sixteen-hour days she'd pulled all last week.

"How's Krishan doing?" I popped my seatbelt open. "I haven't spoken to him in ages."

Priya glared at my abrupt change in topic. Neither her dad nor her brother Krishan had been happy about Pri's decision to leave a steady paycheck and benefits doing I.T. at a large insurance company and go freelance, but they were also fiercely protective of the baby of their family. Krishan, a lawyer, had sat me down when Pri started working for me with a list of employment conditions until Geeta stepped in and saved me from further harassment.

"Don't you dare call him," she said. "I already had to endure a lecture from Daddy that I wasn't eating enough at our last family dinner. Krishan is worse. He'll demand a log of all my working hours and a sleep journal."

"Tough love, baby. Remember, your client needs you more than you need them."

"Yeah, yeah." She smooched my cheek. "Call if you need me."

"Will do and thanks." I gave her another half of a cinnamon bun. "Laters, Adler."

"Laters, Holmes."

Balancing the tray in one hand, I ducked out into the freezing rain that was sluicing down. My toes were numb and I sped up in anticipation of the lovely heat awaiting me inside.

"Ashira." A fleshy red-faced man stepped out of the Greek restaurant to stand under its broad awning. The front window sported an Untainted Party decal of a fist squeezing a drop of blood. For a secular political party, they were impressively zealot.

"Vasilios." My heart sank at the sight of the middle-aged owner and I fumbled my key into my building's lock. The white metal door seemed dingier than usual and someone had kicked a dent into the corner. "In kind of a rush here."

"Maybe you could talk to your mother? Put in a good word for me to cater the next Party fundraiser?"

Oh, Vasilios, oversized portions of lamb and roast potatoes did not possess the correct cachet, not to mention, way to gender stereotype.

I drew myself up to my full five-feet-eight inches and poured every ounce of disdain that I could into my voice. "You want me to ask Talia, a Senior Policy Adviser with the provincial Untainted Party, about catering?"

Just because I didn't subscribe to the Party's racist views (or whatever hatred of Nefesh was, since the argument over appropriate wording had been going on as long as the hatred itself) didn't mean I'd stand for his sexist assumptions.

Vasilios stepped back. "No?"

I smiled thinly. "I didn't think so."

Unlocking the door, I climbed the long, narrow stairwell as fast as my poor leg allowed, darting glances over my shoulder as if that smudgy thing might suddenly loom up behind me. At least I was no longer greeted by the smell of vinegar and bleach now that my former neighbor, Mrs. Hamdi, had moved into an old-age home.

There were only two suites above the ground level storefronts and I hurriedly unlocked the door on the far side of the tiny landing.

The two-bedroom apartment that Priya and I shared had a weird layout, and only really got sunshine on one half, but it boasted original fir on the floors, windowsills, and doorframes, and was, most importantly, a vaguely affordable rental unit, which here in Vancouver was a rare commodity.

I double-bolted the front door, sidestepped the hurricane of Pri's belongings scattered throughout the apartment to test that the windows were firmly locked, and only then toed out of my motorcycle boots, lining them up by my closet before collapsing on my neatly made bed. I let the warmth of my baseboard heaters seep into every icy part of me.

As it was mid-afternoon, my room had hit its darkest point. Later when I was trying to sleep, I'd be blinded by the security light on the building across the alley that made every night feel like an alien abduction and gave me some really interesting dreams. For now, I cocooned myself in the gloom, munching on cinnamon buns directly off the tray and cataloguing my possessions alphabetically: alarm clock, book, comforter, all the way to zipper, a self-soothing habit I'd fallen into in my youth.

Once I'd finished, I looked at the large tapestry entitled Paris in the Moonlight, that was made up of abstract geometric shapes suggesting the Eiffel Tower at night. It dominated the wall across from my bed. I'd inherited it from my grandparents along with a cream antique sofa with carved wood trim and tufted upholstery. Neither were at all my style, but they'd grown on me enough to move them with me when I'd finally left home.

My freak-out abated, I then, to paraphrase Sherlock Holmes, eliminated the impossible. Since it was doubtful that I suddenly had some great ability to see evil creatures that no one else did, I deduced the improbable: that the entire episode had been some weird post-concussion anomaly and all I'd witnessed was a plain old heart attack.

Solid ground firmly in place once more, I pulled out my phone and dialed. "Hey, Talia."

"Ashira, are you getting ready?" My mother issued instructions to her assistant about what time to bring her car around.

Today was Friday which meant...

Oh, shit. The gala.

Talia's years of maintaining a positive attitude with my Nefesh father's schemes had abruptly evaporated the day he abandoned us. Adam Cohen had been a Charmer—literally possessing the magic ability to charm people—and when he'd left, she'd slotted magic firmly under the category of manipulative things she refused to buy into, like religion. She finished her law degree, joined the burgeoning Untainted Party, and quickly became one of its major players.

Her political career wasn't due to some fervent belief in the purity of human blood so much as it was an expression of her frustration and bitterness with her marriage and a determination to make sure that "appropriate checks and balances were kept on magic."

I understood her, I just didn't agree. Shitty people were shitty people. Magic was irrelevant as a factor. Plenty of Mundanes were criminals or plain dicks.

Talia had been sending me weekly reminders of this gala, since all her colleagues would be in attendance with their families and I was expected to be the dutiful daughter for the cameras.

I could play the concussion card to get out of going but then I'd have to listen to her bitch about how she didn't need me to support Party values, but she did expect me to support *her*. That was the last thing I felt like doing, but I had questions about the tattoo, so what was the lesser of two evils: deal with my mother after the day I'd had or bail and wait even longer for answers?

"I'm coming," I said. "But I want five minutes alone with you tonight."

"Fine," Talia said. "In return I want you to meet Josh Millstein. His father is considering a large donation to the Party and has been complaining about his son's inability to meet a nice Jewish girl."

"Two out of three ain't bad, I guess."

"Fake it, darling. The way you do your general love of humanity."

"Unfair. I like several people very well."

"Do we have a deal?" she said.

Everything was a negotiation with her, but to give my mom credit, she didn't lie to me or play games. She'd been very clear about those rules after I'd come out of my coma and surgery.

"Deal. I'll see you later."

"Wear the dress I sent over." She hung up.

I eyed the garment bag hanging in my closet like it was a striking cobra. Inside was a black-and-white sheath dress that Talia had deemed appropriately demure. She wasn't wrong. When I'd tried it on, I'd looked like a boring penguin.

Any other time, I would have worn the dress as the path of least resistance, but tonight I was itchy and off-kilter. There was no way the tattoo was the end of this story. Something was coming, and whatever it was, I intended to meet it head on.

The game was afoot and this dress was toast.

Chapter 3

Two hours later, I glided into the well-heeled throng gathered at the Vancouver Aquarium located in Stanley Park in a floor-length, deep red gown that plunged daringly to my tailbone in the back and hugged my curves in the front. Even though I'd never admit it and be forced into more nightmarish shopping free-for-alls, I was grateful to Priya for "encouraging" me to buy it at a film and television industry wardrobe sale that she'd dragged me to.

My waves floated past my shoulder blades, hiding the shaved patch of hair with the tattoo, while my only jewelry was my bubbe's—Talia's mom's—diamond-studded titanium stacking rings that I'd inherited along with the tapestry and sofa. I wore the shimmeriest touch of gold on my lids and a pop of red on my lips.

I even had red-painted toenails peeking out of the shiny black sandals that were the only heels I'd ever found that didn't irritate my leg. Generally, I had to be cautious even with these if I didn't want to end up hobbling around, but so far so good.

I checked my coat, stepped into the large circular foyer, and rolled my eyes.

Fundraisers weren't just social outings, they were military campaigns. More than one poor event planner had suffered a nervous breakdown curating and divvying up space to entertain—and court—both Untainted Party members and the Nefesh elite.

Since tonight's fundraising benefited a local non-profit that provided financial assistance to out-of-town families with kids undergoing treatment at Children's Hospital, both communities wanted to help out. Or smile politely and then quietly compete to see who could be more charitable than the other.

The lobby was Switzerland. No arguments, no insults, no magic. It was as much an area for the two groups to play nice as for the rest of us Mundanes to take a break from the two extremes.

The design aesthetic here was simple: other than the large underwater photographic prints in rich colors, the rest of the space was white and sparkly. White linens covered tall bistro-style tables, the white floor tiles gleamed, and hundreds of white fairy lights had been strung up, providing the only illumination. Light piano music added to the overall soothing effect while photographers circulated, getting shots for the local papers and various PR pieces for Party and House use.

Curious as to how the rest of the space had been divided, I ducked into the darkened room with the six-foot-high tropical fish tank that beckoned from my right. Techno music with a broody edge flowed through the speakers, perfect for both the large shark tank that anchored the length of the opposite wall and the steampunk-clad acrobats magically dancing and swirling high up in the center of the room. The occasional fireball tumbled above our heads before bursting into showers of red and black sparks that waterfalled harmlessly down.

A server dressed in a similar steampunk vibe offered me a bland-looking cake ball.

I raised an eyebrow.

"Wish balls," he said. "They'll be whatever flavor you want."

"And?"

"And nothing. No mood-enhancing food tonight."

In that case, I helped myself. One of my favorite flavor duos burst on my taste buds and I moaned.

The server peered at me. "Not a chocolate moan. Too earthy for vanilla or lemon." He tapped a finger against his lips. "Aha! Bacon and maple syrup."

"What gave it away?" While there were Nefesh mind readers, they were rare and tended to be heavily medicated. This guy was too upbeat.

"I know my moans, honey." He batted his lashes and moved on.

I headed into the long gallery that housed the Pacific Canada and Treasures of the BC Coast exhibits whose tanks showcased good Canadian fish from various national habitats. A string quartet with members of the Vancouver Symphony Orchestra played a lively little number as written by a long-dead white guy, and the servers were polished in crisp black-and-white, carrying trays with exquisitely plated high-end appetizers. The lights were low, but inviting. Everything was in impeccable taste.

Oh, and there was my mother.

Giving a chin nod to the octopi chilling in their tank, I headed for her.

Talia was surrounded by her usual group of Untainted Party hotshots, Mundane business leaders, and men who wanted into her pants. I'd never seen her accept any of those offers and I was happier not knowing. For a woman in her early fifties, my mother could have easily passed for a decade younger. We shared our dark hair and pale complexions, but she had gray eyes where mine were dark brown like my dad's. Despite her questionable fashion choices for her only child, she was always impeccably turned out. Tonight she wore a knee-length lace dress in the palest mauve with a pencil skirt fit. Her chin-length bobbed hair was razor straight with nary a strand out of place.

"Hi, Mom." I dutifully air-kissed her cheek, forgoing the use of her first name in front of the general public. One of our many negotiations.

She swept a cool gaze over me. I couldn't tell if the momentary flash was approval for my look or a warning. "Darling, how lovely."

A familiar-looking gentleman with salt-and-pepper hair in a bespoke navy suit flashed a toothpaste commercial smile that complimented his relaxed stance. Probably a performer of some type. "Talia, you couldn't possibly have a grown daughter."

My mother speared him with a dazzling smile. "Thank you, Daniel. You're too kind. And it's wonderful you were able to get away from prepping your upcoming trial to support these kids."

Ah. That's why I recognized him. Daniel Hughes was a well-known local criminal defense attorney and often on TV.

"We should chat," he said. "I heard something that might interest you."

She placed her hand on his sleeve. "How about you get me a drink first? I'm absolutely parched."

He strode off to do her bidding, Talia watching him with an assessing look. When I'd said she didn't play games, I'd meant with me. In her professional life, the woman was a shark, but she was so good that she could tear into a person's soft underbelly and they'd present their own intestines as a gift.

"May I have a moment of your time?" I smiled apologetically at everyone while I pulled her away.

"Five minutes, Ashira. This is a work night for me."

"What do you know about a Star of David tattoo?" I watched for the tiniest sign of guilt or knowledge but she frowned.

"A tattoo? Really?" She turned me around, examining me for the offending mark. "I hope you at least got it somewhere you could cover up."

Yeah, my clit. It could do with some communing with the divine.

"I didn't get one." Willingly.

"Then what are you going on about? Honestly."

"Talia," I said through gritted teeth, "did you tattoo me at some point in my life? Did Dad?"

She peered into my eyes. "Are you high?"

What was it with mothers automatically jumping to that assumption?

"Geez, Mother." As the full moon brought out the werewolf, so my mother brought out my raging fifteen-year-old self. It was a toss-up as to which was more dangerous, though at least werewolves were fictional.

I plucked a glass of Chardonnay off a passing waiter's tray. Booze. Thank gawd.

"Smile, ladies."

On cue, Talia and I pasted on our "happy family" faces.

Satisfied, the photographer wandered off in search of his next victims.

"Joshua!" Talia motioned some dude around my age over. "Keep smiling," she murmured. "Make a good impression."

"Tattoo: yes? Or no?" I took a healthy slug of wine.

"Of course not." She adjusted the neckline of my dress.

She may not have been lying, but she was still annoying. I brushed her hands off and unleashed my sweetest smile, the one I'd practiced in the mirror until Priya had signed off on it.

"Less tooth, darling," Talia said.

I knocked back the rest of the white wine and had exchanged it for a second glass by the time Josh reached us.

Talia did the introductions then moved off, quickly swallowed up by another group clamoring for the usual appointments, dinners, drinks at the club, and even tennis games. My mother handled all requests with unparalleled aplomb courtesy of some freaky social butterfly genetics.

Josh Millstein was perfectly attractive with his blond hair and green eyes, perfectly dressed in a stylish trendy suit, and made perfectly correct conversation, asking about me before making some self-deprecating joke about working at a hedge fund.

I'd have been fooled into believing that he was enjoying himself if I wasn't a cynical bitch trained to assess people's smallest movements. Every time Josh lifted his highball to take a sip, his eyes darted left to a blonde woman in a nearby group. Game, set, and match.

Josh was a dude pressured into a meeting and looking to score elsewhere, an easy-to-read book, not a fascinating puzzle. All the better to wrap this up quickly.

"Give it three more minutes," I said.

"Excuse me?"

I took his arm, twisting it to see the face of his Phillipe Patek watch. "In three minutes, we can part. You can move in on the blonde and I can consider my duties to my mother discharged for the evening."

"I wasn't—"

"Sure, you were. Don't care." There was a certain freedom in not giving a damn about most social interactions.

Suddenly there was a lot more interest when he checked me out. "What if I don't want to go?"

"You do. You want a woman like that."

"And what kind of woman is that?"

I finished my second drink but there was nowhere to put the glass so I twirled the stem between my fingers, studying the other woman. Pretty with a too-bright smile that had an undertone of brittle to it, she laughed with a loud, bird-like twitter at a joke the one man in her crowd had made. "Put it this way, if her life was a horror flick, there'd be credit kill written all over her."

Josh laughed. "And which horror movie woman are you?"

I smiled. With definitely too many teeth. "The last one standing who sent the bad guy to Hell. Now, as our time is up, you'll have to excuse me. I have a man to find."

"Lucky man."

I winked at him. "I'm the lucky one."

That much was true seeing as the "man" in question was Jack Daniel's. Chardonnay was kiddie punch peddled to chicks who couldn't handle decent booze. Or who believed the myth that they couldn't.

Extricating myself from Josh, who beelined for the blonde as expected, I pressed through the crowd to the large Exploration Gallery at the back of the aquarium which was Nefesh territory this evening, and let out a happy sigh, bathed in the spill of soft purple light from the jellyfish tanks. Talia and I had spent many a rainy day at the aquarium when Dad was out of town on "business," and while I loved the entire place, this room was my favorite.

And now it was underwater. Light filtered down through magic waves that rolled from one side of the ceiling to the other to crash and break against the wall without spilling a drop on the guests.

An unmanned ice bar was set up to my right, lined with icy stalagmites fused in deep turquoise and silver. Their tips morphed into chilled shot glasses that rapidly filled with liquid. Whenever someone snapped a glass free, the stalagmite grew a new one.

I'd never share this with my mother, but no matter how much money Mundanes threw at an event, they could never compete with Nefesh productions. Even some of the younger Untainted Party members in the previous gallery looked longingly this way.

Tempting as the shots looked, I bypassed them for a bar serving highballs and ordered two fingers' worth of Gentleman Jack with three ice cubes and a splash of water. Exactly the way Sinatra drank it back in the day.

It was a work night for me as well.

Talia had footed the bill for my ticket plus dropped that dress off along with an envelope that contained my taxi and drink allowance. She'd stopped bitching about me spending it on alcohol after I'd shown up with a purse full of juice boxes to some Untainted Party event. Because really, being around her crowd generally required a gentle buzz to keep me from punching people over their racist politics, their judgments on my chosen "profession" instead of following in my esteemed mother's footsteps, or the inevitable "Talia, you can't possibly have a daughter that age," that left me dying to tell them to pucker up a bit more because there was still some ass left to kiss.

Drink in hand, I made my way to my favorite tank containing a myriad of small, translucent jellies floating languidly. The anger that had been stoking for hours eased into a warm radiance.

My mother had no clue about the tattoo and my father was no longer around to ask. I'd exhausted the obvious, but that was to be expected. Where did I go from here? Narrowing down *when* I'd been tattooed would help to find the *who*. Old photos were pointless because even as a toddler I'd had a full head of hair and if the tattoo already existed, it would be hidden.

I really didn't want any of the hospital staff to be behind this, and especially not Dr. Zhang, the surgeon who'd operated on my leg. He'd been emblematic of everything positive and healing at a time when all color had leached from my life. He couldn't have betrayed me like that. I crossed my fingers that I could strike him off as a suspect, but I had to pursue this hospital angle.

It was better than a dead end. I toasted the jellies with my highball.

"A woman with a back that would make a goddess weep and a taste for whiskey untainted by Coke. A rare dichotomy." The low smoky voice curled through me, all illicit decadence.

I grinned evilly, turning to the speaker with my glass extended. "If you start right now, you might be able to blame the fact that you hit on me on your 'drinking your boozy heart out.'"

The gobsmacked look on Levi Montefiore's face was priceless.

"Why are you wearing that dress?" He waved his hand at it.

Even with the shoes that raised me a couple inches above my five-eight height, he towered over me by a good four inches and a skyscraper's worth of arrogance.

"I left my sackcloth and ashes at home. Sorry to disappoint. You drinking yourself out of total humiliation? No?" I shrugged and finished the whiskey before thrusting the glass into his hands. "Do a woman a mitzvah and take this away while you troll for the night's entertainment elsewhere."

Levi handed the glass off to someone else. Not even a waiter. Just some random person perfectly happy to do his bidding. That was the way of the world for the Head of House Pacifica.

To be fair, he played to his strengths. His black hair was cut slightly longer on top than the sides, swept away from his face in a classic side part that emphasized the slash of his cheekbones and a jawline sharp enough to cut. Much like the words that came out of his unfairly full and sensuous lips.

Odes had been written to his ice-blue eyes and of their unknowable depths that changed from the deepest navy to a mercurial storm. Granted those odes were inked on bathroom stalls in glittery pen, but exist they did. I liked to add disclaimers to them in thick marker and ground those flights of fancy in cold, hard truth.

I was one of the few breathing humans who didn't go into a dead faint at his proximity, though I did often wish for someone to kill me when I was around him.

Combined with the gunmetal suit that hugged his long, leanly muscled frame to perfection and made me reconsider my stance on Josh's tailoring, Levi exuded effortless power—and ego. It didn't hurt that he'd invented some virtual reality tech when he was in his early twenties and sold his company for a sum that would have made even an ogre reasonably attractive in the eyes of many.

People had been waiting to see what the boy wonder would do next, but no one could have predicted he'd challenge the previous Head of House Pacifica for its leadership.

Or that he'd win.

Pursing those lips that rumor had it were almost as talented as his fingers, Levi regarded me with a suspicion usually reserved for small unattended packages in airports. "Are you undercover?"

"In a floor-length 'come fuck me' red dress with no visible panty line?"

His eyes flicked to my ass, then away dismissively.

I counted to ten in my head, visualizing pushing him into the jellies and watching them sting him to death. "If I *was*, would you declare this gala Nefesh territory and mess up my case?"

"If you didn't have the right to work it, then yeah. In a heartbeat."

There it was. Levi's absolute refusal to recognize that not everything was as black-and-white as House rules made it out to be, and the reason I hoped Charlotte Rose's Rogue status didn't end up penalizing me in addition to her.

"The husband was Nefesh," I said, "but his wife, my client, who he was cheating on, was Mundane. I had every right to get proof of his infidelity." It was pointless to fight Levi, but that job last month could have opened the door to better gigs for me had I not been sidelined.

He refused a honey goat cheese and raspberry phyllo cup from a polite server. "It's too dangerous for Mundanes to go after Nefesh."

Having never met a goat cheese appy I didn't like, I accepted one. "Mundanes are dangerous, too. We have these things called guns. They kill people. No magic required." Hot damn, these puppies were good. I licked goat cheese off my lip. "And here's another revelation. While we were both assholes when we were younger, the difference is that I grew out of it."

Levi's eyes darkened, the corners tightening, but when a couple called out a greeting, he had his charismatic smile in place. He dropped it as soon as they moved on. "No, the difference is, I became responsible for an entire community while you kept thinking you should be allowed to do whatever you want."

Whatever I want? I couldn't remember the last time I hadn't conducted myself according to someone else's rules, fighting to be taken seriously, fighting to make a name for myself when it felt some days like the entire deck was stacked against me.

Anger rose up hot and thick enough to taste, wiping away all leftover raspberry sweetness. The room swam, the perfume and cologne cloying in this packed space. My heart pounded in my ears but I choked down my retort. Were our respective statuses represented via totem pole carving, I would be the poor schmuck on the bottom just trying to hang on, while Levi, as House Head, would be the capricious god up top plotting how to complicate my life yet again.

I stomped off, zigzagging to try and get through the press of people, but he followed. "Go away, Levi. I'm not in the mood for your insults."

"You're flushed and clearly dizzy. Maybe rethink your plan to become a functioning alcoholic," he said wryly. He grasped my elbow, propelling me through the crowd to the exit.

They parted like the Red Sea for Moses. Just once I'd like to see this guy break a sweat.

The cold night air brought everything into a sharp clarity, but I remained lightheaded and goosebumps dotted my skin. Colored lanterns cast warm, inviting pools of light in the darkness but they did nothing for the actual freezing temperature.

The chatter back in the aquarium faded to a dull buzz, since all the sane people had opted to stay inside. Holding the skirt of my dress with one hand, I lurched over to the viewing platform high above the dolphin pool, keeping to the shadows.

Levi strolled behind me, heat rolling off him.

Head bowed, I stopped in the middle of the platform, gripped the cold metal railing, and flinched because I'd caught a jagged part of the railing's seams. I tried to speak, tried to move, but I was paralyzed. My insides twisted, radiating a stabbing pain that built and built and then burst like a supernova, hot and sharp.

Fire blazed through my body, a searing agony that lit up every nerve ending. Had I not been clutching the railing, I'd have fallen because my legs had turned to Jell-O. There was a mild tug and then a punch that felt like a multi-armed giant was bashing its way out from inside my skull.

Violent shudders wracked me from head to toe and I screamed, but no sound came out.

A tiny drop of blood beaded on my finger. I sucked down a harsh breath, mesmerized by that drop that was so red and earthy.

"Ash." Levi's irises were no longer merely blue but the electric wild skies after a storm. They practically glowed and, between them and the glare of the moon, I had to look away. The overpowering smell of the saltwater from the dolphin pool below made me gag, but was tempered by the mild musky sandalwood scent of Levi's cologne.

"You're not having a seizure, are you?" he said.

Why did he have to be such a dick?

From one blink to the next, the bloody smear on my finger morphed into a solid shaft about eight inches long with a bulbous end that I instinctively jabbed Levi back with.

"Did you just—that's—that's a dildo," Levi stuttered. "You hit me with a magic dildo?"

We both stared at the offending item in my hand.

"It's a sword," I said.

"It's a fucking cock that you conjured up," he growled. "You're Nefesh?" His expression darkened in fury.

Maybe I was actually unconscious and all this was some kind of fever dream?

"As if," I said. "I thought I'd liven up this snoozefest with a giant dick. The sword, I mean. Not you. I've been carrying it in my dress this whole time waiting for the right moment to spring it. Hilarious, huh?"

Okay, as lies went it was admittedly somewhere between "the check is in the mail" and "I won't come in your mouth" for believability, but logic and coherent reasoning had fled in the face of the weaponized penis.

"Right. You carried it in your floor-length 'come fuck me' dress with no visible panty line," Levi said darkly.

"I have a bra." Stop talking, Ash. I white-knuckled the dildo. If I really had magic, *this* was what I produced? Okay, bright side. I could become a vigilante, going around giving the bad guys of my city a good dicking.

I stepped backward, wanting to get the fuck out of Dodge so I could unscramble my brain and figure out how I suddenly had magic, but I was trapped between the railing and a hard place.

Levi grabbed me by the shoulders. "Answer me!"

Panic flooded me, my pulse spiking. One second, I was standing in front of him, the next, I moved with the lithe swiftness of a jungle predator and tossed him to the ground, my knee grinding into his chest and a glinting red dagger poised at his throat.

A dagger that the dildo had transformed into, its blade sharper than any steel.

Oh good, I wasn't a one-cock pony. A hysterical laugh burbled out of me.

Levi pushed up to dislodge me but I held him down, which really shouldn't have been possible, and twisted the knife against his skin. There was a faint rasp as the blade scraped against his light stubble.

What was I doing? I scrambled to my feet, clutching the blood dagger, and pressed the tip against his shirtfront. "Are you going to kill me?"

His face puckered in distaste. "In this suit? It's Armani. But I do want to know exactly what the *fuck* is going on."

Excellent question, but I didn't have an answer. In fact, there were so many I didn't have that I could barely keep track of them.

The pounding in my ears, the buzz of magic thrumming

through me, it was all too much. I lost what little hold I had. The blade disintegrated into blood, splooshing out on Levi, and turning him into one of the promgoers from *Carrie*.

So much for the Armani.

Chapter 4

In the fairy tale version of my life, my Cinderella mad dash would have gotten me home safe but sooty, with only the loss of a shoe. But reality was cold and harsh: I'd lost zero shoes (just most of my dignity), and Levi was no prince.

I crashed through the aquarium's front doors. In my first piece of luck today, a sole yellow taxi idled in the distance.

The parking lot was impossibly stretched out as if seen through a tunnel, the trees weird piney fingers stretching to the inky clouds, and the sounds of cars and guests grotesquely distorted into a harsh rumble. How much blood had I left behind on Levi's shirt and could I bill him for it? Woozy, I staggered toward the taxi, arm half-outstretched as if the driver could hear my whispered plea to wait.

A dark sleek limo pulled up to the curb.

"Get in," Levi said from behind me on the sidewalk.

I ignored him, stumbling forward.

He strode toward the cab.

"That's mine," I whimpered, the world swooping and lurching around me. Kicking off my heels, I snagged them by one finger and attempted to speed up. It was imperative that Levi not get my taxi, because I was scared that if I didn't get out of here I'd remain trapped in some weird Ash in Wonderland version of my life that was at odds with every single thing I knew about myself.

Magic didn't just show up. It might skip a generation or two but you were born with it or you didn't have it. Full stop.

My blood sang as my magic settled in my bones, but the rest of me was upended. What kind of mutant was I?

Get home, get Priya, and get answers. The stress of today's events squeezed my chest in a tight band, but I put one foot in front of the other, assuring myself that if I could return to familiar surroundings and my best friend, I could find a plausible explanation.

Please let me find an explanation.

Levi bent over to speak to the driver through the open passenger window. A moment later the vehicle pulled away with great haste, its taillights a red blur fading into the night.

I curled my nails into my palms, the cold from the concrete seeping into my feet.

Before I could call Lyft, Levi strode back to me and pointed at the limo.

"I don't get in cars with strange men," I said through chattering teeth, moving away as quickly as possible. So, slightly faster than a tortoise.

"You've known me for years." Both he and the damn limo glided alongside me.

"Strange. Not strangers." I briskly rubbed my arms, having forgotten my coat in my sprint out of the gala. "You've got blood all over your shirt. You could be a serial killer."

Except now he didn't. Right. Illusion magic.

He skewered me with a supremely unamused look. "I want answers."

"Forty-two, Miss Scarlet in the pool room with the wrench, and General George Washington."

"About the fact you're a Rogue."

"Don't forget that I'm also 'on the lam.'" I dropped into a terrible southern redneck accent. "I'm headin' for the county line."

A muscle ticked in his jaw.

I patted his cheek. "Careful, Leviticus." I used my old nickname for him that he despised. "You might break something."

"Get in the damn limo." His voice and his expression were both carved from granite and infused with all of the power as Head of House Pacifica. It may have been one of the smaller Houses globally, but it wasn't one of the weakest. Not under Levi.

Intellectually, I'd known he was the big boss, but I'd never been in his presence when he wore it like a mantle of absolute authority. His power rolled off him, sucking all the oxygen out of the night.

My lungs shrunk to the size of peanuts and I struggled to drag in a breath. This wasn't my childhood nemesis who'd graduated from making Frankenstein jokes about my leg to firing the first strike during finals of our university psych class by switching out my double espressos for decaf.

This was a man I didn't want to cross because I'd lose. Badly.

"Fine." I pivoted to get in the limo, but Levi caught my shoulder, draping his Armani jacket over me. It was warm from his body and smelled like him. Remarkably, it was blood-free. I wrapped it more firmly around myself. "Compassion?"

"Hardly," he scoffed. "Can't have you dying before I torture you."

I settled myself on the leather seat that contoured perfectly to my ass, still shivering despite the jacket and grateful for the blast of heat in the car. Dumping my heels on the floor, I wiggled my toes, sighing in delight.

The limo was such a smooth ride that if I hadn't been watching the passing shadows of trees glide over the tinted glass, I wouldn't have known we were moving.

Levi opened one of the side wood panels and removed a bottle of Jack Daniel's Limited Edition Number 27 Gold and two tumblers. He poured a splash of liquid in both and handed one to me. "Sip."

Even one tiny taste spread through me like molten honey.

He considered me over the rim of his glass. "Were you banking on me showing you mercy when you got caught?"

"Heaven forbid." I took another sip of perfection, savoring it. I'd never been able to afford this premium whiskey. "How long have you known me? About fifteen years? Five of them spent together every summer at camp. You really think I'm so talented I was able to deliberately hide magic all this time? And why, huh? What possible motivation could I have?"

"Your mother."

Shit. If my magic cost her her position? Even I wasn't sure how far Talia's motherly love extended. "Yeah, that would have been a good one."

He rolled the glass between his long, elegant fingers, the Tennessee whiskey gently swirling. "But you're right, you're not that talented. At the same time, if you haven't had magic all these years, then explain to me how you're the exception to the fact that *all* Nefesh are born with magic *and* how you possess blood magic when that doesn't exist?"

Blood magic? Fuuuuuck. I tossed back the rest of the drink.

"I'm a special unicorn?" I held out my glass for a refill but Levi swept it away.

"I take my position as House Head very seriously. And

that means enforcing laws that will keep my people safe. I've got no tolerance for Rogues." He set both our glasses down on a tiny pull-out table with a preternatural gentleness that unnerved me, an overcompensation for the dangerous glint in his eyes.

I swallowed. Levi's anger was a cold storm front buffeting me. And some of that probably stemmed from a sense of personal betrayal but I hoped he had some mercy for Rogues, both for myself and Charlotte Rose.

"You've got two chances," he said. "Slim and none. Convince me that you haven't been Rogue all these years or I'll prosecute you to the fullest extent of the law."

The Girl Who Lived. That's what Dr. Zhang had called me when I'd come out of surgery, my bloodied Harry Potter T-shirt cut off my body and later burned. At first the moniker had been a cute nod to the book, but somewhere in my later teens it had hardened into an iron-willed determination to follow my own path. Live on my terms.

And I had, but too much of living had been about surviving. Yet in this moment, despite how surreal this was and all of Levi's threats, I felt more alive than ever. After spending years on bottom-rung cases, I now faced the biggest mystery of my career: myself. A thrill fizzed through my veins and damn if I didn't want to say "challenge accepted" in the boldest way possible, like waving a flag at a bull.

I brushed some dirt off the hem of my dress. "I'll make you a deal."

"This isn't a negotiation," he said.

"You think anyone is going to believe that you knew me all these years and didn't know about my magic? 'Why did you keep her off the books, Mr. Montefiore? Was she running black ops for you? Or were you simply making exceptions for a friend?'"

"Your point?"

"Tonight was as much a shock to me as to you. I want the chance to unravel this mystery." I twisted around on the seat and pulled up my hair.

His breath warmed my neck. "I don't give a damn that you've found religion."

"I didn't. Someone inked that on me and I only found out earlier today. Hours before I discovered that I had magic." I let my hair tumble back down. "I don't know why or how it never manifested before, but I want to find out. This may be a point of law for you, Levi, but it's my life. I'm a damn good private investigator. Let me put the pieces of this puzzle together, because what if I wasn't the only person this was done to? That would have huge repercussions for your House."

House Pacifica headquarters came into view. Located smack dab in the center of downtown on some of Vancouver's priciest real estate, the long seven-story building was shaped like an "S" laying on its side. The glass managed to catch and reflect light in such a way that it was never the same color from morning to night. In dark clouds it took on a deep silver color, while a summer sunset would turn it a brilliant orange-pink. Right now it was obsidian black, immutable and enigmatic.

The limo turned into a driveway. A parking gate built seamlessly into HQ slid open and the car descended into the depths below the building.

"Do we have a deal?" I said.

"No. I don't take kindly to blackmail. Or half-baked lies. Tell whatever story you like."

The next hour was a blur. I was booked on suspicion of being a Rogue and tossed in a holding cell. My protests fell on deaf ears—as did my demands for a phone call. They'd taken away my small handbag with my wallet and iPhone. Also my shoes. As if self-harm via a chunky wedge heel was a serious risk.

The only things I'd been given were a Gatorade and a bag of cashews because, apparently, I'd looked dangerously pale. Well, no shit. Birth a freaking knife out of your blood and see how lightheaded you felt.

I sat on the bolted-down bench, poking at the scab on my palm where I'd cut myself on the railing earlier. I couldn't even blame Levi for not believing me. Magic always adhered to a specific set of rules. "One of these things is not like the others" did not apply.

Yet I refused to rot in here; I was the only one with the motivation and ability to clear my name. Bail would be my first major hurdle. In the plus column was the fact that I had no priors, not even a parking ticket, with a business based in the community. That should qualify me, but the big minus was that they might decide my mother's resources made me a flight risk. I laughed bitterly.

Levi finally returned along with Miles Berenbaum, his Chief of Security. Unlike the Nefesh police chief who reported to both Levi and the Chief Constable, who also oversaw the Mundane forces, Miles worked directly for Levi and was exceedingly loyal.

And wasn't it just perfect that two of the most powerful people in this city were the same popular best friends that my grandparents had sent me to Jewish summer camp with every year in my teens, just wielding influence on a different level?

The cell door clattered open.

I held my hand out to Miles. "I want my phone call."

"You'll get it," he said. At six-foot-four, he was a couple of inches taller than Levi. Dude must have had his customary uniform of black pants and black long-sleeved shirt specially made for him, because that bodybuilder frame of his decimated any puny off-the-rack clothing. Even though it was the middle of the night, his dark brown eyes were clear and his blond hair was as meticulously buzz cut as ever.

If anyone had hospital corners on their bed, it was Miles. He was as reserved as Levi was charismatic—to people other than me—and while I'd never seen him catting around with anyone, it wasn't for lack of offers.

He moved into my personal space and jerked his thumb to the ceiling. "Up."

I grabbed hold of my dress fabric so I wouldn't step on it, though the hem was filthy and I'd managed to rip a side seam when I'd grappled with Levi at the aquarium. Rest in peace, dress.

"About time." I grimaced, the stench of rotting flesh and feces assaulting me. Geez dude, fix your diet.

A smudgy, oily shadow flowed out from Miles at a slightly faster speed than it had with the Green Thumb Employee, bobbing from side-to-side as if assessing Levi and myself for its new accommodations.

My heart stuttered a beat. Miles wasn't my favorite person but I didn't want him dead once that smudge broke free. I also didn't want to find out whether Levi or I would be the new recipient of that abomination, but damn, using my magic would only cement my Rogue status.

Fuck it.

Ripping the scab off my palm, I squeezed my fist to call up a drop of blood, then working on instinct and adrenaline, I magically teased it into a silky thin red stream. I fired the ribbon over Miles' shoulder and into the shadow, where it forked into red branches, anchoring the smudge in place.

That was crazy cool, but the feeling that a million wriggling maggots had surged from the smudge to infest my soul, not so much.

I shrieked.

Charlotte Rose's admonition that the House was experimenting on people replayed in my head. Was this it?

But then Levi shouted, "What the fuck?"

Miles glanced back and jumped about three feet.

"Don't move!" I yelled.

Straining against my branchy grip, the smudge arced over Miles' head like a wave, stretching out for its new victim. It was still connected to Miles, which was a good thing, because the second it disengaged fully he would drop dead. I didn't know if he could accidentally tear himself free and I was determined not to find out.

Spearing the wave with more branches, I stopped it in its tracks, the smudge thrashing against its restraints.

Levi stepped toward it, stepped back, and balled his fists. "Get it out of him."

"What do you think I'm trying to do? Give it a facial?" I said.

"It's in me?!" Miles hurled fireballs over his shoulder. "Where?"

The fireballs passed harmlessly through the smudge to scorch the walls and ceiling of the cell, thin tongues of flame lapping along the seams.

Cursing with the inventiveness of a man whose reality was unravelling, Levi grabbed a small fire extinguisher off a mounted bracket outside the cell and doused the fires, yelling at his righthand man to calm down. Personally, Levi yelling at me would be the least calming thing I could think of, but Miles was vibrating in place from the force of keeping himself in check.

Dark clouds swam through my vision, arms shaking and eyes watering from the atrocious stench. Terror pierced my soul as I stared directly into the heart of this mass that was sheer wrongness. I fell into its endless night, a puny speck against a devouring fiend, my only shield this newfound magic I didn't understand.

The smudge still flowed out of Miles becoming more

entangled into my magic branches, but it had slowed to a trickle and would soon be free of him.

Time was running out.

I swayed, dangerously close to passing out from blood loss. Once I did, the smudge would kill us all.

Levi caught the underside of my arms to bolster my grip. "How do we stop it?"

I was about to give off some snarky retort to the effect that I didn't know. Except I did.

Scraping deep for the last vestiges of my energy, I poured more magic into it, shuddering and convinced that writhing maggots swarmed me, but pushing through for one last assault.

In an act that was both beautiful and totally unnerving, white clusters bloomed all over the branches and devoured the smudge.

Just ate it right up, yum yum.

The smudge was gone, leaving only a shocked silence and a decimated jail cell.

Spent, I sank to the floor, wrapping my arms around my knees, my head down, willing away that creepy maggoty sensation still crawling over and inside me because otherwise I was going to tear my skin off.

"It's gone?" Miles finally said in a hoarse voice.

I glanced up. His expression was pinched and he was rubbing a trembling hand over his sleeve. "Totally gone," I said.

He caught himself on the next pass of his sleeve and dropped his hand to his side. "Thank you."

"Can you walk?" Levi crouched down beside me, and when I shook my head, scooped me up in his arms.

"Where are we going?" My voice was a scratchy rasp.

"To talk." His voice was soft, but I had no doubt that if he didn't like my answers, I'd be right back in that cell.

Chapter 5

A subdued but otherwise unharmed Miles offered to take me from Levi, but Levi shook his head and carried me into the elevator where Miles pressed seven. We silently glided upward past the first two floors where all police activity was centered and the next four dedicated to House corporate affairs.

I barely had the energy to hang on to Levi, but the brush of his shirt against my cheek and the steady beat of his heart banished all thoughts of the maggot sensation from my mind. Being carried wasn't the worst hardship.

Levi had a really good chest. He'd showered and changed into a casual sweater and jeans, which lessened his status as big bad Head but broadcast his masculine appeal like it was a neon sign. He wore no cologne, bearing only the faint trace of a shampoo with an earthy lemongrass scent that unknotted some of the tension in my muscles.

I considered letting go of him and bringing back those maggoty heebie jeebies because Levi as a source of comfort was completely unnerving, but he cradled me so firmly but gently against him that it seemed a shame to disturb the equilibrium he'd achieved, so I merely adjusted my arms around his neck, taking advantage of the shift to study his stubbled jaw.

His face was harshly rugged, but that only emphasized the magnificence of those piercing blue eyes and his lush lips.

"You dying?" he murmured.

"You wish."

The corners of his lips quirked. "Then you're checking me out?"

"Just finding your jugular in case you get handsy."

Levi laughed softly.

The elevator slowed to a stop with a soft bing. We turned away from the rest of the now-empty executive offices and strode through heavy glass doors into Levi's private domain. I may have wondered once or twice what it looked like up here in His Lordship's castle and it didn't disappoint.

One side of the long curved space boasted floor-to-ceiling windows that looked out over the twinkling lights of Vancouver's skyline with a slice of dark water and North Shore mountains beyond. Pale gold walls boasted a host of original art, which seemed random. I recognized an Escher, and another that had to be a Dali, but there was also a snowscape with a figure sitting under what appeared to be lined-up arches until a second glance revealed the play in perspective of the columns. Intriguing.

Levi carried me like I weighed nothing past a long conference room and the unmanned reception desk, his footfalls silent on the richly polished wooden floor planks.

Miles pushed open Levi's dark office doors and we entered the inner sanctum. While one wall had that same ten-million-dollar view, the opposite one contained a gorgeous mahogany bookshelf packed with books.

The furniture was all wood and leather, with a Persian rug in brilliant reds and blues taking the edge off the masculinity of the room. The sleek monitor on his desk was top of the line.

Comparing my office to his was like asking me to choose between Moriarty and a brand-new Ferrari: no matter how much sentimental value my car had, I'd choose the blinged out, fully functional version in a heartbeat.

Levi set me down on a leather sofa by the fireplace which crackled with actual wood logs which meant it had been grandfathered in, since only gas fireplaces had been allowed in Vancouver for some time. He ordered Miles to get me a juice from the staff kitchen.

While I waited, I studied the large photograph of a road running through a green landscape that hung over the mantel. The ground rose up in the center of the photo to split in half, effectively turning the road into a half-open zipper.

I snapped my fingers. "Illusions."

"What?" Levi said.

"Your art collection. It's all about illusions. Like your magic." Small talk was normal. It was easy. What was neither normal nor easy was thinking about how my magic had just eaten that thing up, how I'd orchestrated it all on instinct.

Miles returned and handed me a bottle of orange juice, lowering himself into a sturdy club chair with surprising grace. "What the hell was it?"

Levi idly set one of those desktop pendulums in motion that was the preferred stupid toy for eight out of ten executives. "Show Miles the tattoo, then start at the beginning and walk us through this."

I uncapped the bottle and chugged half of the juice back, desperate for the electrolytes. "You believe me now?"

He propped a hip against his massive wood desk that was turned around so he could watch the skyline as he worked at his large monitor, instead of facing the office door like most CEO's. I wondered if he daydreamed, staring out at the vast sky, putting aside his empire for a stolen moment or two.

"I don't know what to believe," Levi said. "One second, I thought you were attacking Miles, the next you'd speared some blurry black shadow that I hadn't even seen until your magic touched it. That I've *never* seen before." His gaze went flat and distant, but he shook himself out of it. "You say you're not a Rogue, but you sprang into action without hesitation. For all I know, you could have called that thing up in the first place."

I scrubbed a hand over my face, bone-weary. "It was instinct, not experience or training. I saved your lives tonight and I can prove it, but you'll have to hear me out."

Levi and Miles exchanged a long, wordless glance, then Levi nodded.

I told them everything, even coming clean about the Charlotte Rose case and asking for clemency for her. Might as well use my power for good. Levi promised to talk to the in-house counsel about options.

Miles examined the tattoo after I explained the circumstances of its reveal.

"I'm gonna call in Mols," he said to Levi.

"Who's that?" I placed the empty orange juice bottle on the floor.

"Tattoo artist friend of ours."

Levi steepled his finger together. "That okay with you?"

I shrugged. "If she has any insights on it, sure."

Miles fired off a text while I continued with the story up to the death at Green Thumb.

"Call them and verify it," I said. "Because whatever killed that guy and jumped into the woman was the same type of thing that flowed out of Miles. If I'd been behind it and wanted Miles dead, I wouldn't have lifted a finger to stop it and since you couldn't see it, you'd never have known it was me. Unless you think I had some other nefarious agenda in mind?"

"No," Levi said after a beat too long.

"Bite me." Levi's disbelief was this tangible weight crowding in on me. If a potential client was giving me this bullshit, I'd have been out the door and down the elevator already. I couldn't do that with a House Head, but I was damned if I didn't want to follow company policy.

"Find out if there have been any other sudden heart attack deaths." Levi instructed Miles and motioned for me to continue.

I got to my magic's appearance at the aquarium, and Miles laughed when he heard about the dildo. "That might be the greatest thing I've ever heard," he said. "Next time, take photos."

"There's not going to be a next time," Levi said.

Miles winked at me. "You could make serious bank."

My mouth almost fell open. Miles had a sense of humor? We hadn't had a lot of direct interactions since our camp days, but he'd always struck me as so serious.

I scrambled to get back on track with my story. "I can't explain why my powers didn't manifest earlier or why it's blood magic since I'm not some weird fetishist."

While there were many types of magic, they all stemmed from the same basic idea, going back to when magic had first been released in the world in the seventeenth century.

As all Canadian students learned in their magic history unit in grade eight social studies, ten Jewish men, purported to be descended from each of the Lost Tribes of Israel, had banded together in the 1600s. Ten was a symbol of good luck and power in Judaism. It was the number of commandments, the number of righteous individuals required by God in Sodom to avoid holy wrath, and the number of men (bar mitzvah'd males over the age of thirteen) to form a minyan for traditional Jewish public prayer. Women need not apply.

Being devout practitioners of Kabbalah, these men wanted to become one with the divine, or, in their terms, achieve the fifth and highest plane of the soul, Yechida. They just didn't want the years of studying it took. Like many a con, it fucked up big-time. Instead of only the ten of them achieving full union with their god, Yahweh, the magic they brought into our world as a whole was rooted in the first level of the soul, Nefesh.

Shoulda sent ten women to do the job.

"In Kabbalistic terms, Nefesh is the animal part of the soul, correct?" I said.

"Right." Levi pushed on a wooden wall panel to reveal a bar fridge filled with nothing but water bottles. Would it kill him to have Coke on tap? "Similar to Freud's idea of the Id. Impulses, basic human drives, pleasure principles. Which isn't surprising since Freud was well-versed in Kabbalistic philosophy."

Ugh. Levi was smarter than I generally gave him credit for. "Then correct me if I'm wrong." I caught the bottle of water that he tossed at me. "Boiled down, magic, like these impulses, stems from our attempt to find whatever is pleasurable and avoid that which is painful, developing through childhood. It's the instant gratification of our wants and needs, be they food, safety, love, or whatever, and it manifests in a fuckton of ways."

"Exactly," Levi said. "Though people's abilities vary according to how much they train and develop them."

"Regardless, I'm not jonsing for blood," I said. "I don't even like vampire stories." Keep your blood-sucking fiends with melanin issues; my fictional love was and always would be Holmes.

Reason, intelligence, deduction.

"Maybe not consciously," Levi said. "But did you end up having a bunch of blood transfusions back when..." He cleared his throat.

"When in my rage that Daddy Dearest had abandoned us, I went joyriding in my mom's car and totaled it? Why yes, Levi. I did have a bunch of transfusions then." I uncapped my water and took a sip to clear the bitter taste in my mouth.

"Blood would have meant life. Pretty strong desire," Levi said.

"But I was already thirteen and the magic would have taken form much earlier than that," I replied. "Not to mention, oh yeah, I didn't have any of it before yesterday."

"There are rare cases where extreme trauma influenced the magic. Changed the nature of it."

"You're not listening to me. There. Was. Zero. Magic." I squeezed the bottle so hard that water splashed out over my fingers. "Besides, other people have been in accidents. Why aren't there any other cases of blood magic?"

"Coincidence that you know that or covering something up?" Miles said.

I dried off my hand. "Professional curiosity. I'm interested in noteworthy crimes. Back in the 1980s, there was a case in London where a serial killer claimed to have blood magic. Freaked the cops right out, because they were imagining evil wizard movie crap. It turned out he didn't and he was just a sick fuck, but the press had gotten so frenzied that Nefesh historians had to squash the panic, stating there were no recorded or anecdotal cases of blood magic. Ever."

Levi slammed his hand down on his desk. The sound cracked like gunfire and I jumped. "It's magic. There aren't exceptions to how it works. You had to have been born with it. You somehow hid it and the accident changed it."

He sank into his desk chair, swiveling around to present its high back. Poor guy really wanted this in a nice package, tied up neatly with a bow.

I gentled my voice. "Think logically about this, Levi. If there are no exceptions, how come I was the only one who saw the smudge initially shoot out of Miles? It wasn't visible to either of you until my magic revealed it. I was the exception initially. There's also no way I hid magic from you all this time. I didn't conjure that thing up and you know it. Something happened in the last twenty-four hours that made me magic. I just don't know what yet."

Levi swiveled back around, swearing under his breath in Italian. I tended to forget he'd moved here from Rome as a child, since he'd lost his accent. "Was this the same thing that killed that other man?"

"Same type. Exact same entity?" I shrugged.

A petite black woman in her forties with a giant red mohawk poked her head in the door.

"Mols," Levi smiled warmly. "Come in."

Miles stood up and hugged her. Their size disparity was so huge, she all but disappeared in his embrace. Huh. I wouldn't have pegged Miles for a hugger but this wasn't sexual either. More like hugging a favored aunt.

"Hi, Mols," I said. "I'm Ash."

We shook hands. She wore long sleeves, long pants, and thin gloves. A Van Gogh.

"Can I see the tattoo?" she said. Once more, I pulled up my hair to show the Star of David and she ran her gloved finger over it, poking and prodding. "Huh."

"Is that the technical term for your findings or…" I drifted off as Mols sat down and took my hands in hers. "Why do I feel like I'm about to get a terminal diagnosis?"

"I'm a Van Gogh," she said.

"Yes, I deduced that. How is that relevant?" I looked at Miles and Levi but they appeared as confused as I was.

"You understand that I'm well-versed in creating magic art?"

Van Goghs were remarkable artists who tended to dominate whichever visual field they were in, but at the price of creating art that tortured them. Their magic, their passion, was a subset of fire magic, and the more they lost themselves in their work and created greatness, the higher the chance of them bursting into flame. Given the long sleeves and gloves, Mols had already experienced some burns. They healed faster than non-magic people, but the scars never completely left them.

I wasn't sure the cost of their magic was worth it, but they certainly produced beautiful art.

"I do," I assured her. "Why?"

"That Star of David isn't just a tattoo," she said. "And those black lines aren't ink. This star was magically burned into your skin as a ward. An incredibly powerful one. I've never seen anything like it."

Ward? Oh. One piece slotted into this puzzle. It would have had to be powerful if it had suppressed my magic. That was the only explanation that fit. I touched the tattoo. There was no scarring and everyone believed it was ink. The Van Gogh who'd done this to me must have had unrivaled precision and control.

If I'd gotten the ward as a baby that could be why I had no memory of magic, but what prompted it? Did my parents see that I had blood magic and get scared? No, I couldn't see my parents being freaked out by this. My father finding a way to use it, on the other hand? You bet.

"How old is the tattoo?" I said.

"It's hard to pinpoint because it was under your hair," Mols said. "Could have been ten years, could be thirty."

What if I'd gotten it at some later point? Where had my magic been up until then? Every new piece of information only deepened the mystery, and instead of saying something that properly summed up my curiosity, all my exhausted brain could come up with was, "I'm only twenty-eight."

Because that was the salient fact here.

"Okay." Mols held up her gloved hand. "Could be

twenty-eight years. But the ward was broken recently, wasn't it? There's a fresh scab slashed through it."

"I hit my head." And then magic filled my world.

Growing up, I'd envied kids with magic. Though I wouldn't have admitted it on pain of death. Their lives seemed filled with a promise that mine had lacked. Now it turned out that I could have had that adventure and I'd been robbed.

Where might I be now if I'd had magic all this time? *Who* might I be? A master Nefesh detective solving fascinating puzzles?

What kind of special douchecanoe took it upon themselves to deprive a kid of their future?

I jumped to my feet. "Get it off me."

Mols looked at Levi.

"It's not his body," I said. "It's mine and I want this fucking ward off me. Now!"

"You heard her," Levi said.

Sometimes the moments that changed our lives hit us with the force of a speeding car, other times they were the gentlest of tugs. Removing the tattoo took Mols mere seconds. A violent shiver rolled through me and my insides rearranged themselves like they'd been slightly off-kilter all these years.

The ward was gone and for the first time in my life, I was truly and fully myself.

"How do I find who did this?" I gripped the top of the sofa.

"I have no idea," Mols said. "I've worked with tattoos and magic for years and I wouldn't know where to begin."

"You were telling the truth." Levi stood up stiffly. "As Head of House Pacifica, may I extend my apologies? Any charges about you being Rogue will, of course, be dropped and—"

I winged my water bottle at his chest. "Fuck your

charges. Fuck your House. And most importantly, fuck you." I grabbed my shoes and bag that Miles had brought with us.

Miles stepped sideways into my path.

I pivoted sharply to face Levi, my hands balled into fists and my breath coming out in harsh rasps.

His eyes darted between Miles and me for a long moment. "She's been through enough. Let her go."

Chapter 6

Throwing the money that Talia had given me for cab fare at the bewildered taxi driver, I sprinted up the stairs to my apartment and tore the ruined dress off, kicking it into a corner before showering and slipping into my coziest fleece pajamas.

"Pri?" I whispered, pushing her door open. Careful not to trip on the dark lumps on her floor that were probably shoes, I sat down her bed.

She yawned, cracking a bleary eye open. "What time is it?"

"Really late or really early. Can I sleep here?"

She brushed a strand of hair out of my face. "Want to talk about it?"

"Not yet."

Priya pulled the covers back and I crawled in beside her. I expected to stay awake rehashing the night's events, but my friend was giving off heat like a furnace and her sheets smelled like sunshine and sleep claimed me.

She didn't push me to talk the next day, for which I was profoundly grateful.

We made coffee in comfortable silence, Priya washing

our cups as soon as we'd finished. For all that her shit was strewn everywhere, she was fanatical about staying on top of clean dishes and laundry, whereas I kept things tidy but would happily ignore dishes and laundry until circumstances became dire.

It wasn't until we'd reached our office on the outskirts of Gastown on Vancouver's Downtown Eastside and my triple shot of espresso had kicked in that I was up to the task of sharing everything that I'd gone through last night.

Cohen Investigations was part of a shared space on the second floor of a five-story walk-up heritage building with a ton of vintage charm in its exposed brick, original oak floors, and cool steel cross bracings that ran through the building, allowing it to sway in an earthquake when the Big One hit. It didn't matter that my office had a view of the alley or that the cockroaches were currently winning our ongoing war, every time I walked in, I smiled.

I was about to tell Priya everything, except who should I find waiting for me in the common reception area? Charlotte Rose.

She slouched on one of the sofas wearing some weird fuzzy cap with bunny ears, but as soon as she saw me, she jumped to her feet. "This is your fault!"

Priya raised her eyebrows at me and I shrugged. "Why don't you come into my office?"

Without waiting to see if she'd follow, I crossed into the frosted glass office door with my business name stenciled in gold.

Spaghetti western music played in my head as I sat down on my squeaky chair. Every encounter with the damn thing was a high noon showdown. I prayed the Crazy Glue held on the wonky wheel because tipping over sideways was not an experience I relished enduring a third time.

Priya set up her laptop at the IKEA desk next to mine, while Charlotte Rose took one of the moss green wingback chairs set out for clients. I didn't bother opening my ancient MacBook, snagging a pen out of the ceramic mug that said "Baker Street Boys" in order to take my preferred longhand notes.

"Meryem is missing because of you," she said. "The House took her."

A dull pounding danced a samba in my temples, leaving me with no patience for conspiracy theories. "When?"

"Yesterday. We were supposed to meet at midnight and she didn't show. She always shows. And her phone is off, which isn't like her."

"Maybe she couldn't sneak out like you did," I said.

C.R.'s lip quivered then became a sneer under those floppy bunny ears. "Forget it."

"Wait," I said as she stood up. "Sit down. I'm sorry. I had a crappy night but that's not your fault. Tell me what happened."

"Mom contacted House Pacifica last night. It put me on their radar and they took her to get back at me."

Priya subtly pushed a note across her desk. It was a drawing of the earth revolving around a little Charlotte Rose stick figure. She'd nailed the bunny ears.

I tamped down on a grin. "First of all, what did the House say?"

C.R. bit her lip. "Nothing yet. I don't think. Mom left a message. But Meryem—"

"Yeah, Meryem may be missing, but that doesn't make the House responsible. Bad shit happens."

Damn. Meryem was Nefesh so I couldn't take this case. Oh, hang on. Hell yes, I could. And I would because those smudges were out there feeding off people. I vowed to do everything possible to ensure she lived to give the finger another day.

"Give me a dollar," I said.

"Why?" Charlotte Rose said.

I rolled my eyes. Of course she wouldn't know this. And I should have known better than to entangle myself in this further but— "Just do it."

She dug around in her pocket and handed me a gold coin. A Canadian one dollar, known as a loonie after the loons depicted on them.

"There." I placed the coin on my desk. "Now you've officially retained me and have client-P.I. privilege."

"I don't have a lot to pay you, but I can give you my babysitting money."

"How about we worry about that after we find Meryem? Tell me everything you know about her."

An hour later, I had all the details about their nauseatingly cute courtship and very little useful information. Meryem didn't like to talk about her family, but C.R. confirmed she wasn't living with them. She'd been living in a youth shelter or crashing with friends.

Young, magic, and alone. A tasty meal for the modern smudge-about-town.

"Why do you think the House is experimenting on people?" I said.

"This kid at my school? His brother's friend's boyfriend was at his dealer's place when these guys showed up and took him."

Nothing like a trusted source. "What was his magic?"

Charlotte Rose frowned. "He wasn't Nefesh."

"Then why would the House want him?"

"Because they experiment on Mundanes, too."

"The boyfriend said this?"

"No. The boyfriend was found dead." She gave me one of those scathing "keep up" eye rolls.

"Of what?" I rooted around in my desk drawer for some Tylenol and dry swallowed a couple.

"Heroin overdose. But see, that's the proof. Because he

only ever smoked pot." She lowered her voice to a dramatic whisper. "It was a cover up."

I nodded sagely, pretending to write a note on my pad while really drawing a hangman.

"Who else except the House has that kind of power?" C.R. said.

That was the million-dollar question. I sighed. "I don't know, but we'll find out."

The interview wrapped up soon after.

"Did I give you enough information to find her?" C.R. turned big, worried eyes on me as I escorted her to the office door.

"Yeah. You did great." I patted her shoulder. "I'll keep you posted, okay?"

The second the door shut, I turned to Priya. "Whatcha got?"

"Meryem Orfali." Priya turned her laptop to show a school photo that was maybe a couple of years old of a girl with a shy smile wearing a headscarf. "Turkish. She came over with the other magic refugees in the big purge five years ago."

The men who had released magic into the world may have been Jewish, but they had come from countries as diverse as China, Afghanistan, France, and Russia, because by that point, the bloodlines of the original Ten Lost Tribes flowed through every race and religion. As a result, so too, did the magic.

Nowadays, magic, found in about ten percent of the global population, was pretty much everywhere with a fairly even divide between men and women.

I used the stack of unpaid bills on my desk as an elbow rest. "So what happened between then and now? Because the girl I met wasn't playing dress up. Or down, as the case may be."

Priya's fingers flew over the keyboard, her gold rings

catching the light. "Give me a bit. I need to suss out multiple sources."

During the forty-five minutes that it took Priya to amass a more detailed profile, I sent three reminder emails for payments, ate two packages of discount ramen noodles in the shared kitchen, i.e. breakfast and lunch, and disappointed Bryan, the insurance agent who rented one of the other offices, when I failed to have satisfactory answers about how Priya's aunt's dog's kneecap surgery had gone.

A rabid dog lover, Bryan looked so anxious about the animal's condition that I trudged back into my office. "How's Reeses Puppycups?"

I resented even saying the stupid name.

Priya glanced up with a wide smile. "Is Bryan asking? The vet had hoped that she could fix it by loosening the tissue on the inside of the patella, but they also had to stabilize the tibial tuberosity with pins."

I stared at her hard, then turned back to Bryan, hovering in the reception area. "The dog is fine."

He threw me a thumbs up and retreated into his office.

Priya was snickering when I came back in so I blew a raspberry at her.

"If you're quite finished demeaning the help?" she said. "According to Meryem's immigration records, she was shipped here to live with her maternal aunt and uncle, both Mundanes, when she was eleven. Aunt died about a year ago."

"Any priors on the uncle? Reports of abuse?" I sat down, dancing C.R.'s coin over my knuckles.

Priya shook her head. "No. But there is a donation record in his name to the Untainted Party."

"Fuck. I'd have gotten out of there, too." Poor girl. Even if her immediate family was still alive back in Turkey, she couldn't return home. She'd escaped a country that was fanatical against Nefesh and then lost the one person here looking out for her well-being. "What's her magic rank?"

"What was your assessment of her abilities?"

"Hmm." I considered opening the bills littering my desk. For about a second. Running my own business was no easy matter. Some days the actual casework took up the smallest fraction of my time, while the rest was a precarious balancing act to stay afloat. I didn't have the energy to navigate that today. "Coming from a country known for its persecution of Nefesh, Meryem wouldn't have been trained in her powers. And I doubt any training happened after she arrived. Not with that uncle. She did generate a good blast of wind but there was no finesse to it. More like she threw everything at the wall."

"So to speak," Priya said.

"And she didn't try again. Even factoring in the sonic weapon, a well-trained elemental could have attacked again. Two out of five. Maybe three but that would be pushing it."

"Good guess. Two." Priya closed her laptop and folded her hands. "Tell me what happened last night?"

I grabbed a handful of darts from the mounted holder and planted myself in front of the dartboard hanging on one wall. Other than a framed photo on my desk of Priya and myself in our university graduation caps and gowns, it was the only personal item in here. "We should come up with a plan for Meryem."

"We will, but you need to talk this out."

I threw my first dart and launched into my tale, picking up from when she'd dropped me off at home and taking her through the events of last night. "Essentially I have blood magic because a powerful ward on my head designed to suppress it was destroyed."

She shrugged.

"That's all I get? How about a gasp that I have magic at all? Or some pearl-clutching at it being blood magic?"

"Eh. Name one part of your history that isn't fucked up."

I blinked twice, then laughed. "Trust you to put it all into focus. Je t'adore, Adler."

Priya tossed her hair. "Mais bien sûr, Holmes. I'm extremely loveable." She grew serious. "How are you going to determine who's behind the ward?"

A couple of bills toppled off the desk and I lunged to grab them. I wasn't enough of an asshole to take C.R.'s babysitting money, but that didn't mean my grown-up responsibilities could be pushed off forever.

People viewed the world through one of two filters: trust or certainty. Trust was a shell game. That's where I came in. Life was messy and complicated and full of mysteries, large and small. *Is my husband cheating? What did she do with my grandmother's ring? Is that leg cast for real?* I got answers so that clients in the "Fool Me Once" category wouldn't get fooled again and shut down those trying to pull a fast one: be it on an insurance company or a loved one.

And yes, sometimes, the truth was hard to hear, but it was always better to know. Answers, no matter how upsetting, trumped unanswered questions because they brought closure. Answers equaled certainty.

Answers equaled control.

It wasn't altruism. Humanity sucked, but not everyone deserved what they got. I loved sniffing out clues and methodically putting the pieces together until the full picture was revealed, and if my skills eased someone's anxiety, then win-win.

Speaking of, if I didn't ease some well-paying anxiety soon, I was hooped.

Sighing, I sat down at my desk and straightened the pile. "First let's focus on Meryem. We'll take a two-pronged approach. If you—"

The office door opened and Levi strode through like he owned the place, wearing an exquisitely tailored wool coat, a leather briefcase in one hand and a dry cleaning bag dangling from the fingertips of his other.

I bristled. "We're closed."

"Good." He sat down across from me. "We won't be disturbed. Hey, Priya."

"Levi," she said coolly.

He grinned at her, his blue eyes sparkling with mischief as he shrugged out of his coat. "Should I expect payback for arresting Ash?"

"When you least expect it. Yes."

"Duly noted." Levi handed me the bag. "You left this behind at the Aquarium and as they aren't in the second-hand clothing business, I took it upon myself to retrieve it. You're welcome."

I smoothed out the plastic-wrapped wool trench coat and hung it off my chair. "Thank you, Mr. Montefiore, for your overwhelming benevolence. Now if that's everything?"

"Not by a long shot." He opened the briefcase and handed me a manila envelope. "Papers. Sign them."

"Is our divorce final? At last." I pulled the documents out and scanned them. "Registration forms," I said in a flat voice.

Levi chucked me a Montblanc pen. It hit me in the chest and bounced onto my desk. "Brilliant powers of deduction."

I scribbled my signature on the damn documents because legally I had no choice in becoming part of House Pacifica, then thrust them back at him, along with his rich dude cliché pen. Levi may have thought he was bringing me under his control, but he'd just ensured that any Nefesh case was mine for the taking. I almost threw a victory sign. "We done?"

"No. I want to hire you."

Fat gold dollar signs danced around his head, but I kept my cool and leaned back in my chair, which creaked disturbingly. "Hire one of your lackeys."

"This is a sensitive job."

"And you trust *me* with it?" If my eyebrows shot any higher they'd have liftoff.

"Least of all. But your skill set makes you uniquely qualified."

Ah. He wanted me to investigate the smudge. This could be huge. Except he was going about it in his typical high-handed way. Let him work for it.

"Give me another backhanded compliment, baby. I get all shivery."

Levi removed a small white bakery box from the briefcase and slid it across my desk. "A peace offering."

I opened the lid. A jelly doughnut.

"Only one?" Priya said.

"I didn't know you'd be here."

"Uh-huh," she said snippily and left the room.

Ooh, Levi was going to pay so badly. Even he looked concerned.

"You think a jelly doughnut is going to smooth things over?" I said.

"They're your favorite."

"Says who?" I mean, yeah, they totally were, but how did he know that? Was he stalking me?

He held out his hand to show me the tiny silver scar at the base of his thumb. "The fact you stabbed me with a fork when we were sixteen to get the last one."

"Youthful exuberance. That still does nothing to convince me I should work for you. Or what this case even is."

"Destroy those smudges and find whatever or whoever is causing them."

"Why me?"

"Because you're the only one who can see them." Called it. "I don't want to cause mass panic by asking around if anyone else can. The situation is delicate and I don't want

76

knowledge of smudges going beyond you, me, and Miles, for now. And Priya, obviously."

"Took you long enough to believe me."

"I believe you aren't responsible for those things. Hence why I'm here." He loosened his death grip on his briefcase.

"You hate this, don't you? All your Nefesh cops and security and you need me." I couldn't have stopped my smirk for all the money in the world.

He flexed his hands against my desk. "Yes or no?"

I grinned at him. "Say 'I need you, Ash. Your investigative skills are unparalleled and your magic puts mine to shame.'"

"This is the opportunity of your lifetime."

True, but by his own admission, there was no one else he could turn to. If Levi wanted my skills, he could admit my competence instead of acting like I was doing him a favor with my magic party trick. "I'm full up. Too bad. So sad."

Levi stuffed the documents in his briefcase. "This is all a game, isn't it? All about how clever you are to solve your cases. Well, this isn't about puzzles, it's about people and the fact that something out there is preying on them. But I guess you'd have to respect and care about them to understand that."

"You are so out of line." I toyed with one of my darts, resisting the urge to nail him with it. "I care about people enough to do everything to give them the truth. To give *all* people answers and closure and assistance, where your so-called caring only exists for Nefesh. And if you want to talk about respect, I haven't seen a whole hell of a lot from you over the years. Don't know if it's 'cause you pegged me as the weird fucked-up kid and never got past that or I was Mundane or what. But you've judged me at every turn."

I threw the dart across the room. It bullseyed into the board with a satisfying thunk. "You want respect from me? Earn it."

Our silence was charged with a tension so thick, the air practically crackled with it.

I took a breath.

And then three more.

Levi was insufferable, but I couldn't fault him for caring about his people. Maybe he'd come to the same conclusion about me.

"I—" The two of us spoke at the same time. I motioned for him to go first.

"If you take this case to help the Nefesh community, *our* community," he said, "I promise to treat you with the courtesy and respect you deserve."

Priya returned with a steaming mug of coffee, her eyebrows raised at Levi's words. She sat back down at her laptop, not even pretending to work. She sipped her drink and watched us like we were a mildly interesting movie trailer.

"Who would I report to?" I said.

"Me."

Working directly for Levi. That oughta be interesting.

Nefesh had kept their abilities hidden for the first several hundred years. Witch hunt was an understatement. Not only was anyone suspected of having magic rounded up, tortured, and killed in gruesome ways, they took out the entire family for good measure. Eventually in the late 1800s the first Houses in Europe were founded. As a young country, Canada didn't get Houses until after WWI. House Pacifica's rule originally only included British Columbia, but during the latter part of the twentieth century, it expanded to include the Yukon, the Northwest Territories, and Nunavut, once that province was created in 1999.

Levi expanded it further in the first couple years of his leadership. He folded the weak House that governed Nefesh in the prairie provinces into House Pacifica, extending its rule from the west coast all the way to the Ontario border, where House Ontario took over, which ruled both Ontario and the maritime provinces. The third and final House in Canada was Maison de Champlain in Montreal, named after Québec's founder, Samuel de Champlain. It governed all of Québec.

Geographically speaking, Levi was Head of most of the country, though he acted like he ruled the world.

Could I expense "body bag" as a line item?

"Let me be clear," I said. "I am not your lackey or your employee. I am a free agent and not at your beck and call." Modeling for Priya how to set boundaries.

He spread his thumb and forefinger slightly apart. "Little bit, you are."

Pri smirked at me.

"Also, you're going to train with me," Levi said.

"Excuse me? No deal." I wasn't going to take a pounding from him on a regular basis. Argh. Phrasing!

"No? Call up your magic. Right here. Right now."

"Okay, well. It requires blood." I found a safety pin in my drawer and half-heartedly poked at my skin. Grimacing, I tried again. And again.

"I'm embarrassed for you." Priya dug a letter opener out of her drawer. "Want me to try?"

"Hush you. Aha." I managed the tiniest pin prick and then thought really hard at the drop of blood.

Nothing happened.

"The training is non-negotiable." Levi put on his coat. "You've got powerful magic and no clue how to consciously control it. You hurt an innocent person and House Pacifica is on the line. Therefore, as the most powerful person in my House and the most capable of handling anything that goes sideways, I'll train you."

I opened a new tab on my computer, typed something in and spun it around to him. "Here. The definition of 'respect,' since you're failing out of the gate."

"I don't want anything to happen to you either which is why I will personally oversee your training. Better?"

"Marginally."

"That's another thing. Don't tell anyone about your magic," he said. "Right now, it's our element of surprise. I don't want to blow that."

"I signed the papers. My magic is going to be part of the House records as soon as one of your inspectors verifies it and determines how powerful I am."

"And isn't it too bad that the registration department has been swamped with a weeks-long backlog to process and who knows when that might happen?"

"Playing fast and loose with the rules? That's so unlike you."

"I do what I have to in order to protect my community. You in or not?"

"Fine. I'll take the case."

We shook on it.

"I'll see you at HQ this evening at 8PM. And don't be late." Levi threw me a shark's smile and gathered up his briefcase. "Welcome to House Pacifica."

Chapter 7

After sharing half of the jelly doughnut with Priya, I set her searching for all missing persons' records in the past six months across the country. If a pattern emerged, I could cross-check it against Nefesh heart attack victims and see if there was a conclusive tie.

Talia had left me a message saying that she saw me run out of the gala last night, that my entire behavior had been aberrant, and to call her. Fun as that sounded, my masochism quota for the day was filled by tonight's training session.

I headed over to the youth shelter where Meryem stayed semi-regularly. It was a short walk away from the office, located in a drab concrete building in a part of the Downtown Eastside that had yet to feel the effects of gentrification.

The bright sunflower mural that greeted me inside the front doors didn't make up for the eye-watering stench of burned coffee and wet dog. It was great that shelters like this existed and far better for the kids to be here than sleeping on the streets, but the line between this and slipping through the cracks once and for all was too damn thin.

The harried workers had little time to speak to me. Meryem had barely been missing a day, which in this world didn't qualify as missing at all. These kids often weren't seen for weeks at a time, plus this population was quite transient. I gave them my card and asked them to call if they heard anything.

The few kids hanging around the lounge eyed me suspiciously. I'd get no traction there.

I headed outside, looking around for the smoker's hangout and some possibly more receptive—or bribable—kids, when I found something better: a small skatepark located a block over.

Vancouver had a fair number of these scattered around the city, though there wasn't much to this one, only a couple of small skate bowls. Ignoring the riders pulling out their best moves, I scanned the edges of the park for a potential informant.

A kid squatted by a flight of stairs, a can of spray paint in hand. She had a partially shaved head, a short, stubby ponytail, and a giant Anarchy symbol sewn on her coat. Seemed like the kind of person who Meryem "Fuck the patriarchy" Orfali would be friends with.

I ambled over to her, watching her tag the stairs. "Malice in Wonderland. Clever."

She filled in one edge, not bothering to look at me. "Fuck off."

"I'm looking for my sister. Meryem Orfali. You know her?"

She stiffened, almost imperceptibly. "Nope."

I squatted down next to her. "I get the whole freedom of expression angle and making art, but graffiti isn't a victimless crime. It attracts other kinds of crime, makes residents feel unsafe, reduces property values, and drains tax dollars in clean up. It's also considered property vandalism under Canadian law."

She faced me for the first time. "What's your point?"

I held out my hand for the can.

Scowling, she shoved it at me.

I shook the can, smiling at the familiar rattling sound. "Rusto fat cap, huh? You do a lot of bombing?"

Her eyes practically bugged out of her head. "Uh, yeah. It's a pretty good nozzle for thickness and coverage."

"Quicker fill-in, gets some nice flare on lettering." I depressed the tip, falling back into the flow and strokes like I'd done this yesterday and not years ago. The fumes were both nauseating and comforting. "For me, it was about putting my mark on something. Leaving evidence that I existed."

Everything I'd said about graffiti's negative effects was true, and if I was caught, it could affect my P.I. license, but there were no cops around, and at the moment, the only thing concerning me was Meryem. If doing this got me my first lead, I'd risk it, because my gut was telling me that my missing person and these smudges were linked.

Besides, Levi could hire Graffiti Busters to remove this.

The rattle can was an extension of my hand, the letters blossoming into life.

"For me, it's about leaving a message for someone else to know that they aren't alone out there," the girl said quietly.

"That too. I'd see someone's tag and it was like getting a signal. So I'd answer back. Kind of a 'hey, I'm out here.'" I lowered the can, nodding in satisfaction at my work: Baskervillain. The tag I'd gone by in my teens. A bit on the nose for a raging adolescent, perhaps, but subtlety was wasted on the young. This tag was a vast improvement over those first shaky ones and I puffed up at the form and ability that I displayed even after all this time.

But there was sorrow in viewing my work as well.

Tagging had been my way to connect to others in my dark years. I wasn't sure how successful I'd been, because that anger and hollowness had lasted a long time, and maybe it never entirely went away. I was so lost in my thoughts I missed what the girl said.

"Sorry?"

"Meryem," she said. "Are you really her sister?"

I shook my head. "I'm a P.I. Name's Ashira."

"Rebel."

"Hey, Rebel. Good to meet you. I'm helping Charlotte Rose find her. She's Meryem's girlfriend."

"The princess." She shrugged. "Though she really cares about Mer."

We sat down on a patch of grass, the spray can on its side between us.

"Did you see her last night?" I asked.

"Yeah. A bunch of us were hanging out here. Mer was killing time before she had to meet Charlotte Rose. Then this guy showed up. He was..." She frowned, struggling for the right word.

I gave her time, watching two dudes try and ride the rails, and wincing at their spectacular wipeouts. The sound of wheels over concrete was a soothing white noise. I'd never ridden myself, not with my leg, but I'd spent a lot of time in parks like this one.

"Intense," Rebel finally said. "I'm used to dealing with pervs and druggies, but this guy was super focused. And he had a weird purple birthmark under his eye. Super creepsville."

"What was he doing?"

"I dunno. Handing out flyers."

"For what?"

"All-ages after-hours party he invited us to."

"Did you go?" I said.

"Nah. We were chilling here." She pulled a crumpled piece of paper from her jacket and handed it to me.

The flyer was written in crude marker and poorly photocopied. The only interesting part of it was a heart with a crown and scepter next to the words Queen of Hearts Productions.

"Was he ever around before?

Rebel shredded a few blades of grass. "Couple weeks ago? Pushing another party."

"Anyone take him up on his offer?"

"I think Gabe did. Not sure. I haven't seen him around since then."

"Gabe usually pull disappearing stunts?"

She popped the lid on her spray paint can and shoved it in her pocket. "I'm not his babysitter."

I waved a toonie, a Canadian two dollar coin, so that its edges glinted in the sunlight. Rebel's eyes flicked to it. That's right, look at the shiny and answer my questions. "How soon after Birthmark Man was here did Meryem leave?"

"About twenty minutes?"

Easy enough for him to have stuck around waiting for one of them to peel off on their own. His presence could be a coincidence, but I didn't believe in coincidences when something bad was going down. Not coupled with Rebel's sense of him and that rumor of Charlotte Rose's about the pot-smoker being snatched. It could be an urban legend, but what if there was a grain of truth to it?

"You really think she's missing?" Rebel said.

"I hope not. But if she is, I'll find her."

After I bought Rebel a hot meal, and snapped a photo of Baskervillain which I sent to Priya along with the message "amazed I didn't choke on my own sense of cool," I grabbed Moriarty and drove over to the party space, which was a glorified term for this rundown warehouse. Oddly, the lot was surrounded by security fencing with signs proclaiming that the grounds were patrolled twenty-four hours a day.

What was in here?

I strolled casually around the block sussing out any

85

cameras. There weren't any, though there was a freakishly tall guy in a jacket with West Coast Security emblazoned on the back. I couldn't see his face, because his baseball cap was pulled low, but given his rigid stance, I'd bet he was ex-military.

Curious and curiouser.

Since I didn't want to attract attention, I crossed the street to the grimy convenience store selling long distance phone cards and bongs, spending long enough browsing the chips display to note that the guard completed one circuit, including a walkthrough of the warehouse, every six minutes.

What a yawn-fest of a job.

As soon as the guard began the loop once more, I scaled the fence on the opposite side of the building in the alley, a three minute timer on my phone running. Half the loop. My leg barely even tweaked climbing the chain fence thanks to the summer I'd spent breaking in to an outdoor public pool after hours.

By the time I hobbled across the yard to the back door of the warehouse, I was down to thirty seconds. The guard would be rounding the corner any second now.

I tugged on the warehouse door but it was locked, so I ducked behind a particularly odiferous dumpster, the hand that was clamped over my mouth and nose a futile gesture.

Seconds later, there was the jangle of keys and the creak of hinges. I waited until the last second to catch the door before it locked. Holding myself still until I heard the faint slam of the front warehouse door moments later, I slipped into the dim interior.

Spent glow sticks and discarded water bottles littered the floor with a couple of sagging couches in one corner. Between them and the grimy bathroom, they promised an interesting variety of STIs. I quickly moved to the small office with some battered office furniture. It didn't contain a computer and the top drawer only had paper clips and a couple of loose orange wristband tickets. Printed on them was "A Night in Hedon," with an H in a circle.

It teased out a half-buried memory of one of my parents' rare fights. I'd been hiding in the shadows on the stairs outside my bedroom, listening to my father convince my mother that this trip to Hedon was absolutely necessary.

Mom had protested that it was too dangerous, but had finally acquiesced. Dad had come back missing a rib and Mom had given him the "told you so" silent treatment for a week. One thing about Dad, he could have gotten his way right from the start but he never used his Charmer magic on either of us.

I stilled. What if he had? Was he simply a Charmer running petty cons, or did he charm us into believing that's all he was doing because there was something bigger at stake, like my magic? Was that why he'd disappeared? Was it because of me?

He wasn't here to ask and now wasn't the time to spiral out in guilt.

I blinked myself out of my stupor.

That had been the first time I ever heard of the Nefesh black market, but it wouldn't be the last. Now it was my turn to visit Hedon and connect the dots between these parties and the black market itself. They could be merely borrowing the catchy name, but I doubted it.

A door slammed. Shit. The guard was back. Jamming the wristband into my pocket along with the flyer, I hid behind the office door, praying he wouldn't come in and find me. His footsteps grew louder and louder, his boot heels echoing off walls.

Did my breathing always sound like Darth Vadar's?

The footsteps paused directly outside the room.

I peeked out through the crack in the doorframe and stuffed my fist in my mouth to stifle a scream. Not only was he taller than I'd pegged—almost seven feet—the guard's face was all wrong. His features were simplistic carvings in a clay face.

I fumbled for the switchblade in my pocket. Flicking it open, I pushed up my sleeve and nicked my forearm. Icy sweat trickled down my spine and I was assaulted with doubts of my ability to call my magic, but with the first bead of blood, I channeled my fear into a wordless command.

Nothing happened.

The guard pressed his abnormal face to the crack in the doorframe.

Swallowing hard, I pressed back out of his sight, weak with relief when the magic rose fast and furious inside of me.

With absolutely zero telegraphing, which was massively rude of him, the guard ripped the door off the hinges and grabbed me around the throat with his clay fist.

My brain stumbled on how smooth and glossy his fingers were. Also on the lack of oxygen. Stabbing him did nothing except score some marks on his clay skin.

The thing stared at me with a disquieting lack of interest and squeezed my windpipe harder.

The world tunneled down to black pinpricks; my lungs burned. I scrabbled on tiptoe against the ground and, fighting to stay conscious, pried his fingers off my throat.

A shaft of pain blazed up my injured leg when he dropped me, but I grabbed the discarded door and hurled it at him, loving this enhanced strength. The corner embedded right in his schnozz and I used the precious few seconds while he tugged it free to get a head start.

My magic hadn't done shit for my speed, but I stayed a few feet ahead of the lumbering ape, though my shoulder blades prickled like mad and I tensed, bracing for another grab. I bolted out the back door and hurled myself over the fence, not stopping until I was safely inside Moriarty with all the doors locked.

My leg was screaming at me but it hadn't given out and I was still alive. The best possible outcome. I popped some painkillers, then sat there, phone in hand, hesitant to search the net. Either there'd be no results matching what I'd seen, in which case I was going to feel incredibly foolish for imagining things or…

There were almost one hundred and fifty million search results for "living clay man." I hit pay dirt on the eighth one.

A golem. I had seen a freaking golem.

How? And why? And most especially, what the fuck? Of all the things that had happened to me in the past couple of days, this was the one that broke my brain.

I checked my throat in the rearview mirror to find it was a mass of bruising. Where was super healing when I needed it? Pulling up the collar of my leather jacket like some throwback late 00's preppy and artfully arranging my hair hid the damage, but damn. Golems, really?

One thing was certain, there was no way I was going to Hedon after that reality up-ender. I wanted an errand that was familiar. Predictable.

Vancouver General Hospital was a sprawling complex in midtown Vancouver, and despite the excellent care provided there, being on the campus always made me feel like I couldn't breathe.

This place was too tied to both the physical pain from the crash and the emotional pain that had driven me to it. Maybe if Priya had a kid one day, I'd manage to get through the front doors without bile rising in my throat at the smell of disinfectant and baked-in food. As always, as soon as I walked inside the main tower, my skin went clammy and my ears rang with the shouts of nurses racing me down a hallway, the lights a blur from my concussion and blood in my eyes, before I'd fallen into a coma.

Just because VGH was safe and predictable didn't mean it was easy for me to return there, but one way or another, this visit would provide a clearer timeframe for when I'd been tattooed.

I took a steadying breath and went to find my former surgeon.

His booming laugh reached me before I found him at the nurse's station in the Intensive Care Unit.

I cleared my throat. "Dr. Zhang?"

He looked over with a polite smile that turned to genuine affection when he recognized me. "The Girl Who Lived."

"Hey, Doc. Still telling the same old jokes?"

The nurse, who was too young to have been there back in my time, nodded good-naturedly, and Dr. Zhang huffed. He'd shrunk since I'd seen him, but the intelligence and compassion in his eyes hadn't dimmed a whit.

"Can we talk?" I said. "I won't take up too much of your time."

"You already took up too much of my time when you were thirteen."

He escorted me out of the ward, which had been renovated in the passing years. The horrible yellow had been replaced by a soft cream, the entire space far less institutional than it had been.

It didn't put me at ease.

"What did I tell you when you were discharged?" he said.

"That you never wanted to see me again."

"Yet, here you are." He spread his hands wide. "Still stubborn."

I smiled. "I prefer tenacious."

His eyebrows rose. "Oh ho. Who got herself a fancy vocabulary? You fulfill those Sherlock Holmes dreams of yours?"

"Trying to. I started my own private investigation business."

"Good for you." He pulled a key ring out of his doctor's coat and unlocked his office door, motioning for me to take a seat.

It was small, cramped, and filled with photos of patients. Every single one of us had to take a picture with him with both of us wearing fake mustaches. Mine was still pinned to the same top corner of his corkboard. Stupid though it had been, I'd rocked that Luigi 'stache.

My stomach twisted. Don't let it have been him.

Dr. Zhang sat down behind his desk, his fingers folded primly. "How can I help you?"

I gave him the condensed version of the tattoo cover story, and yes, he stared at me like I'd lost my mind. Good thing I didn't mention the golem.

"Crashing a car into a wall wasn't exciting enough for you? Decided to add some other bizarre life goals?"

"Well, business is slow so I'm trying a new strategy," I said. "You and I do a little under-the-table deal for chloroform. We dose up rich targets, I'll get a shady artist to ink them, then bam! I offer my services to track down who did it. Thought I'd perfect the workflow on myself first. Whatddya think?"

"Needs improvement." He called up my file, studying the screen. "I don't personally remember any tattoo, but I was more focused on your leg."

"It was under my hair. Could it have been missed?"

He dug deeper into my medical records and shook his head. "There was trauma and some burns on the back of your scalp. It was thoroughly examined while we treated you and would have been noted down. Sorry I couldn't be of more help."

Between the blood transfusions in emergency on the way to the operating room, the orthopedic surgery to put the rods in my leg, my brief coma, and all the post-op care in the ward for a week and a half afterward, I'd been pretty out of it. But if there was no mention of a tattoo when I'd been brought in, then my stay at VGH was the most logical time for the ward to have been burned on without me noticing.

Much as it felt like a knife to my heart, I couldn't cross Dr. Zhang off as a suspect, but I could cross off my father and that made up for a hell of a lot. I hadn't had the ward or my magic prior to the accident and Dad was gone by that point. It didn't lessen his betrayal in leaving us, but it didn't compound it into emotional devastation, either.

"This was very useful," I said. "Thank you."

"Good. Now get out of here and don't let me see you again." He gave me a lollipop and ushered me out.

Orange lollipops were the bomb. I called Priya on my way back to Moriarty. "Anything on your end?"

"No," she said. "The search is a bust. No pattern to any missing person reports and if kids like Meryem are being targeted, there might not be anyone to file a report for them. Hang on. My latte is up."

"Where are you?"

"Higher Ground. I craved one of their cinnamon buns and they have the tall tables that are perfect to work at. What did you find?"

"Maybe a lead with some company called Queen of Hearts Productions. They're throwing all-ages after-hours parties. Could be using these smudges on marginalized teens, testing for something. We need to know what these things do, other than kill people when they jump." I bit into the candy, the sweet orange flavor crunching between my teeth.

"The parties would be a good ruse to lure them in," Priya said.

I left out the golem part of my day because there was no reason to upset Priya. Let her continue to live in her "ignorance is bliss" bubble. I sure as shit would have liked to.

"Since the missing persons thing is a bust, can I please

get you on something else?" My visit may not have provided clarity on Dr. Zhang's innocence, but there had been enough of a hands-on examination of me when I was rushed to the hospital that the ward wouldn't have been missed. "I've got a timeframe of just under two weeks when I could have been warded. Three days of coma and then all the post-op recovery. Someone must have noticed my magic and then brought in this mystery tattoo artist. Find my patient record and get a list of names of everyone involved in my care."

"What I am looking for?"

"Signs of guilt or complicity. Calling in sick during that period. Complaints from other staff about their behavior. Anyone who unexpectedly quit or asked to be transferred. And… start with Dr. Zhang. We'll go from there. I'll be home after my training session."

Priya cackled. "Getting all sweaty and grapply with Levi. Have fun."

She hung up, both getting in the last word and putting that image in my head. I licked the final bit of lollipop, weighing my fundamentally anti-social tendencies against the benefits of breaking in a new best friend.

Bah. She could stay, but on a probationary basis. I pulled out my car keys, then dropped them with a curse because they were burning hot. No, it wasn't the metal, it was me. Heat poured off red, blistering skin. "Fucking fuck balls!"

My earlier cut burst open, blood beading on my arm.

Tapping into a primal desire to not become Crispy, the eighth dwarf, I smeared the blood on my skin like a salve. I felt incredibly foolish and didn't really expect this spur of the moment idea to work, but it not only repelled whatever magic I'd been hit with, it slithered over me like a shield. Not a cool shield that looked like body armor, mind you. No, mine was exactly what you'd expect from being slathered in blood: sticky, smelly disgustingness.

Plus, leaves and pollen were starting to stick to me, so

now I looked like the serial killer version of Pigpen. Swipe right for me.

I advanced on my assailant. Bald and wrinkly, I'd have placed his age somewhere in his seventies though with every inch of exposed skin covered in tattoos, unless I read them like tree rings, it was hard to get an exact number. "My mystery Van Gogh, I presume."

He tackled me, grabbing my skull to keep it still. The skin on the back of my head where the tattoo had been, suddenly warmed and tingled. The fucker was trying to burn another ward into me.

"Oh, no, you don't." I elbowed him in the throat as hard as I could.

Coughing, he fell off of me. "They'll kill me if they find out I betrayed them," he wheezed. "But it wasn't my fault. The magic was too compelling. I couldn't refuse."

"Who will? What magic? Mine? What are you talking about?"

"If they find out about you, they'll know I did it." He burned a diagonal line on me. The first line of the Star of David.

My blood shield should have stopped any further warding, but I was tapped out and it had gotten patchy. Unable to hold his magic at bay any longer, I pressed the button of the sonic weapon still in my pocket. Work smart, not hard.

He slapped his hands over his ears, his magic assault on me abruptly stopping.

I dug my knee into his back. "Answer my questions."

He refused to talk, so I cuffed him with my handy magic suppressors that hung from my belt loops, which I'd brought along in case of any trouble with the Nefesh youth when I'd been asking about Meryem. Then I frog-marched him into Moriarty's passenger seat.

This blood powers asshattery needed an instruction manual because it took me five minutes and a whole bunch of straining noises that sounded too much like taking a shit to make the shield disappear. I wiped myself off as best I could with most of a package of baby wipes, then scrabbled at my glove compartment for the box of chocolate-covered almonds and a stick of stale beef jerky left over from a stakeout last year. Expiration dates were only a suggestion, right?

I devoured all of it in a rush, my lightheadedness only slightly abating. Blood loss sucked. "Ready to talk yet?"

The Van Gogh stared stubbornly out the window.

Where could I stash him? I only had a half hour until Levi expected me. Ooh. Levi's charming jail cells.

First things first. If I didn't eat something more substantial, Levi and I weren't both coming out of our training session alive. I stopped by one of the Japadog carts, home of Vancouver's famous Japanese hot dogs, and ordered two of their signature dogs with teriyaki sauce, mayo, and seaweed. I scarfed the first one down right then and there, taking the second with me in a white to-go bag.

The Van Gogh didn't get one. Men who assaulted me were not fed in thanks. I left him in the car. With the windows rolled up.

The beefy security guard manning the desk in the lobby of House Pacifica could only have looked less welcoming if I'd had leprosy and was dropping diseased body parts.

Sure, my hair was a mess but I'd hidden the bruising. His attitude was uncalled for.

I crossed the gleaming marble floor inlaid with a black "HP." Sadly this was no Hogwarts, though I'd bet the guard was Slytherin all the way.

"I'm here to see Levi." I glanced over at the glass doors to the central Nefesh police department across the lobby but didn't see any of the asshole cops I'd had the misfortune to run into over my career.

"Is Mr. Montefiore expecting you?" the security guard

said. His eyes darted out toward the building's front door, his fingers tapping a rapid staccato on the desk. There was a rectangular bulge in his shirt pocket. Past your smoke break, dude?

"Standing weekly appointment." I leaned on the desk. "You ever try rope play? Big guy like you, probably carry a lot of tension. Takes a bit of getting used to but the high works wonders. Pure bliss."

He turned florid. "Mr. Montefiore would never—"

I tsked him. "Don't yuck someone's yum. And I never said he did. Because if hypothetically I was a dominatrix here to do a little Mary Poppins and bondage, I'd certainly never be unprofessional enough to disclose that fact."

Hard to say if it was the guard practically choking on his tongue, the prickling feeling between my shoulder blades, or the hand clamping down on my shoulder that first alerted me to Levi's presence.

The security guard snapped out a salute. "Evening, Mr. Montefiore."

Kiss ass.

"Hi, Evan. Sorry about her. I'll take it from here," Levi said.

"Seriously, dude," I said to Evan. "Rope play. Think about it."

Levi was already manhandling me toward the elevators, so I threw a wink over my shoulder at the guard.

He mouthed the words "House Cat" at me. Uh, okay?

I was about to demand clarification, but the elevator door slid shut, sealing me in with grumpypants, and the moment was lost.

Chapter 8

Before Levi could hit the button for the seventh floor, I pushed P2 where I was parked. The one floor available for guest parking. "Quick detour."

A muscle ticked in his jaw. "Do you have any filter whatsoever?"

"Where you're concerned?" I laughed. "Oh, that wasn't a rhetorical question. Then no. Hot dog?" I offered Levi the bag which, in the least shocking move of the century, he smacked away with long, uncalloused fingers. They weren't soft, though. His hands projected strength and capability, as did the firm line of his shoulders. This was a man who handled the problems laid at his door.

I mentally slapped myself. Or his hands were just hands. Hands that had, not ten seconds ago, visited harm upon my peace offering.

"No need to damage the wiener, bud." I took it out of the bag. Why waste a perfectly good Japadog?

"You told a member of my staff that you were my dominatrix. Do you understand how unprofessional that is?"

"First of all," I said around a mouthful of delicious teriyaki meat, "I only hypothetically said it. And second, you're paying me to get results on this smudge. You want me to change my behavior toward you, that's a whole other negotiation. One you can't win."

Levi stuffed his hands in the pant pockets of today's expensive suit and rocked back on his heels. "Bet I could."

"Your competitive streak requires an intervention. We've discussed this sickness of yours. It doesn't lead anywhere good." I finished the dog and wiped my hands on the bag, earning a grimace from Levi. "Someone may be using raves to lure marginalized youth with possible ulterior motives connected to the smudge. I'm looking into it."

"Anything comes of it, let me know. Immediately."

"Aye, aye, captain."

The elevator doors slid open, depositing us in the surprisingly well-lit parking garage.

I led Levi to my car and flung the passenger side open. The still-cuffed Van Gogh glared balefully at us.

"I brought you a present," I said.

"Looks like you regifted."

I pinched his cheek. "Humor, Leviticus? I'm all verklempt. My little boy is a man."

"What's his connection to the smudges?"

"Nada. This is the Van Gogh that tattooed me."

"Not my problem," Levi said.

"I can't exactly bring him home. Hold him in one of your jail cells."

The Van Gogh mumbled something behind the duct tape sealing his mouth so I ripped it off. As painfully as possible.

"You can't throw me in a cell," the Van Gogh said.

"Sure, we can. You assaulted me and I'm pressing charges. Book 'em, Danno." I moved my hair aside to show the bruising. It was a great visual. The golem had come in handy.

Levi stilled.

"I didn't—" the Van Gogh protested, but he was cut off by Levi none-too-gently hauling him to his feet.

"Enough." Levi's tone was sharp enough to cut. He was handling the problem I'd laid at his door with a menacing edge. I kind of wanted to tease out this aspect of his personality and see how deep his darkness ran.

But that would have been unprofessional.

We left the Van Gogh with the cops and I gave my statement, playing up my fear as a poor Mundane victimized by this random act of violence.

My luck held in that the cop that assisted me was a stranger, and thus, sympathetic to my complaint, if confused about why Levi hovered over me, tapping his foot impatiently the entire time. I barely got to finish signing the statement before His Lordship dragged me into the elevator.

He hit the button with more force than necessary. "Are we quite finished with all your personal business? Can we return to the case you were actually hired for?"

"What's got you so touchy?" I said. "That senior citizen is a menace. He assaulted me and could harm other Nefesh. I'm doing a public service by letting him stew in jail for a couple nights. Then, when he's cooled off or freaked out, either works, I'll have a heart-to-heart and listen to the little canary sing."

"I've had to rearrange my plans due to the delay." Levi stepped into the open elevator.

"Poor baby. You pushed a booty call? I'm happy to cancel my training so you can go have your regularly scheduled sex. I am a giver, after all."

Levi reached across me to hit a button, and I swear given how close his elbow came to my face, he'd considered jabbing me. "I pushed an important meeting. You're a pain in the ass and until you can control your magic, you're also a thousand times more dangerous than that Van Gogh."

"High praise indeed."

Levi pinched the bridge of his nose, but the doors opened on the seventh floor and he pasted on a bland expression because there were still a fair number of employees working late.

"Do you keep standard slave driver conditions?" I rearranged my hair to once again hide the bruises. "Five minute pee breaks every twenty-four hours?"

"Of course not. No breaks and I toss the bodies when I've milked every ounce of work out of them."

A middle-aged man stuck his head out of his office door, his face suffused with relief. "Levi, thank you so much for getting Melinda in to see that cardiologist so fast. They told us it would be six months for an appointment."

Levi clapped him on the shoulder. "She'll beat this."

The man lit up in fervent adoration. "Yeah, she will. Thanks to you."

As we walked away, I gagged. "Levi Montefiore, the good and benevolent."

"Don't forget universally beloved."

"Ever considered that there's a fine line between 'Levi' and 'evil' and you're trying too hard to prove otherwise?"

"At least I try."

"Levi, hold up." The same man jogged over to us. "Forgot to tell you that the Attorney General can't meet later. I rescheduled us for tomorrow."

The Honorable Troy Grant, of Musqueam heritage, was widely touted as the front runner to lead the Liberal Party in the next federal election. If he won, he'd be our first Nefesh Prime Minister, joining leaders like those in Britain, Japan, Mexico, and New Zealand, to name a few. Vancouver lay on the unceded territories of the Musqueam, Squamish, and Tsleil-Waututh First Nations and it made sense for Levi to strengthen ties with this influential politician, but I'd never been witness to him engaging in the same types of power schmoozing I associated with Talia.

How did Levi win people over? Did he lay out methodical and irrefutable arguments? Did he engage in a delicate dance of charm and negotiation? He didn't have a reputation for bullying people to get his way, our contentious acquaintanceship notwithstanding.

My curiosity stemmed solely from having to work with him.

"Problem?" Levi said.

"Huh?" I said.

"You were frowning at me."

I shook my head, motioning for him to continue.

Levi shot me a suspicious look before turning to his employee. "Make sure Troy's been briefed on Mr. Abel's upcoming parole hearing because his entire case was badly mishandled and he deserves to have the facts re-examined free from Mundane bias."

"On it." The man walked away.

Levi was righting an injustice, I was the reason his meeting got pushed, and I was bitching about him helping me. Way to look like an asshole, Cohen.

"Where are your workout clothes?" Levi pressed his hand to a scanner to unlatch a security door, then steered me inside to the private gym for him and the executives who worked on this floor.

"Do I look like I work out? Wait, don't answer that. We're only training my magic, which does not involve sweating."

The room was the size of a small school gymnasium with basketball hoops and a number of stationary bikes set up in one corner. A set of open blue doors led to an equipment room. My stomach sank into my toes. It was high school Phys. Ed. class all over again.

Levi slapped a plastic package into my hands which contained a gray T-shirt and matching sweats, both with

"House Pacifica" written in discreet script. I shook out the clothes and held them up. Exactly my size.

"Been perusing my measurements, have you?"

"Wishful thinking, sweetheart." Levi's voice was a rough purr that caressed my skin and curled inside me with a flutter. He raked a slow, lazy gaze over me that made my nipples tighten.

It was such blatant game playing that I rolled my eyes and told him a thing or two about the difference between selling it and slathering on the bullshit.

Or at least, that's what I'd meant to do, but my lips parted with a breathy exhale. Fuck balls. I grimaced, intending to make a crack about dust in my throat but Levi's eyes snapped to mine, blazing with a brilliant blue heat.

Big deal. We were having a moment of chemistry. As attractive breathing humans, it was hardly statistically surprising and should have only lasted a second before we looked away.

Except this was Levi and me. Neither of us was going to back down from a challenge, even if it involved the most unthinkable act imaginable. A coiled anticipation tugged between us, growing more and more loaded as both of us waited for the other to crack first and close the distance.

A door slammed out in the hallway and I stepped back as Levi jerked a thumb at the far side of the gym. "Get changed."

Why was I even seeing him as a sexual possibility? I'd spent my life decidedly not seeing him that way and had been much happier. This better not be some cat-in-heat side effect of my magic because that would suck so hard.

I glanced at Levi's lips again, then scowled. Tossing the sweats to one side, I fell down on some padded blue mats. "I've had a very trying day and I'm exhausted, so can we get on with this?"

"The old man kicked your ass, did he?"

"Get real. I handled Baldy fine. The golem took it out of me."

Levi made an impatient noise. "You can't be serious about anything, can you?"

Fuck it. I didn't have the energy to convince him. "Let the torture begin. But first answer me this. What's a House Cat?"

Levi released a rope hanging from the ceiling to let it dangle free. "Use your powers of deduction and extrapolate."

"A tame pet." With a longing glance at the mats, I pulled off my motorcycle boots and lined them up neatly.

"Think Internet."

"A forum dedicated to the care and feeding of domestic felines." I stood up.

Levi grinned wickedly. "Sure, that too."

Ew. Please no. This man did not need any more ego stoking. "People having sex in cat onesies?"

"You would look ridiculous in cat ears," Levi said.

"Not me, you jerk." I rolled my shoulders back to stretch them out.

"Too repressed for anything other than lights out missionary style?" He nodded as if he'd always believed that about me.

"Anywhere, any way."

He cocked an eyebrow. "Less talking, more warming up. You'd do anything to get out of training, wouldn't you?"

"I wouldn't do you." There was only one reason the guard would have mouthed those words at me. "It's a House groupie, isn't it?" I sighed. "As Head of a House, you have one of these forums devoted to your rather dubious charms?"

Levi jerked his finger upwards.

"Five?" I massaged a tight spot in my neck.

Many more insistent jerks upward.

"Fine. I get it." I scowled.

"I'm a catch," Levi said.

"Normal people would be embarrassed. Not brag about it."

"My feelings on the matter exist in direct inversion to yours. On all matters, actually."

"Is that what this is about?" I tugged on the rope. "You know I would never willingly try this and make a fool of myself, so of course it was all systems go?"

His expression softened in contrition. "I'm sorry I was an asshole to you about your physical limitations when we were younger. I wouldn't do that now."

Part of me believed him, but part of me clenched the rope like a noose, lost in memories of whispers about my freak status that had followed me for years after the crash. I rubbed my thigh with my free hand.

"Ash." Levi pried my fingers loose from the rope. "When you manifested your magic, you were able to pin me down. You're not weak. This training is as much about cataloguing all your new abilities as it is helping you control your magic, okay?"

"Then allow me to sum up. Enhanced strength, manifesting solid objects out of my blood, and creating this shield thing, though it's still a little rough and not yet available for public viewing. Also destroying smudges. Magic catalogued. Next?"

"I'd like to see for myself. And since you could never do the ropes course at camp…" He handed me the rope.

Sighing, I stared up at the top. "I have to bleed to access my powers."

"Want me to punch you in the nose?"

"Ha. Ha." I pulled my switchblade out of my pocket, folding my jacket before placing it next to my boots.

Levi frowned at the knife. "You shouldn't need to cut to call up your magic. It's inefficient. Powers don't work that way. Your magic is a part of you. Call on it."

"It's *blood* magic and I've only been able to use it when I was bleeding."

"Did you try without it?"

"Give me my freaking training wheels, Levi." But I hesitated. It was one thing to cut in the heat of danger but standing here in a gym and deciding where to wound myself made me feel oddly vulnerable.

"Allow me."

I handed him the blade and he made a precise incision in the crook of my arm that I didn't even feel.

"There. You're bleeding." He put the knife in his pocket. "Do you sense your magic now?"

"Yes." It vibrated in a slightly ticklish way through my body like a light switch had been thrown. "I'm ready."

"Finally." Levi positioned me with my arms overhead and the rope falling down the center of my body. "Wrap and lock." He made a few adjustments. "Use your feet."

I climbed that rope like a boss—in my mind. The reality was less impressive. I did climb it, but I was a fumbling, grappling mess.

"That was not pretty," I said, once I'd slid down.

"Again. And this time, don't use your feet. Let's test your upper body strength."

"Not happening."

"You're right. You're too feeble."

"That's the lamest reverse psychology ever." It wasn't easy, but I did it, for the first time ever. "Told you. I'm stronger."

"Possibly. Or I pissed you off enough to get off your ass and climb, and you were being wimpy all those times at camp."

Blue. That would be a nice color for his body bag.

He led me over to a wooden archery target and handed me four small throwing knives. "Next test. Fine motor skills and accuracy."

Balancing them in my hand to test their weight, I planted myself in a solid stance and bullseyed all four.

"For the record," I said, "that wasn't magic. That was my ten thousand hours playing darts. How do you think I kicked your ass at the water ball toss that night?"

We butted heads over me running sprints.

"Put away your stopwatch," I said. "I tested it earlier. I'm a slow runner but at least I can run. My leg doesn't give out on me now. Are we done?"

"Not by a long shot. Time to test your control of that freaky blood magic."

"If I was a guy, you'd think blood magic was cool. Dudes who bleed for a good cause are heroes. It's only women's blood that freaks people out. Deal with it."

I'd gotten up in Levi's space and he pushed me back a few steps. "I don't give a shit what gender you are. Blood magic isn't supposed to exist."

He really couldn't get over that. Then again, I was still struggling on the golem front. I'd half convinced myself I'd seen a basketball player with a growth disorder and a bad fake tan.

"Fair enough," I said. "I'm sorry for the crack."

"You are?"

"Yes, Levi. You're right. My magic is highly unusual. Like, riddle me this. People don't get multiple powers. So why did I? And how does strength fit in to blood magic?" There had to be a logical pattern here. "That first night it manifested, I called up a dagger—"

"Don't forget the dildo," he said.

"Wow. You're really dwelling on that. Scroll through your little black book and hook yourself up, man, stat. Anyway, I also nuked that smudge that came out of Miles. What if my love of logic and reason and justice gave me magic to root out unnatural shit? Ooh. What if I'm a magic ronin here to save the world?"

"Technically, you'd be a samurai because Lord and Master standing right here."

I made a big show of looking around.

"Not to mention, you're hardly a Chosen One, Buffy."

"Who said anything about being a Chosen One?" I said. "I don't believe in destiny crap and I have no desire to have the fate of the world on my shoulders. That said, I do believe in my awesomeness that humanity is desperately in need of and could potentially join fellow ronin. We could have bowling shirts."

"Your dubious fashion choices aside, you can manifest solid items out of your blood, which means you can manipulate it. How far can you go?"

He ran me through a number of tests. I couldn't turn my blood poison or transform it into a gas or a bomb. "Solid matter," I finally said. "That's the extent of it."

"What about on other people? Make my blood stop flowing."

"Permission to kill you? Yes, please!"

Yeah, it didn't happen. I failed to do anything to Levi's blood.

He patted the top of my head. "It's important to know your limits."

"Sure." I was exhausted from all these trials.

Levi took off his jacket and shirt, revealing a cream fitted tank top. Folding it carefully, he eased out of his Italian leather shoes and set everything neatly aside, our clothing habits identical. "Last test. Miles didn't fight you when you destroyed the smudge, but the next person might and you could have to subdue them. Strength is vital to close contact fighting, however, even the strongest man can be taken down. Knowing how to use your strength and not have it used against you is imperative."

We headed back to the mats. Oh, to have a nap.

The tests were a disaster. I could barely get a hold on

Levi before he slipped free and tossed me down. Ten minutes in and I was sweating. Twenty and my back was bruised, every defeat a painful reminder of my own inadequacies.

Levi had hardly broken a sweat. "You're giving up."

"You're too slippery." I pressed my hands against my sides, heaving.

He flung me down again. "Quit making excuses. I always pegged you for a fighter."

Wait, what?

He prodded me with a toe. "Get up."

I dragged myself to my feet. This was useless. I was tired, sweaty, and I couldn't do this. I'd always been a tactician, the brains behind the scenes. I just wasn't built for combat.

"Snap out of whatever self-defeatist loop is playing in your head." A smudgy shadow slowly uncoiled itself from Levi like a peacock's tail.

My breath caught. If I didn't get to kill Levi, this magic fuck certainly didn't get the honors.

"What the—?" Levi yelped as I plowed him down.

"Stay still," I growled, straddling him. I called up my blood magic and fired a silky ribbon into the smudge that forked into branches, anchoring it.

Levi grit his teeth together, his body taut. He was fighting me as much as the shadow, but I kept him pinned down, the forks growing denser and ropier until they bloomed into white clusters.

The smudge vanished in an instant and I frowned. That's not what had happened last time. Nor was there any maggoty sensation, and come to think of it, the smudge had never uncoiled before either. It flowed out of people.

Why had it behaved this way? It was gone, which was good, but nothing about this situation made sense. Holy hell, was this a different type of smudge? Or was this what happened when it fed off a level five Nefesh like Levi? I patted Levi down, desperate to ensure I'd actually destroyed it.

Levi pushed me off of him. "Told you, you could do it."

"Something is off." I examined the mats for evidence of what had transpired.

"There was no smudge." He pointed to himself. "Illusion magic, remember?"

I frowned, not computing.

"You needed something to jostle you out of your defeatist headspace, so I made you think you saw a smudge, knowing you'd fight it, and get a win. You pinned me and held me." He looked pretty pleased with himself.

A buzzing noise filled my brain. My body tightened, a red wash rolling over my vision. "You played me?"

He blinked. "No. I was trying to help—"

I decked him, my fist connecting with his jaw so hard that his head snapped back. It was a terrible punch and I hurt my hand in the process, but thanks to my increased strength, it did the job. As I pulled my arm back, I realized there was no longer any cut on the inside of my elbow. "Another illusion?"

I slammed him against the floor.

"You don't need to bleed for your magic," he gasped. "You just need to believe in yourself."

"Shut up." I pressed my forearm across his throat. It felt like a shard of glass had slashed something soft and vital inside me. Oh right, that was Levi's breathtaking betrayal.

"Ash," he ground out, turning purple.

I wasn't a mark.

His heartbeat pulsed through my fingertips and I itched to take it.

Not his heartbeat, his magic. It smelled of oaky aged amber scotch and chocolate, and my mouth literally watered at the thought of stripping it from him, my body clenching in yearning.

His magic was an inviting siren's song.

Levi pressed my switchblade into my side. "Let go."

The prick of pain brought me to my senses. I would never rob someone of their magic, so why did I want to?

Why did I know that I could?

Despite my horror, it took every ounce of willpower to release him. I grabbed my stuff and ran out of there without another word.

This was supposed to be a straightforward training session. Levi would be a hardass, I'd bitch, probably humiliate myself a few times, and then come out of it with a new practicable skill, like a solid right hook, not stealing magic.

Levi was right. I wasn't a ronin.

I was a supervillain.

Chapter 9

"Pri?" I locked the front door behind me.

Voices and laughter floated out from the living room so I did what I did best, which was veer toward my bedroom hoping to evade them.

"Ash? That you?" Priya stepped into the hallway, her "two glasses of wine" flush in full force. "What happened to your neck?"

"Run in with a hostile. All good."

"Come meet Arkady."

I edged closer to my bed. Unlike Priya, who thrived in a crowd, I preferred to recharge in a quiet space, and right now my internal energy bar was blinking red. How could Levi have done that to me? "I don't want to intrude on your date."

Priya laughed. "He's gay."

"Everyone needs a hot, unattainable person in their lives and I have come to bless you with me. Arkady Choi, at your service." A man with chin-length black hair sauntered into the foyer and shook my hand. "Pronounced Ar-KAH-dee, and not like I'm a video game. Though I am good for hours of fun. I also don't house pairs of animals so for the love of anything holy do not shorten my name to Ark."

Arkady was slightly younger than us and about six feet tall. He sported a shit-ton of tattoos peeking out of his short sleeves and, with his arms braced over his head against the doorframe raising the hem of his shirt, a set of abs that were more cut than glass. He possessed that feline grace I'd seen in martial artists, and combined with his long-lashed dark brown eyes and full lips, he may have been the most beautiful man I'd ever seen.

I mistrusted him instantly. "Why are you in my house?"

He pulled a face. "You're right. She is a ray of sunshine."

I balefully divested myself of my jacket and boots while Priya shrugged without an iota of remorse.

"I love the bruises. So badass." Arkady took my arm and escorted me into my living room.

I'd slip out after I'd gotten some answers about who he was, since I couldn't in good conscience leave Priya alone with some unknown entity.

Our sleek modern sofas, coffee table, and bookcases from a high-end Montreal design company were way above Pri's and my paygrades. We'd inherited them in Talia's last redecoration spree, but we put our stamp on the room with throw cushions made of vivid sari fabric that Priya had brought back from India. Photographic prints of a red phone booth on a London street, sunset over the Colosseum, and dazzling white homes with blue doors in Santorini hung on our walls. Reminders of our travel goals.

Arkady pursed his lips, looking me up and down. "Tell me you own leather pants."

No, but maybe I should stock up if I was going to be bleeding on a regular basis. Blood was hidden on leather better than on denim, right? "You didn't answer my question. Why are you here?"

"I'm your new neighbor, pickle. Keep up."

"Did you just call me a brined cucumber?"

"Well, I wouldn't presume to call you Holmes. Not yet, anyway. We'll save that for next week when we're fast friends." Arkady beamed, revealing a dimple in his right cheek.

"You and Pri have gotten very cozy for someone who didn't live here this morning."

Priya grinned, sitting with one leg tucked under her in her pink minidress and black tights, already refilling their wine glasses. "I'm keeping him."

Yeah, I'd figured, since she'd tidied up the books that tended to spill off the shelves, from our old university textbooks, to her sci-fi novels and my Sherlock Holmes collection, gifted to me by my dad shortly before he took off. Nor was there any trace of the jumble of computers, cords, chargers, adaptors, and various other electronic odds and ends that usually cluttered up the coffee table. Her interest in a person was measurable in the amount of cleaning attributed to their presence. Interestingly, Kai had not yet warranted this level of tidying.

Arkady dropped onto the sofa, sprawling out like it was his regular spot. "So you're a private investigator?"

Priya patted the overstuffed comfy chair next to hers. I sat down and took a sip of her wine.

"Enough about me," I said. "What's your deal?" Because it's a pretty big coincidence that a chatty new neighbor shows up wanting to be friends when I'm uncovering this tattoo mystery.

"Usually, we get to know each other first with what might best be categorized as small talk before our late night easing into the soul-searching questions, pickle." Arkady snagged a pitted Kalamata olive from the small bowl full that Pri had set out and tossed it in his mouth. "Or has it been so long since you've met a new friend that you've forgotten?"

I wasn't on the clock, I was in my own home, and I didn't have to be "on." I didn't have it in me to slip into my glib "Ashira Cohen, P.I." self that I wore out in the world because I was too damn raw. Still, a hot rush of embarrassment speared through me. I tugged my cuffs over my fists, pretending my sleeves were the most fascinating things in the world. I was hollowed out like a deflated balloon and past the point of hitting home runs with my social interactions. I just wanted my bed.

"Sorry." Arkady scrubbed a hand over his face. "Mom despairs because she's never managed to entirely correct my broken filter. You look like you've had a rough day and maybe it would be helpful to hang out. We don't know each other, but I'd like to be friends with my neighbors."

It was possible he was telling the truth. Arkady didn't have any noticeable tells: biting or licking his lips, grooming gestures like straightening his cuffs, or a forced smile.

Once I'd announced my desire to be a detective when I grew up, my dad made up a game to help me better read people (and not get taken advantage of). It was his way of contributing to my dream. He didn't know about the technical or scientific parts of being a private investigator, but he did know reading and working people.

Walking through the business district, Dad would point out a misaligned button on someone in a three-thousand-dollar suit and ask me what it signified, or while at 7/11 getting Slurpees, he'd have us eavesdrop on the customer explaining why they were short a few cents and see if I could spot tells to uncover any lie.

Reading people wasn't a skill that came naturally to me, like it did for him. It had taken me years of practice observing people to get to the point where I was more successful than not.

However, that was with a clear head and no emotional involvement, and not me still reeling from the training session and Priya nodding with her "be nice" look involving her raised eyebrows and wide eyes. She wanted us to be friends with Arkady, which meant having to give a damn about this particular social interaction to make her happy.

That was clouding my bullshit-meter.

"How about this? I'll accept your apology if you give me a second chance at small talk?"

"Deal." He held out the olive bowl but I shook my head.

"Are you new to town or just the building?" I said.

Arkady picked up his wine. "Been in Vancouver about a year now. And my deal?" He winked. "Is that I'm twenty-four and both my parents are Korean-Canadian. Dad was the ambassador to Russia when I was born, hence my name. Mom was a surgeon who worked at an NGO while we lived there. Moved a few more times because of Dad's postings until we landed back in Ottawa in my late teens." He grimaced. "A city obviously not suited to my particular brand of je ne sais quoi, so like all good Village People, I went west and am trying to make it in the Nefesh MMA league out here."

"Earth elemental," Priya said.

Instead of weight categories, the Nefesh MMA League or NMMAL was divided by magic types.

"Scrawny Asian kid who never seemed to be anywhere long enough to fit in." He pulled a smooth stone from his pocket, rubbing it between his thumb and forefinger. "Always gravitated to rocks, caves, what have you. They were so permanent."

There was a wistfulness to his voice that belied the brash sassiness he'd displayed up until now. I smiled sympathetically at him and topped up his wine.

Then I caught myself. Evoking sympathy was a great way to make a connection with someone you intended to con. Was he genuine or was this a good mask?

I pointed to the stone in his hand. "Does that one have any special significance?"

Under Arkady's bright chatter, my fears over this desire to forcibly rip out Levi's magic and possibly his still-beating heart washed away. I had no such desire with Arkady.

After he left, I collapsed on the sofa, watching Priya gather up their dirty glasses.

"I appreciate you hanging out the entire time," she called out from the kitchen. "He's fun, right?"

I grunted something non-committal, but vaguely affirmative. Yawning, I debated getting up, but I was comfy, and enough time had passed that I wanted to talk to Pri about Levi. "His Lordship has sunk to new lows."

Priya returned and perched on the arm of the sofa. "How so?"

I told her about Levi's deception.

"Maybe he meant what he said about getting you out of your head?"

"Or maybe he's a snake so high on his own power that he thinks he has the right to fuck with people under the guise of helping them. Illusion magic. Enough said."

"In that case, I'm amazed you only punched him."

"I almost didn't. I…" I hugged a pillow to my chest.

Priya nudged my leg. "I love you and I'm not going to judge you for anything you tell me, you know that, right?"

"Yeah." Being friends since we were fifteen, we'd seen each other through some dark times. She'd supported me through the worst of my anger, and I'd pulled her back into the sunlight—literally—when her asshole ex had blown up their engagement two years ago and plunged her into a deep depression. If one of us killed someone, the other would be there with shovels and battery acid, while in times of celebration, we'd have "Shoop" queued up, chilled Prosecco in hand.

"I wanted so badly to rip his magic out and I could have

done it, no problem. Ever since I got my powers, I'm like Neo after watching those training videos in *The Matrix*. Abilities readily available for me to access."

"Some things are instinctive with Nefesh," Priya said, "but they train and develop their powers. Yours sound like some kind of pre-programming that you call up as needed."

"I hate that. It makes me feel like I'm at my magic's mercy and I'm some kind of mindless vessel." I plucked at the decorative button on the cushion. "The weird thing was that I wasn't taking Levi's magic for myself, I just wanted to tear it from him and destroy it. What the fuck kind of Moriarty move is that?"

"A lot to unpack there. But before your face gets stuck in that mopey Eeyore look forever, remember that you didn't take his magic. More importantly, you *chose* not to take it. Doesn't that prove that your moral center is intact and you get to choose how to use your powers? You're like an A.I. instead of a toaster."

I raised my head from where I'd cradled it in my hands. "Is that supposed to make me feel better?"

Priya snapped her fingers. "Doesn't House Pacifica have a library? If anyone can answer some of your questions, the librarian probably could."

"Good idea. Thanks, Pri."

"Any time." She picked up the empty bottle and headed into the kitchen, leaving the cardigan she'd been wearing earlier on the floor.

I stayed awake long after she went to bed.

According to the Van Gogh, tattooing me had been an act of betrayal. Why? Because my magic should have been allowed to run free? If someone was interested in my powers and they realized it was back, would I get a party in my honor or a bullet to the brain? Was there some slayer out there hunting me now that my abilities had resurfaced?

On the plus side, being target numero uno might be a

good push to update my wardrobe. I could have a signature color.

Magic was magic. It wasn't inherently good or evil. I would be in control of how I used it. Though I'd be the lamest badass ever if I had to ask my foes for a time-out while I cut myself. Levi got to be right about this one thing: bleeding to access my magic was impractical.

Time to take the training wheels off.

When I was in grade ten, we'd had this sexual health class where the speaker had said we needed to know our bodies. Not necessarily in a sexual way, but to visualize all of ourselves. She'd urged us later that night to use a mirror if necessary, and look at all the parts we generally didn't, so that we were at home in our body and took ownership of it. It was stupid and beyond embarrassing, but I'd done it.

The part I'd lingered over most wasn't my vag, it was my scar. Up until then, I had done my level best to ignore the long gash on my thigh, but that night I accepted it. It was the same now. I had this magic but I had yet to fully accept it. Take ownership of it. I couldn't just cross my fingers and hope for it to come out when I panicked.

I closed my eyes and took a centering breath, seeking out the magic that swam through my veins with a pins and needles faint tingling. I visualized gathering it up and drawing it through my palms into the shape of a sewing needle. Starting small.

There was nothing. Not even a pinprick's worth. Again and again I tried, until I was so flushed with exertion that I'd peeled down to my bra and underwear.

I shook out my hands. So far, my magic had manifested three times and in all three, I'd reacted instinctively out of fear. Was I overthinking this? I fixed the image of the needle in my head and a second later, it lay in my palm. It was more like an uneven, oversized child's rendition of a needle, but it was solid and sharp. I kissed it. Cold, hard, and dazzling red. "Oh, you beauty."

Looking around the room for inspiration of what to manifest next, I decided on a coaster. A small round shape. It took a few tries but I mostly pulled it off.

Nice party trick, but every time I manifested something it ran my battery down that much more, so there was no point in creating items that didn't serve a practical purpose. Better to concentrate on weapons.

After a couple of hours practice, I reliably produced picture-perfect needles on demand. Also, a pair of throwing stars and two small daggers, all made of blood. I didn't bother with guns because that was a complex procedure versus a sharp blade. Too many moving parts that I would inevitably get wrong. Better to stick with simple weapons, easily visualized and produced.

I was less successful at making the items vanish after I'd produced them.

I stood up to stretch and the world swung around me, my legs buckling. I ass-planted on the sofa. Slowly, I made my way to the kitchen, downed half a carton of orange juice, and ate a handful of salty peanuts, riding out the blood loss until my breathing had evened out and my heart rate dropped down to normal. I wasn't used to having magic and definitely wasn't used to the toll it took.

This was something to be a lot more mindful of in the future since my blood fueled my power. There had to be some magic mechanism to compensate for the blood loss and keep me relatively topped up. Bleed a regular person enough to fill a few dagger-sized molds and they'd be dead pretty damn quick, but even with my fancy blood powers I still felt like trash after a few manifestations. Fainting in the middle of some magic battle would suck.

Did certain actions take more of a toll? Killing smudges wasn't too bad, producing too many physical items was more exhausting. Would that change with practice or did I simply have to learn the relative costs of different actions? Magic wasn't just about knowing what I could do, it was also about safely working within the boundaries of my power.

Lots of new things to think about.

I placed the needles and daggers in an empty Chinese food container, marking them "SHARPS. DO NOT TOUCH."

There was one other thing to test. Healing. My blood shield had protected me against magic attacks, but could magic retroactively fix me? I rubbed blood on my bruises like I was a fancy lady with an expensive cream. I'd deal with the weird factor if this worked.

By the time I'd finished, the sun was pale gray streaks against the night sky. So much for a good night's rest. The most I'd get was a cat nap, but I was exhausted and exhilarated and crashed hard.

On the sofa.

In the same underwear I'd been wearing.

And my blood home remedy.

I woke up drooling, face down on the couch with the decorative button stuck to my forehead. My mother had left me three more messages. I texted her that I was fine, just very busy. After a moment's reflection, I sent a second text.

Me: *Do you have cancer or something?*

Talia, Destroyer of Egos: *Are you still high? Call me immediately.*

If she wasn't experiencing concern due to a fatal diagnosis, then my first instinct had been correct: the call was to ream me out.

Me: *So busy.*

I checked the sharps container. It was empty save for the second dagger I'd made, but when I checked on it after coming back from the bathroom, that too had disappeared. I consulted the time on my phone. I'd made the knife about four hours ago, so that was the extent of these weapons' shelf life. Good to know.

Unfortunately, the bruises hadn't gone anywhere, though this newfound strength had bolstered my leg, because after last night I should have been debilitated, yet there was nothing worse than a twinge.

A fragile stalk of hope took root in my chest. Might I live a relatively pain-free life?

After a quick shower, I contemplated my clothing. What was appropriate for projecting a "don't mess with me" vibe in Hedon while not coming off as overly aggressive? I tried on everything I owned, including that horrible dress that Talia had bought me to wear to the gala and a unicorn onesie that was part of a misguided Halloween costume. Finally, I threw on skinny jeans and a deep blue sweater with a metallic sheen to it. I tied my hair into a simple knot at the base of my neck and applied on a ton of mascara and light gloss. The only accessory I wore was the bruises.

Since breakfast was the most important meal of the day, I made coffee, scarfing down a croissant of questionable freshness while the brew gurgled away into the pot. Soon as it was ready, I downed my first two cups then poured some into Priya's favorite mug, the one with "I turn coffee into code" written on it, and brought it to her in bed.

"Mmghgmg." She pulled the pillow over her head.

Setting the mug down beside her, I said, "Java's up. If I don't come back from Hedon, I bequeath you all my worldly goods. Take good care of Moriarty."

I got another mumble and a thumbs up extended from beneath the covers. Good enough. After stashing a few of her protein bars in my leather jacket, I jogged down the stairs, emerging on the street to a beautiful spring day.

Fat fluffy clouds drifted cheerfully across the bright blue sky and the remaining snow on the North Shore mountains glinted in the sunlight.

Darting down the side street to where Moriarty was parked, I called Miles.

"This number is unlisted," he said.

"Most people go with 'hello,' but you do you."

"You report to Levi. Go bug him."

"Nope. You're my new bestie. Besides, I need the Head of Security."

He sighed. "For what?"

"A way into Hedon."

He laughed and hung up.

I hadn't expected it to be that easy, but now I had his location. Thankfully, he wasn't at House Pacifica, but at his townhouse. Naturally, Priya and I had amassed our own database on persons of interest, Nefesh and Mundane, in this city.

I knocked on Miles' door until he answered it with a growl. "How did you find me? Was it that coder friend of yours? The Pink Menace?"

As Head of Security, I wasn't surprised that Miles knew about Priya, especially since she worked for me, but he had met her exactly once and he remembered her enough to give her a nickname? Interesting.

I ducked under his arm. "Nice boxers."

His physique was impressive but it was too jacked up for my tastes. I preferred someone more like—nope.

Miles grabbed my collar and turned me around to face him. "What happened to your neck?"

"Work-related injury. Hedon. How do I get in? Skip ahead five steps and spare me the useless arguments."

"I have to clear it with Levi." Muscles exploded on muscles when he crossed his arms. "FYI? He's going to say no."

"One little love tap during training and the boy gets pissy? I'm not asking for permission. You willing to live with the consequences of me not solving this case as fast as possible and destroying those smudges roaming our streets?"

The silence stretched out. Was it possible I'd misjudged his concern for the greater good? No. Levi would never allow him into the inner circle if that was the case. This was Miles pulling attitude.

"Wait here." He lumbered down the hallway. Ten out of ten for those tight glutes of his.

The foyer was devoid of all personal touches. There was nothing to clue me in to the personality or psyche of this home's inhabitant. Maybe that was the point.

Miles returned shortly with a dented token coin stamped with an H. It looked like a gag gift.

"If you're messing with me, I'll set the Pink Menace on you."

"Try it." He bared his teeth.

I swiped the token away. "Pleasure doing business with you."

After a special bout of coaxing to get the fucker to start, Moriarty and I headed downtown. This early on a Sunday, there was plenty of available parking alongside Harbour Center, a tower which housed both the downtown campus of Simon Fraser University and a revolving restaurant with 360° views of the city.

I stood in line behind the tourists waiting for their turn in the glass elevators that crawled up the outside of the building along the forty-plus floors to the restaurant. After the group ahead of me took forever to find the discount coupon for their admission, I finally reached the cashier and presented the token.

She stared at me blankly. "Twenty dollars. Visa, MasterCard, cash, or debit."

I slid the token closer.

"Visa, MasterCard, cash, or debit."

"It's kind of *hedonistic* today," I said.

The woman leaned out around me. "Next!"

The couple behind me tried to shuffle past but I stopped them. "I'm not done."

"Do you want me to call security?" the cashier said.

Doubt slithered through me. I could have been wrong about the entrance being here since I'd learned it eavesdropping on some drunk Nefesh private investigators a couple of years ago and the woman was reaching for the phone.

No. This was the right place.

"One please." I handed her the token, folding her fingers around it.

She regarded me coolly, then replaced the receiver. "Elevator on the left."

An elevator that went up the outside of a building in order to enter a dangerous magic black market. I was positive I'd be in there alone, battling monsters whispered about in the dead of night that hurtled from the darkness to devour you.

Instead, I was wedged in with a large, boisterous Greek family. Halfway up, after several people had stepped on my toes, I checked hopefully for any vents dispensing poisonous gas. Two thirds of the way up, when I was squished in the corner doing a partial backbend while the Greeks took their one millionth selfie against the Vancouver skyline with the superb view of the water beyond, I prayed for a ninja assassin dropping from the ceiling.

And when we reached the top as the same saxophone muzak piece of shit looped around for the third time, drilling into my brain like a dental procedure without the Novocain, monsters might have been the better alternative.

I stepped into the welcome area. Before me was a revolving door that led to the restaurant. The tourists went through it, their animated chatter falling away.

Other than the door to the restaurant and the elevators, this space was all windows and sandstone tile with no doors or portals. I clicked my heels together three times. "Hedon. Hedon. Hedon."

Ah, well. It had been worth a shot.

"Ash?"

I stiffened, the smell of Old Spice and lemon candies causing a lump in my throat, and turned around slowly. "Daddy?"

Adam Cohen's hair was more gray than brown now, as was the stubble that he never managed to totally shave clean, but the way his eyes lit up at seeing me hadn't changed a bit. "Little jewel!"

He hugged me, his arms strong and safe and the entire world making sense for the first time in so very, very long.

I wrenched free. "This is a trick. You aren't here."

He scratched his chin, his expression crestfallen. "You have every right to be mad, my girl, but it's really truly me."

"Yeah? Where have you been?"

He shrugged with that lopsided smile that always preceded him dancing around the truth. "Here and there."

My heart clenched. This wasn't my dad, this was the monster I'd been expecting. Every detail conjured up the instant I thought of it. "Good try. But you're a little too pat. A little too exact."

"What?"

"You. Adam. Or whatever you are. You're not my father. So what do you want?"

"You have to pay the price of admission."

"I did. The coin."

He laughed, the hearty sound cutting straight to my heart. "That was a test to weed out the unworthy. And the price is nothing so extreme as you're imagining. A simple game."

"Rigged, I suppose."

"Not at all. Fall backwards into my arms and let me catch you."

"Let me fall, more like." I toed the floor to gauge how painful my landing would be.

He held out his arms.

Whatever. I'd play this stupid game. Except I couldn't make myself face away from this image of my father. A certainty filled me that if I did, he'd stab me in the back. Either literally or figuratively and disappear again. It didn't even matter that this wasn't my dad. He looked like him and he smelled like him, and I once more tasted the bitterness that no amount of spearmint chewing gum could get rid of in the months after he'd left.

My throat closed up on me and my body tingled, alternating between hot flushes and clammy chills.

"Don't have all day, little jewel."

Swallowing hard, I forced myself to think of Meryem. I could do this for her. I had to. Millimeter by millimeter, I shuffled around so that my back was to that atrocity. That grotesque joke that wasn't my father but hugged like him. A hug that my heartbroken thirteen-year-old self would have killed to experience one last time.

My vision narrowed, the memory of a concrete wall zooming up to meet me, and I jerked hearing the screech of twisted metal, a million shards of glass and hot metal pouring down on me like rain drops.

I breathed my way through it and told myself what I always told myself when this happened, in hospitals, in near-misses at rush hour, in the dead of night:

I am not a mark.

I whipped around and threw the blood dagger I'd called up directly into Adam's center mass.

He looked down at it, eyes sorrowful and shocked, then wavered and disappeared. I tucked the knife against my back under my leather jacket with shaking hands and a heavy heart.

A low grinding noise made me start. The revolving door

had started up behind where Adam had been, slowly moving dividers that alternated between tables with bright linens from the restaurant and a foreign night with a crescent moon.

I should have felt a thrill of victory as I stepped into Hedon, but all I could think of was Adam's sad eyes, how he'd looked down at his solar plexus and my knife without blame, only regret.

Go me.

Chapter 10

Imagine one person's magic was a single melody. Listened to by itself or in small numbers, magic could sound beautiful. But all at once? It was a mess.

That's what Hedon was, a deafening cacophony of magic and noise that made no sense. Ever evolving, rumor had it that the black market had been carved by the most talented of Nefesh architects from spaces stolen from reality and stitched together. It resided in the pockets outside our normal world, accessible globally to those in the know, but existing nowhere.

It defied all logic and I despised it, even without its foundational magic that bitch-slapped me so hard that I gagged and sat down on the lip of the weed-choked fountain in this tiny plaza, with no sign of where I'd entered. I closed my eyes, taking the shape of this magic that smelled of axle grease and vanilla ice cream inside me, letting us get acquainted. I couldn't unravel or seize the magic from the market's bones, nor did I want to, but if I didn't push this waterfall down to a manageable dull roar and quash this nauseating overload, I wouldn't be able to function.

It took some time before I no longer wanted to vomit,

but eventually I stood up on unsteady legs and took stock of my surroundings.

Hedon possessed a drunken, listing quality, from the stalls and shacks thrown up haphazardly to the sticky velvet night that caressed my skin. This world was awash in neon, or rather the magic equivalent thereof: an electric blue ramen bowl floated above a simple kiosk while a pair of dragons made of light swooped and belched fire above a penthouse far in the distance.

Two narrow crooked roads veered away from the plaza. I went left, wandering through a street crowded with people haggling for wares, the scents and smoke of grilled food making my stomach rumble, and the whizz of motorcycles over cobblestones vibrating up through my toes.

The fashions were as over-the-top as the architecture. There was an androgynous person in a ballgown wearing a monocle and with a live frog on their shoulder manning a stall selling bones and beauty potions, an elderly Asian woman standing on stilts and wearing steampunk goggles as she dished out glistening noodles in rainbow colors, and a biker gang in gas masks and brass-studded body stockings hawking gold coins that evaporated into a deadly poison through body heat.

I followed the road about six blocks to its end. No one that I asked about Queen of Hearts Productions was willing to give me an answer. They either ignored me, fearfully told me to go away, or became outright belligerent. I was about to double back and take a side street I'd passed, when a man with white hair, even though he was probably in his forties, and a white suit that even the 1970s didn't want back, stepped away from the wall, grinding his cigarette under his white boot heel. "Looking for the Queen?"

"Unless I'm late for a very important date," I said.

White Rabbit Man failed to get my reference, but come

on. This Alice in Wonderland second-rate cosplayer couldn't be serious.

"Sure," I amended, when he continued to stare at me, dead-eyed.

That was the last thing I said before he knocked me unconscious with a blast of electricity.

I woke up unceremoniously slumped in a hairdresser's chair. My hand flew to my head but my locks were present and accounted for. Sadly, so were a pair of magic-suppressing handcuffs around my wrists.

The salon's red-and-white tiled floor matched the red walls and three stylists' chairs in white. Only one other chair was occupied: by a plus-size woman in a stylist's cape, her hair being encased in foils by a reedy hairdresser whose long nails clacked against the brush used to apply the dye. A person in black tactical gear with mesh obscuring their face stood in the corner standing guard. The same heart with a crown and scepter logo as the Queen of Hearts Productions was stitched on their upper arm.

"You're disturbing my beauty regimen, blanquita." The customer's Spanish-accented voice was honey over steel.

I had the craziest urge to curtsey. And physically hold on to my head. No. It couldn't be... could it? I stood up. "Sorry, I wouldn't want missing kids to interfere with your dye job."

The stylist gasped, her plastic bowl of hair color splatting to the ground.

The client placed a stiletto on the floor and slowly repositioned her chair to look at me. Her thickly lashed large violet eyes sparked and her pouty lips compressed into a thin line. She had crow's feet, making her older than I'd originally thought. Maybe in her early fifties. "¿Qué dijiste?"

I swallowed at her hard tone, but awkwardly retrieved the flyer from my pocket and thrust it at her, the handcuffs jangling. "You're kidnapping marginalized youth."

She took it between her thumb and forefinger like a soiled napkin, gave it the barest glance, and laughed huskily. "Sí. I'm diversifying my business interests into kids' parties and abduction. Do you have any idea who I am?"

"Someone with pretensions of royalty?"

The stylist gasped, now on her knees cleaning up the fallen dye. "Show some respect for the Queen of Hearts, ruler of Hedon."

"I'm not good with authority. Ask my mom. Look, House Pacifica knows about the smudge and isn't going to stand by and let you do this."

"Que es un 'smudge?'" She waved away the stylist.

The woman scurried through a red door, holding the towel she'd used to clean up the mess and leaving me alone with this glamorous lady who drove my instincts into high alert more than the creepy bodyguard in the corner did.

The Queen ripped off the cape, revealing a red wrap-around dress that hugged her curves and popped against her bronze skin. She waited for me to continue with the patience of a lioness stalking its prey in the high grass.

I explained about the smudge, creatively rearranging details so as not to put Miles or the House in a position of weakness.

"How did you see those things?" The last vestiges of her amusement fell away, her eyes darkening with cunning and the promise of retribution.

"I didn't. It was Levi Montefiore."

"Because of his illusion magic?"

I nodded. Sure. Let's go with that.

"What do you want from me?" she said.

"If it's not you, then do you know who's behind it? You don't have to get involved, I just need a name so that I can stop them."

"They implicated me when they put my name on their flyer. It's my business now."

"That doesn't really work for me," I said.

A dozen pairs of scissors rose out of their disinfectant liquid to quiver in mid-air, their sharpened points directed my way. The guard's hand was raised as if they were conducting an orchestra.

I called up my magic, but I was as dead as a downed phone line. Stepping sideways didn't help either, because the scissors repositioned themselves to follow me. "There's a missing girl that is very much my business. And since she's registered with House Pacifica, that makes it their business. Now, we can work together quietly, or I can reach out to all the other Houses and see which other ones this affects. Then we'll come back en masse, barging into your affairs until we get the information we need."

The speech would have gone over a lot better if my hands weren't cuffed in front of me, but I was gambling on the collective Houses being a sufficient threat.

The Queen studied me for a long time, but I met her stare, steely-eyed and chin up. She nodded at the guard and the scissors glided back into their containers. I let out a pent-up breath.

"I'll do you one favor, but you have to choose," she said. "You can either have someone connected to all this or the location of your papá."

"You're the one who called up that fake Adam?"

She gave a one-shouldered shrug. "Call it a magic alarm."

"Or a magic mindfuck."

"I like to know who's entering my domain for the first time. What do you choose?"

"Even if you could find Adam, why offer this? Do you give everyone what they want? How big are the strings attached to that offer?"

"You are very suspicious, chica." She brushed a foil out of her face. "No strings. I'm very good at unearthing things that are in my interest, and you have become very interesting to me."

That was… disturbing.

"This is a one-time offer," she said.

The decision should have been a no-brainer. Why would I even want to see my dad again? He couldn't help me with any of this and, moreover, he'd made his feelings for us abundantly clear. But what if he'd run into trouble? What if the reason I'd never been able to find him was because he was dead? That he'd meant to come back and couldn't? For years, I'd clung to that thought like an addict, and with her offer, the need to know roared to life, digging its hooks into me.

I could finally have closure and put my past to rest. Or, I could be given a lead that would require further investigation, since she wasn't promising to get me those actually responsible.

Get the one answer I'd been denied all these years or ask questions to help someone else?

Her tapping foot ticked off the seconds. She stopped, the sudden silence clearer than any buzzer that I had to choose.

"My father doesn't matter," I said.

"Bueno. What price are you willing to pay?"

I crossed my arms as best I could with the handcuffs on. "First of all, you said I had a choice and I chose. And second of all, what kind of cockamamie business are you running that you set terms after the agreed-upon negotiation and never mind, you're a criminal."

"I prefer visionary." She motioned me forward and unlocked the cuffs, the mild arch of her eyebrow enough to make me nod that I'd behave. "That part is still a favor." She smiled like the cat who swallowed the canary. "But I'm guessing you want to leave Hedon?"

I rubbed my wrists. "What do you want?"

"Show me your magic. Montefiore sent *you* for a reason."

"That's a second date move. I'll take my chances getting out of here." My magic danced inside me and I curled my fingers into my palms to keep it from bursting out.

She smiled. Too many teeth. "I insist."

"I don't have any," I said. "Though the cuffs really added a rock and roll punch to my outfit."

The Queen jangled the cuffs menacingly. "You're lying."

"Ashira Cohen. Check the House database. I'm not in there." I showed her my P.I. identification which marked me as Mundane. She might come after me once Levi decided to enter my magic into the records, but I'd deal with that when the time came.

"That makes you even more interesting," she said.

"You have no idea. Now, I showed you mine and I'd like to leave."

She inclined her head regally. "Await my call. Oh, and Ashira Cohen?"

I turned around, eyebrow raised.

"You and I are going to spend some quality time together. Soon."

"Can't wait."

My exit from Hedon was an anticlimactic elevator ride, but oh goody, my life was livened up by Levi's stupid mug. He sat on Moriarty's hood, his hair a raven's blue-black in the sunlight with a pair of shades obscuring his eyes. He was the picture of cool and unaffected in his camel trench coat, his long legs stretched out.

I sat down beside him, leaning back on my elbows with my face turned up to the sky, grateful to have made it back to the light.

"I'm sorry about last night," he said.

"Words many a woman has heard from you."

"You were scared of the smudge. But afterwards, even though you were mad, you also looked terrified. If that was

134

because of me, I sincerely apologize." He took off his sunglasses, his remorse clear.

"I'll accept your apology for mindfucking me instead. What happened after wasn't about you." I shook my head at his inquiring look, not ready to discuss my dark side wanting to rip out his magic.

His eyes drifted to the bruises on my neck, then back up to my eyes. "Hedon was useful?"

Miles was such a tattle tale.

"The Queen of Hearts was useful."

Levi fumbled to catch the sunglasses he'd dropped. "You just waltzed in and saw the Queen?"

"Pretty much. She finds me interesting."

"That's not a good thing. Do you know how she got her name? She consolidated her power in the underworld after a string of beheadings. In one night, all the other players were gone. There was never any evidence tying her to it, but the next morning she was top dog."

I exhaled slowly, the sunlight infusing my soul. "That's probably true and I'm sure it bolsters her position for people to think that, but that's not what the moniker refers to. Or not entirely. Pro tip. If you ever take that elevator ride to Hedon for the first time, be prepared to face your heart's deepest desire."

"I thought the way in was fraught with monsters."

"When it's the Queen seeing into your heart? It is."

He looked like he wanted to probe more deeply, but all he said was, "You okay?"

I shrugged. "I survived."

"You do that a lot."

I braced for some sarcastic sneer but there was nothing but admiration as he gazed down on me. "Don't do that. It's unnatural. We're still nemeses."

"Moriarty and Holmes admire each other," he said.

"Dude, check your ego. Do you even know anything about Moriarty?"

"He's Sherlock's enemy."

"He's a criminal mastermind. Which takes you out of contention." Besides, I might be Moriarty in the grand scheme of things. "Though you both dislike anyone smarter than you." I batted my lashes at him.

"I'll up my game," he said dryly.

"You're more Watson."

"The boring sidekick? Hardly."

"I'm just saying, you're no Moriarty. Uh, one minor thing. In order to keep my magic a secret, I told her you were the one to see the smudge."

"So if this blows up, the Queen of Hearts is coming after me?" Levi said, annoyed.

"Probably. Scared?"

"No shit, Sherlock. As I should be and so should you. She's incredibly dangerous. And here everything was going so well since I last saw you." He slipped his shades back on. "I knew you were the kind of woman to ruin my day."

"Aww, Leviticus," I said. "Don't tempt me. Properly motivated, I'll ruin your life."

"I don't doubt it. So we're good?" he said.

"Once you clean up the graffiti at the skate park near the youth shelter on Powell Street."

Levi snorted a laugh. "You didn't. Not that stupid Baskervillain handle you used to doodle on everything."

"You have never appreciated how cool I am." I pulled out my car keys. "Is that the only reason you came by? To see if I was okay?" That was actually decent of him.

"No. I came to tell you that my people found the woman that the smudge went into at Green Thumb. She's still alive and I want to keep her that way. Pay her a visit and destroy it." He texted me the details.

"Really?"

"Yes, really. It can't be allowed to exist."

"Not that. I thought you didn't trust anyone else on this."

"I don't. But I can assign grunt work without raising suspicion. This woman needed to be tracked down and the more assistance I can give you, the faster this gets resolved. If anyone else gets hurt, or the press gets wind that the smudge exists, the damage to our Nefesh community could be catastrophic."

"It's not the fault of the community at large. No one blames all Mundanes when one of them blows up a building." I stood up, the keys jangling, but Levi didn't get my hint.

"Not one white person," he said. "But if they're brown? Or Muslim? Works the same way with us. Did you know that Baghdad used to have a thriving Nefesh community?"

"Iraq is one of the worst persecutors of Nefesh. What happened?"

"Back in the 1960's, a Rogue went on a killing spree in a department store. Eighty people dead including a very well respected Imam."

I unlocked Moriarty. "Yikes. Is that when they turned on the magic community?"

"Yeah. The reprisals were swift and brutal. Not only that, they whipped neighboring countries into an anti-Nefesh fervor, which has never changed. We live a very fragile existence."

Levi's sense of responsibility to his people ran deep. It was an admirable quality in a House leader but how much time did he spend ensuring the general impression that his community was safe and strong, not even through magical means, but by inspiring his people to make it so? He was the king on the chessboard, thinking six moves ahead and hoping he didn't sacrifice a pawn.

"You'll do anything to make sure your Nefesh stay safe,

won't you? And now you're stuck relying on a person whose mother is dedicated to upsetting that balance. That can't be easy." I opened the car door, which squeaked in protest.

"I don't believe in the sins of the father. Or the mother. You may be one of the most irritating human beings I've ever met, but I'll admit you give everything to your job."

Warming under his surprising praise, I stilled. "You have a file on me?"

"Like you do with me." Levi's limo pulled up to the corner exactly as he stood up. Damn, he was irritatingly smooth.

"More a napkin with some notes in leaky pen," I said. "Three bullet points, tops."

Levi winked at me. "Hidden depths, baby."

Chapter 11

Noemi Rosen was a mid-level Sensitive, able to detect sound-waves. No sneaking up on this woman. Her hair was shaved down to the scalp without a trace of stubble so she'd buzzed it recently.

I pretended that Green Thumb had sent me to check on her and make sure she was okay after witnessing their employee James' death.

"That was nice of them, but this visit really wasn't necessary." She kept me on her front stoop.

There wasn't that same rotting flesh and feces odor as when the smudge had been in Miles, but if it was no longer inside Noemi, and I was positive it wasn't, then how was she still alive?

"You haven't experienced any odd symptoms lately, have you?" I said.

Noemi rubbed a hand over her head. "Other than hair loss, vomiting, and mouth sores?"

"I didn't realize. I'm sorry."

She smiled. "It's okay. I finished chemo a few days ago and my prognosis is good."

I was all for Noemi's continued health, but where was

the smudge? If I'd stuck around when the light had turned green that day, would I have seen the smudge jump into the next person? Or could the chemo have killed more than her cancer cells? Had that treatment saved her life in more ways than one or had the smudge moved on because of the chemicals in her body?

At least the visit with Noemi allowed me to slot in another piece of this puzzle. James had been a very low level earth elemental, which meant the smudge fed upward since Levi's notes on Noemi ranked her magic higher.

I stifled a laugh. The smudge that had flowed out of Miles had been undecided as to whether to jump into me or Levi, so I was more powerful than Miles and could apparently, give Levi a run for his money. I was totally sharing that fact some time.

From there, I swung by House Pacifica to kill two birds with one visit. HQ's lobby was bustling today and I hurried to the elevator banks to make it into one of the packed cars.

"Yo, Nancy Drew." A voice boomed out from behind me.

The uniformed cops entering the building with their coffees laughed like their burly Staff Sergeant Novak was the world's greatest wit.

"Find any missing cats lately?" Novak smirked. That had been my first case, finding that cat. I'd solved it by dinner, and in the process, had the misfortune of meeting this cop. He was never going to stop giving me shit about it.

"Just your wife's pussy." I jerked a thumb at one of the cops. "Lewis had it."

Novak lost the smirk. "Fuck you."

"Not in any universe whatsoever." I got on the next elevator, scratching my nose with my middle finger as the doors slid shut.

I let out a low whistle as I got my first glimpse of the massive House library, all detailed woodwork, with that glorious smell of warm paper, wrapped in a hushed reverence.

Elke, the good-natured librarian with a slow and calming manner, was happy to assist me.

When I asked if it was possible for magic to only appear after a traumatic event, she confirmed that although she'd never heard of it happening, it wasn't impossible.

As she explained it, DNA, the genetic material that determined our physical characteristics and made us who we were, was also responsible for a number of diseases with a hereditary component, like cancer, diabetes, Huntington's, and Alzheimer's. The risk of inheriting them was passed down from our parents, but recent findings confirmed that DNA wasn't necessarily set in stone.

Researchers had shown that DNA could be modified by our environment during childhood and that these modifications could affect how or when a person developed certain illnesses later on.

"But I'm talking about magic, not disease," I said.

"There are those who believe that, genetically, it's the same thing," she said. "Remember, magic didn't evolve. It invaded us."

I mulled that over. If magic had originally been a recessive gene in me, but the trauma of the crash and surgery had turned it on, that would explain why I'd thought myself Mundane. For all intents and purposes I *had* been Mundane during my childhood.

It also might explain those crazy clusters that had eaten the smudge. The smudge was a magic entity that had invaded a Nefesh host. If I followed the disease supposition then those clusters could be the magic equivalent of white blood cells attacking a disease. It was *blood* magic, after all.

"That gives me a lot to think about, thank you." I said. "One more question. Ever heard of anyone having blood magic?"

"No." Her eyes gleamed. "Does it exist?"

"I'm looking into it."

"Let me know what you learn."

"Sure." Eventually, Levi would have to put my magic on record. Good to know that at least one person would be happy about it.

Neither Miles nor Levi were around to get me access to the Van Gogh. As I headed to the elevator to go upstairs and see if anyone else could authorize it, my footsteps slowed and my fingers drifted up to the single line of the new ward the Van Gogh had burned into me. Let him stew one more day. It couldn't hurt.

I texted Levi that the whereabouts of the smudge that had been in Noemi was inconclusive.

He texted me back when I got home that Miles had paid the Van Gogh a visit but he still wasn't talking. How sweet. Levi had sent his resident badass in on my behalf. Hmm. I wondered if Miles ever freelanced, because there was a pizza delivery guy I'd love to give an attitude adjustment to.

Priya was in the bathroom, angrily typing with one hand on the laptop that was balanced on the counter, while curling her hair with the other. She glanced up at my entrance. "Three pages long. Was he fucking kidding me?"

"Wow." I had no clue who she was talking about, but when Priya got code red mad, she tended to simply include you at whatever part of her ranting she was at. "What did it say?"

She grabbed a set of damp crinkled pages from where they'd been tossed in the sink and shoved them at me.

I got two paragraphs in and winced. One of the partners of the company she was working for had sent an email mansplaining to the female coder what a database was. "Oh my."

She stabbed at a section on page two. "Not only does he fundamentally *not* understand that a database is not a magic box, but he had the gall to tell me that his nephew who got accepted to computer programming in the fall assured him that every single change he wanted could be done. Never mind that I have years of experience."

I placed a hand on the top of her computer. "Would now be a bad time to remind you that the bathroom is a laptop-free zone? Remember, work-life balance starts in the toilet."

"I'm balanced. You're the one with a neck that looks like a zombie gnawed on it. There's arnica cream in the drawer." She used her hip to indicate which one. "Use it."

I slowly lowered the top of her computer but she brushed my hand away.

"I need to fix this one buggy line of code." She savagely ripped the printout into pieces and tossed them in the trash.

"Uh-huh." I uncapped the tube and smeared some arnica lotion on.

Priya unplugged the curling iron and set it on the tile floor to cool. Her eyes flew across the screen, then she typed a quick series of commands, before picking up the laptop and carrying it out. "See? Done. I'm taking the rest of the night off."

"Good." I followed her out.

"By the way, I wrote you an algorithm to narrow down potential hospital employees to a short list of suspects. Should have something for you in the morning."

"You never cease to amaze me."

"That's why you pay me the big bucks. Oh, wait." She grinned at me. "Want to come for a late dinner with me and Arkady?" She detoured into her bedroom to deposit her laptop on her dresser and grab a coat.

"Getting pretty buddy-buddy there, Pri." I lounged in her doorway, turning sideways to let her into the foyer.

"Aw. I'll always love you best, baby." She shrugged into her jacket.

"That's a given. Just be careful. He moves in and wants to be besties? We have no idea who this guy is. Did you know he was in the army? How come he didn't mention it?"

She paused, black ballet flat in hand, looking around for its match. "You did a background check on him?"

"Yes. If a right-wing racist homophobe moved in next door, steps would need to be taken. His story seems legit, but still."

Priya wandered through the apartment holding her shoe like it was a dowsing rod, so I joined in the search, locating it with a cry of triumph under the couch.

"Sometimes you have to have faith in people." She slipped the flats on and grabbed her purse.

I laughed. "No. That's exactly what you don't want to have. Present company excepted. I have ultimate faith in you."

"Not everyone is out to screw you over. Your constant suspicions have narrowed your world."

"My world is narrow because people are just not worth knowing."

"I call bullshit. Either way, you need to branch out from just me." Priya opened the front door. "If you want to join us, we'll be at Park West. Arkady specifically asked me to invite you."

"Another night."

She threw up her hands. "You're always like this. I feel like I'm your lifeline to the world and I'm sick of it, okay? Most people are only out there trying to connect, but you refuse to see that. Your dad wasn't some saint dispelling gospel. He was a con artist who seriously fucked up your ability to have relationships."

I bit back my retort and mentally stepped away from the line that could fracture our friendship. She'd had a bad day.

"Just because I don't feel the need to become bosom buddies with everyone within ten seconds of meeting them doesn't mean that I'm damaged goods. I just don't feel like going out. I'll come another night. Tell Arkady that."

"I'll tell him not to hold his breath." She slammed the door when she left.

After washing off the arnica cream from my hands, I scrounged up some cheese and crackers, and turned on the latest British crime drama released on Netflix. I kept losing the thread of the plot, mulling over Priya's words. She was generally very laid back. I was the door slammer.

People, like puzzles, had varying degrees of complexity. It was a lot easier for me to figure others out than let them get close to me. I had trouble revealing the pieces of who I truly was, because what if I showed them to people and they left? I couldn't fully convince myself that the risk was worth the potential reward.

Sadly, logic didn't trump emotion.

But I didn't want to hurt my best friend. If I was putting unfair pressure on Priya, then I'd socialize with Arkady to make her happy. I was stuffing my feet into my motorcycle boots to join them when my phone lit up with a text from a blocked number. It said "midnight," an address in Tofino on the west coast of Vancouver Island, and a red heart emoji. Another text immediately followed it with an invitation to an auction. No mention of what the auction was for.

The Queen had come through.

I called Levi but it went straight to voicemail, so I forwarded the Queen's text along with a 911.

He phoned me back immediately. "I'll be there in fifteen minutes. Be ready."

"I work alone. I just need—"

"The only way you'll make it in time is with a private plane. And if you want that, then smile and partner up."

"If something shady's going down, they're not going to let in a House Head."

"I won't be recognized." He was impossible.

"Should I wear anything in particular?" I said.

"No. I'll take care of that."

Fuck balls. I'd probably end up in ridiculous heels that were impossible to run in and one of those dresses that gave everyone a free show when I sat down. Plus, I'd have to wear opaque black stockings to hide the scar on my right thigh. "Can't wait."

I'd packed the stockings, some toiletries, and a change of clothes in an overnight bag in case we got stuck on the island, and was braced for whatever fashion nightmare Levi was about to throw at me, when the limo glided up to the curb. I opened the door, then did a double take at the blond man inside. "Sorry. Wrong ride."

He laughed with a silky sensuality. In fact, everything about his slender body was silky, from his golden skin to his rosy lips and eyes that were the blue of an ocean on a hot summer day.

Couldn't be.

But what were the chances of a random limo showing up here?

"Levi?"

"Fooled you." Even his voice was different. Smoother. I liked his regular deep growl. Whiskey, not honey.

"The voice is part of the magic?" I said.

"No. Why waste energy on magic when I can do an impression?"

It was a damn good impression. Openly gaping, I climbed in next to him, setting my bag on the floor. "You look like a Siren." A Nefesh with sexual attraction magic. I took in the open V of his shirt, exposing his hairless chest and his soft, manicured man hands. "A submissive one. That's your cover?"

"No one will think it's me."

They wouldn't. This person was designed to serve and pleasure. My treacherous brain flashed on actual Levi holding me down as he took his maddening time licking down my body and I vowed to spend some quality time with my vibrator.

Levi poked me. "Snap out of it. You need to be sharp tonight."

"You surprised me, is all. I figured that any disguise would involve you going as a big bruiser."

"This is better. We'll be completely underestimated."

"You going to glamour me as a Siren, too?"

Silky Levi grinned wickedly at me. "Not quite."

He held up an ice bucket.

"Whoa." The reflection staring back at me was a woman in her sixties with silver hair pulled into a sleek chignon, a face so tight that if I smiled too broadly it might crack, and makeup that had been troweled on. "Got some GILF fantasies you want to share?" I thrust my hips at him. "Ooh, grandma."

"Mock all you want. People will see us and simply see a rich old eccentric with expensive tastes." He made a ruby necklace and ring set appear on me. The clustered jewels were showy, pretentious, and fussy.

"Do they come with my own Brinks guards?"

"Like I'd let you near the family jewels."

I snorted.

"They're excellent likenesses," Levi said.

"And excellent visual clues for people to latch on to should they need to describe me."

Levi booped me on the end of the nose. "Correct."

"Calm down there, sugar rush. You're positively giddy."

"I don't get to use my magic much these days." His expression grew distant as he stared out the window to the passing streets. "If I'd known how much being House Head involved playing politician…" He exhaled sharply. "It's good to flex that muscle. We'll keep these faces on so we get used to seeing each other like this."

I snapped my fingers. "We need names. I'll be Lillian," I said in my poshest British voice, and you're my arm candy, Santino, recently arrived from Rome."

"We're not doing accents," he said.

"The impressions were your idea. We proceed as planned." Still using the ice bucket as a mirror, I ran my hand over Lillian's hair, but felt my slicked back ponytail. Though if I looked down, I saw her leather sheath dress and heels, not my jeans and motorcycle boots. I jerked my head up. "That's a vertigo-inducing disconnect. I see the illusion but feel my real self."

"You get used to it."

"What do you see when you look at me?"

"The illusion I created. It's how I know the magic is working."

"What about touch? Does that break the illusion?"

"Not at all. You can feel the truth under the illusion because it's you." He gestured to my hands. "May I?" When I nodded, he put them on the side of his ribcage. "See. This person feels thinner than I would."

"That's really cool." I patted him down.

"Getting handsy?"

I shrugged. "If you wore that face, I might." Blech. No.

His amused expression smoothed out to a bland poker face. "The only caveat is that you have to stay relatively close with no doors or walls between us. Otherwise the illusion will fall away."

The driver opened the limo door.

A sliver of moonlight lit our way across the tarmac to the small plane silhouetted against the open hangar door.

"Given the size of your ego, Leviticus, I thought you'd have a larger plane." I hefted my overnight bag onto my other shoulder.

"Think *hard* about it, do you?"

"But seriously. This is the House plane? I'm under-whelmed."

"I'm not fueling the jet for a forty-five minute flight," he said. "I rented this."

At a moment's notice. Oh, to be rich. "Not under your name, I hope."

"Damn. Should I not have used my personal Visa? No, Ashira, it won't be connected back to me."

I marched up the stairs. "Ooh, how duplicitous. So you keep spare aliases around? Juggle families in various cities?"

"You have your secrets, I have mine," he said loftily.

Suddenly I wanted to know those secrets, the rush of discovering them and what he would do to hide them.

I stepped into the empty cabin. "Where are the attendants to cater to my whims?"

There was no lounge or TV, just eight leather chairs, admittedly wider than in cattle class, arranged in two facing groups of four.

"More private this way." Levi sat down and fastened his seatbelt.

I sat down across from him and stowed my bag under my seat, snapping in my seatbelt as the pilot announced our takeoff.

Once we'd achieved our cruising altitude and there was nothing to see outside except more nighttime, I turned to Levi. "You want the game plan?"

"No, I want to tell you the game plan."

"You have real control issues, you know that? You hired me. That means I come up with the plan."

"Porco cane. Fine. Dazzle me."

"Information gathering. Until I say otherwise."

"And then?" Levi said.

"A careful analysis of next steps."

"So winging it," he said.

"Pretty much. Why, did you have something different in mind?"

"Mine was more a detailed analysis of next steps."

"Such a shit. Is your magic going to interfere with mine at all?"

"Shouldn't. Why?"

I flexed my fingers and called forth my magic. "Here. Add this to your disguise."

Levi barked a laugh at my faithful reproduction of the dildo from the night at the aquarium. "And you didn't bleed to do it. Look at me being right."

"Go for fifty percent less smug. You'll still be unbearable." I held out the dildo. "Come on, arm candy. Touch it."

Levi picked it up, tossing it in his palm to test the weight. "Big deal. I'll have you know that Santino has a drawer full of these."

"Okay, that's more backstory than I needed, but I appreciate your dedication to the mission."

He handed it back to me. "Make it go away now."

"Don't worry. It'll disappear in a bit." I put it in my overnight bag.

All too soon, the pilot instructed us to make sure our seatbelts were fastened for our arrival at the Tofino/Long Beach airport.

I pressed my face to the window, but couldn't make out anything other than dark blobby shapes during our descent.

A Town Car waited for us outside the small weathered building.

Levi took my overnight bag, as well as a brown leather weekend bag that he'd brought for himself and we exited the aircraft.

The driver opened the back doors and relieved Levi of our bags. "Good evening."

"Good evening, young man," I said in my Lilian voice and widened my eyes pointedly at Levi.

"Ciao," he said in a perfect Italian accent that did syrupy things to my insides. "Payback is going to be sweet," he whispered in my ear, as he helped me into the Town Car.

I blew him a kiss and he flinched. Yeah, that had to be all kinds of old lady creepy.

The driver made sure we were seated comfortably and off we went.

Game on.

Chapter 12

Clouds covered the moon on our drive to the auction in Tofino, leaving little to see along the winding roads beyond the dark press of trees and the occasional "deer crossing" and "tsunami hazard ground" warning signs.

Levi and I didn't speak because there wasn't any privacy barrier with the driver, so instead, I used the time to psych myself up. The situation wasn't ideal. We were walking into an unknown location mostly blind and we didn't know what was being auctioned or what type of danger the other attendees posed. Even if weapons weren't allowed, Nefesh were plenty lethal on their own.

I was smart, could think on my feet, and was confident that I could manage my magic. Plus, I had Levi for backup. Honestly? Going undercover like this was the most exciting moment of my career. Tonight was going to be awesome. I jiggled my foot, riding the buzz. This was the big league and I couldn't wait for my turn at bat. I was going to hit this out of the park and find those responsible for the smudge.

The Town Car turned down a long, narrow driveway and stopped in front of a starkly modern mansion. Built on a cliff, the center section of the U-shaped home was elevated on metal poles.

A slender valet approached the car, asking for our invitation and the QC code allowing entry. There was no other visible security, but considering the flat look in her eyes, she was the first line of defense. She wouldn't be the last.

My stomach clenched as she scanned the invitation. If the Queen had fucked me over, I'd find out the hard way in about ten seconds.

The valet's scanner seemed to take forever to turn from red to green, but it did, and she allowed us out of the car and up the front stairs with a brusque nod.

The foyer was spectacular. A soaring cathedral ceiling rose three stories above us, while white walls displayed an extensive and priceless art collection. The glass wall facing the turbulent waves far below admirably showcased Mother Nature's beauty.

I accepted a glass of champagne from yet another lethal-looking attendant, and then strolled the space with Levi, my expression arranged into as ennui-laden a one as possible.

Lillian was a world-weary bitch.

But I needn't have worried: old lady Lillian and her boy toy Santino didn't draw nearly as much attention as I expected. Mostly because the place was full of entitled douchebags dripping with conspicuous wealth, more than one of whom had their own arm candy.

"Three o'clock." Levi subtly inclined his head toward a man wearing those stupid shuttershades, a fur coat, and his body weight in gold. "That's Thug Money. Registered with House Carmel." The wine-country based House that oversaw Californian Nefesh.

"Five bucks says his real name is Norman and he got his gangsta handle from an Internet generator," I said.

"Well, our boy Norm is drug-dealing scum with level five animal manipulation."

"A Dr. Doolittle. Don't they usually become vets or wrangle animals in the movie industry?"

"He's channeled his abilities in unique ways. He likes to take out the competition by driving his victims into the forest and having local wildlife tear them apart. Slippery fuck. No one can get charges to stick." Levi placed his hand on the small of my back, his head bent close to mine.

It was bang-on body language for two people who were intimate with each other and I was suddenly grateful for the barrier of the leather jacket that I was actually wearing.

I caught sight of the newest arrival and sipped my champagne to cover my shock. "See the man coming in?"

"The 1970s called. They want their outfit back." Levi covertly studied him for a moment. "Or not. Why can I picture him with a neck ruffle and a pocket watch?"

"I know, right?! He even works for the Queen of Hearts. I mean, the wardrobe had to be deliberate."

White Rabbit Man was headed our way so I casually sauntered past him. Well, Lillian did, arm-in-arm with Santino, but the minion didn't register a flicker of recognition.

"Were you testing how good my magic was?" Levi said.

"You noticed that, did you?"

He tapped his head. "I'm more than a pretty face."

"I'll give you this. You're holding this illusion for longer than I thought anyone could."

"This is nothing," he scoffed. "I have impressive endurance."

His eyes danced, and the corners of his lips quirked up wickedly, and I plucked a glass of wine from a tray, chugging half of it without tasting it.

"Who's that?" Levi said.

Every eye was glued to a stunning Asian woman about my age, twenty-eight, with long, lustrous hair, and a body that should have come with a "beware of dangerous curves" sign pinned to her hot pink slip dress. As she breezed past, I caught a whiff of her Chanel No. 5 perfume, which I only recognized because my bubbe had worn it. Guess it was as timeless as she'd claimed.

I was used to feeling invisible. It was a handy skill in my line of work and, my dress choice at the aquarium aside, I didn't generally solicit attention. I preferred to observe. But there was something a bit too uncomfortable about being in my old lady guise while drool practically ran down the chins of the collective males and a number of women in this room.

"Keep it in your pants, Santino love," I warned in my Lillian voice. "Appearances matter. Tonight you're mine."

"Cara mia," he purred in his Italian-accented English. He stroked his hand up my arm and, somehow, I could have been wearing an entire cow and it wouldn't have been enough to protect me from the fizz that rolled through my body. "No other woman holds a candle to your beauty."

I humphed and stuck my nose higher in the air.

Levi laughed his regular laugh, the sound tumbling down to my toes. This was mission giddiness, nothing more.

A bell chimed and a white-gloved attendant with the same flat gaze as the rest of the staff opened a set of doors which everyone obediently filed through. The new room was round and windowless with rows of chairs facing a podium.

I stifled a laugh as the clientele burst into a round of musical chairs trying to get the seats against the walls. Let them pull their dominance moves. We hadn't been invited here for a bloodbath. This crowd was so replete with ill-gotten gains they were practically constipated, and whoever was behind this auction wanted a piece of that.

I took the front middle seat with Levi on my left. The Asian woman sat at the end of our row, her body angled to see as many of the others as possible. It was almost like she was cataloguing the attendees. She kept glancing at the doors as if waiting for someone in particular to arrive.

An expectant hush fell over the room.

After a couple minutes with the only sound the rustling of clothes and the occasional clearing of a throat, an older man with a neat goatee and slicked-back hair stepped up to the podium. Unlike the flashy clientele, this man's attire was understated but of very high quality. He walked with a self-assured stride.

"Good evening," he said in an accent so upper crust that it made Lillian sound like a guttersnipe. "I'm Mr. Sharp. Please consider me your own personal procurer of enigmas, oddities, and wonders the world has never seen. Tonight you are fortunate to be part of a very exciting event. We have some highly coveted items to begin with before we get to the main attraction, so let's ease in with the first lot, shall we?"

The first item up for bid was a skull ring releasing a metal magic that turned the wearer to iron. Death guaranteed. An African woman in a colorful headscarf studded with dime-sized emeralds won it.

The woman next to me commented to her friend that the bidder was the long-time mistress of a powerful dictator. Maybe not for much longer.

The auction moved on to random items like a pouch of brown powder with magic nulling abilities, a mummified eye that allowed the owner to spy on any environment, and a mirror that let you see through walls.

I struggled to remain poker-faced. My brush with the Nefesh world had apparently been superficial at best. Would I have had a different understanding if I'd had my magic all these years? Or even if my father had stuck around? No doubt he'd seen more than his share of dubious artifacts. I snapped my attention back to the auction because I didn't want to miss a second of the proceedings.

As the night went on, I bid on several items to have

some skin in the game, but I ensured that I dropped out before I could win.

Interestingly, the Asian woman had the same strategy.

I nudged Levi when it happened for the third time and he nodded.

"How's your magic holding up?" I whispered.

"All good."

Dang, he wasn't kidding when he said he had stamina.

The penultimate lot before the main attraction was a variety of enchanted swords, with each piece sold separately. A man with thin hair and a suit so shiny it was practically an oil slick bet on every item, the fat diamonds in his multiple rings flashing every time he signaled. He seemed very eager to own the entire collection.

"He's overcompensating," I whispered to Levi. "Probably has pubic lice."

"Why have one STI when you can collect them all?" he murmured.

"Santino, you're terrible."

"You wouldn't want me any other way, Lillian."

Once that lot was dispensed with, and props to Thug Money for his shit-disturbing ploy that snatched the final sword away from the original bidder, Mr. Sharp nodded at the white-gloved attendant.

"That brings us to our final item which is not up for auction." Our self-styled procurer raised his hands at the angry outburst. "You misunderstand. This item is available to everyone." He chuckled. "Well, all present, that is."

The attendant wheeled in a table with a metal briefcase on it.

Mr. Sharp stepped out from behind the podium and unlocked it. He held up a stoppered vial with a shifting shadow inside.

A smudge.

My hand tightened on Levi's forearm. He was slouched

lazily in his chair but the preternatural awareness rolling off him made the hairs on my body stand on end. This was full-on "protector of my Nefesh, fuck with me at your peril" mode.

"What's that?" the woman next to me asked Mr. Sharp.

"Magic. In this case, water elemental magic. But we can supply any type that you like."

An electric charge jolted through the room, everyone reaching the conclusion they'd been invited to draw. That Mr. Sharp held the key to acquiring magic, any magic now within reach instead of limited to being born with one specific type. Mundanes could become Nefesh and Nefesh could hold multiple powers.

Except they hadn't seen what I'd seen. They didn't know that smudges killed and this had to be a con.

"What do we do with it?" a man with a pronounced Adam's apple and Slavic accent said.

"I invite you all to envision a world where Houses no longer dictate the rules in favor of one ruled by the powerful elite," Mr. Sharp said.

"Even Mundanes?" A cunning look crossed the Slav's face.

"Absolutely. This is a world where Mundanes could become a thing of the past."

I barely contained my snort. Yeah, because if they tried to use this, they'd be dead.

"A world where one could have multiple abilities, all made to order." Mr. Sharp smiled. "For the right price, of course."

The room erupted into pandemonium.

"Sounds like a fairy tale," I said loudly in my Lillian voice, cutting through the roar of discussion. The room fell into a tense silence, awaiting Sharp's response.

"I assure you, Madame, it's quite real. Thanks to special technology, my employers have found a way to harness magic. All magic." He tapped his finger against the vial. "With one simple injection? This could be yours."

The crowd relaxed. People loved a good shortcut to power. Especially if it was only available to the privileged few. Idiots. This guy was trying to put one over on them, what did they think he was going to say? Whoops, sorry. Actually it'll kill you super dead.

"I heard House Pacifica was experimenting on people," the Asian woman said. "Is that how you got this?"

Levi's Santino face darkened. I stroked his back until he relaxed, wondering what had prompted her to speak up.

"The fuck would they do that for?" Thug Money scoffed. "He just said this would destroy the Houses."

Thank you, Thug Money, for providing the voice of reason.

"Houses have to operate according to a lot of laws," the Asian woman retorted. "But if the House Head decided to go private…"

"It's the Queen of Hearts," the African woman said. "Rumor has it she's expanding her interests in a substantial way. This fits the bill."

White Rabbit Man didn't react at all.

"That true?" I whispered to Levi.

"There's always that rumor," he said.

"I'm not at liberty to confirm or deny whom my employers are," Mr. Sharp said. Coy bastard, keeping doubt on both House Pacifica and the Queen, and providing two convenient scapegoats for when the goods didn't perform as advertised. He held the vial higher. "This is going to change the balance of power. It's not just magic. It's legacy magic."

The audience gazed up at him in greedy rapture. Hook, line, and sinker to Mr. Sharp.

The doors were flung open.

"If you will follow me back to the foyer, there are a number of attendants waiting to take your orders." With that, he sealed the vial containing the trapped smudge back inside the metal briefcase.

Another guard entered from the door next to the podium. One with a purple birthmark under his eye.

I dug my nails into Levi's thigh.

Mr. Sharp cuffed the briefcase to Birthmark Man's wrist and spoke a few words to him, before the man left through the same door he'd entered.

Levi stood up and offered me his arm. "Lillian?"

"Let them go ahead, Santino. As the good man said, this is available to all."

While we waited for the room to clear out, I checked it for hidden cameras. There was nothing readily apparent so I moved to level two and opened an app on my phone.

Levi raised an eyebrow so I flashed him the screen, keeping it low and partially covered by my hand. It was a hidden camera detector app. Technology was marvelous.

"Tonight was a con," I said. "A cash grab. Smudges don't stick."

"And someone wants me to be a fall guy for when the truth comes out." Levi sat forward, his elbows braced on his knees and his Santino face grim.

"Yeah. You or the Queen. Can you think of anyone who wants to personally target you?"

"All House Heads have enemies, but I can't think of anyone I've so badly wronged that they'd go to this extreme. Or that have the power and resources to do all this."

The hidden camera detector app finished its sweep without finding anything. I glanced out the door. No one was paying us any attention. "Come on. I want to poke around."

There were purple bruises under Levi-as-Santino's eyes.

"You all right?" I said.

"I'm angry and the auction went longer than I anticipated," he said as Levi. His voice was steady and there wasn't any tension in his body. How tapped out was he?

"Can you hold on ten more minutes? Birthmark Man was the one handing out flyers. I want the location of the missing kids *and* that briefcase."

Levi nodded.

We exited out the same door into a back hallway.

The rest of the mansion was eerily deserted. It was also empty, with one unfurnished room after another.

"They rented it for this occasion." I swore viciously, my slim hope that Meryem might be on the premises dashed. "How are you doing?"

Levi made a see-saw motion with his hand. "My vision's going."

I came to an abrupt stop in the middle of the hallway. "What do you mean 'going?'"

"Tunneling. I'll be blind soon. Temporarily."

I almost punched him. "Are you kidding? You shouldn't have come with me."

I meant that he shouldn't have pushed himself, that even if the blindness was temporary it wasn't worth him succumbing, that I'd have found a way in, but that's not how he took it.

His expression hardened. "This has happened enough times that I can manage. Finish up and we'll go."

He clearly wasn't open to backpedaling explanations, so I peered around the corner. There was one more doorway and then the kitchen, which was the only place with any activity other than the large foyer.

"You want to wait here?" I said. "I can check the last room myself."

"Illusion won't hold if we're separated." Levi leaned against the wall looking dangerously pale, one hand over his eyes.

"We'll be super quick." I put my arm around his waist to

support him. The second the coast was clear, we hobbled to the door and slipped inside.

"This area is off-limits," said a man.

"Perhaps if you marked your powder rooms properly, I wouldn't have to waste my time looking for one," I said in my most imperious voice. Oh, *hel*-lo, Birthmark Man.

"Scusaci," Levi said in his Santino voice. "We were just leaving." He stood straight and steady, looking directly at the guard, without a trace that anything was wrong with him.

One of Levi's shoes flickered from pointy-toed leather loafers to a scuffed Daytona boot.

Shit.

I shuffled slightly sideways so Birthmark Man wouldn't see. Levi was running out of juice and if we were exposed, we were fucked. But this was flyer guy. He was my shot at finding the kids before anyone else got hurt, and I wasn't leaving without that briefcase.

With an apologetic glance at Levi, I manifested a dagger and flung it at the man.

The dagger flew straight and true, but right before it hit him, his skin transformed into rubber. The blade bounced harmlessly off and boomeranged back at me.

"I'm rubber, you're glue," he said.

I yelped, barely scrambling out of the way as the knife sank into the wall next to my head. "*Words* bounce off me to stick to you, not knives, you taunting fuck. Seriously? Insult magic?"

He frowned at me because I'd forgotten to use my Lillian voice.

"Who are you and what do you want?" Birthmark Man glanced at Levi who was listing precariously, but I snapped my fingers to keep his attention on me, skittering back out of reach. A rubber body meant a ton of mass so he couldn't move fast, but we still had no way to hurt him.

"I'm not anyone you want to trifle with," I said in the

British accent. "Where are the kids that you took with those pathetic flyers of yours?"

"Lillian, it's time to leave," Levi said.

"Answer me," I said.

"You can't do anything to me in this form, old woman," Birthmark Man taunted. "I'm invincible."

His magic pulsed beneath his skin, smelling of glue and wet leaves. Not even a grilled steak would have smelled as good right now. I could take it. Just a taste. Enough to scare him into answering. All I needed to do it was blood.

His.

Ducking low, I rushed him, knocking him over. He hit the ground with a meaty splat and I landed on top of him. His body was rubber, but his teeth weren't. A lapse in judgment that was going to cost him. I landed one of my patented terrible punches that hurt my hand and knocked out his front tooth.

He fought hard, dealing a punishing undercut against my ribs, and bucked me off him. I caught hold of the briefcase and snapped it free of the cuffs, tossing it to Levi.

The briefcase flew right past Levi and bounced off the wall with a thunk. He stood there, one hand braced on the wall, blinking rapidly, like he was trying to clear his vision.

Much as I wanted to help him, I refused to lose this opportunity.

Birthmark Man and I grappled, grunting. He rolled over, his weight half on top of me, but I kneed him in the groin and as he flailed back in pain, I decked him in the mouth again.

Blood welled on his gums and I surged my red magic into them. His blood was a conduit to his magic and it was like I'd mainlined directly in. I shuddered, my flesh tingling. Warmth unfurled inside me.

The world snapped into sharp focus, like going from Kansas to Oz and seeing color for the first time.

"Lillian," Levi growled.

I didn't move. Dynamite couldn't have shifted me away from this rush.

"Where are the kids. No? Nothing to say?" My blood magic didn't just flow through Birthmark Man, it turned into dozens of tiny hooks, snagging his magic. Making it mine.

His magic swam through his blood in a thick, heavy stream, similar to molasses, though it tasted like it smelled of glue and wet leaves. Even that didn't deter me.

My lips parted breathily and my thighs tightened around his torso. I would have savored it longer but Levi gave a raspy inhale, startling me and causing me to jerk on Birthmark Man's magic, yanking a black smudge partway out of him.

It snapped me out of my trance. Ice cold, I scrambled off him and slammed down our connection. The smudge flew back inside him.

I gasped. What had I done?

What was I?

I turned stricken eyes to Levi to find him staring at me in horror.

Not Santino. Levi.

His clarity of vision lasted one horrible instant, then the light died out of his eyes and he sucked in a harsh breath.

Birthmark Man roared and clubbed me across the head with a rubber fist. The world went blurry, all sound flattening out to an atonal buzz.

Levi's glamour snapped into place and fumbling blindly in my direction, he caught me by the shoulder and hauled me upright.

Our assailant staggered to his feet and pulled out a gun.

"Gun," I croaked. I stared down the barrel with a paralyzing numbness that wasn't enough to keep the aching yearning for his magic in check.

164

A large reddish ant with an overly large head crawled out from the baseboard. Then another. Then a dozen more, marching up Birthmark Man's pant leg.

"Fuck!" He tried to shake them off, but the motion unleashed a flood. They poured from the walls and up his body, encasing him.

The man shrieked and fell to the ground, trying to protect himself.

"Get us out of here. Now!" Levi ordered.

Grabbing the briefcase, I broke into a run, dragging him along with me. It wasn't easy leading someone while sprinting when that person couldn't see and you were bent double with violent muscle cramps that threatened to tear you apart. We almost wiped out twice getting to the end of the corridor.

I looked back before we skidded around it.

The ants were gone, but the man was still curled in the fetal position slapping at himself with broken cries.

"You did that?"

"Guess we're both monsters," Levi said, right before I pushed him out into the night.

Chapter 13

The ride back was as silent as the one to the auction had been but for very different reasons.

Levi was in as bad a shape as I was, sitting with his eyes closed, still blind, still maintaining our stupid illusion for the driver's sake since this was Santino and Lillian's ride.

How temporary was temporary?

I had my arms wrapped around myself, literally attempting to keep my shit together, curled into the door as cramps rolled through me. I was shivering so hard my teeth audibly rattled.

No wonder the smudges I'd destroyed felt so foul. They were atrocities. It was also why they smelled rotten. Without the flesh to anchor them, the magic was dying. These ghostly abominations weren't simply feeding to survive. They were attempting to find a new permanent host.

Smudges were inherent magic ripped from the body.

By people like me.

Blood magic was the "technology" that caused smudges, which meant there were more people out there with this power, living in secret.

Why were they doing this? For the money? For chaos?

Or because taking magic was better than any high, and even through all my shame and self-disgust, I would have sold a kidney for the chance to feel that again.

The driver dropped us off at the Wickanninish Inn, a world-famous resort out here on the edge of the west coast of Vancouver Island. I couldn't appreciate the beauty of the place because I was still in a pained fog, my body spasming like a junkie who'd gone cold turkey from every drug all at once.

I don't know the effect on my body if I'd pulled the smudge all the way out of Birthmark Man, but this coitus interruptus nipped at the heels of my car crash for worst pain ever.

I hissed as a fresh wave of hell rolled through me.

The second the Town Car had pulled away, Levi dropped the glamours and staggered forward.

My relief at seeing him was dizzying, but it was bound up with anger over the monster comment, fear over how bad off he was, and these cravings that rode me hard.

"We're not staying here," he said between harsh breaths. He jerked a thumb to the left, which because he couldn't see was actually the lobby of the Inn. "One property over."

I shoved him down onto a bench, then bent over double, a spasm punching the air from my lungs. Wiping sweat off my brow, I pushed to my feet. "Stay."

Squeezing the briefcase handle hard enough that it bit into my flesh, the sharp bite of pain allowed me to put one foot in front of the other, head inside, and have the receptionist call a taxi.

When I came out, Levi's face was pinched, his shoulders rounded forward. His eyes were still closed.

"When is this going to wear off?"

At the sound of my voice, he jerked up, affecting a "relaxed" position as if nothing was wrong. Other than him looking past my ear instead of into my eyes.

"I'm fine," he said tersely. "I need rest and food and there's both at the cabin."

He didn't want me to see him weakened? Well, I didn't want to feel like his condition was my fault and that I should have seen past his insistence he could hang on a bit longer and got him out of there.

I sat down, stretching out my fingers and toes. My muscles had unwound from burning and seized up to a full-body twisty throb, kind of like an everywhere stomachache. *You wouldn't be so miserable if you'd taken the magic like you were meant to.*

Sure, evil voice. Welcome to the party. Slowly, I fought my way out of this unquenchable need. The cravings and cramps subsided, but no matter how hard I tried to stuff my lingering horror over what I could do into a padlocked box, it squished out in a toxic darkness, its form eerily reminiscent of a smudge.

Levi still wasn't looking so hot.

"Why did you let me search the place?" I said. "If we'd gotten out of there sooner—"

"Had we left, we wouldn't now have the briefcase and one more smudge to destroy."

We wouldn't have found out what I could do.

The taxi pulled in. Levi raised his head in its general direction, but didn't move.

"Come on, babe." I wrapped my arms around him like the clingiest of girlfriends, and bundled him into the back seat.

His body was rigid beneath my hold, but his eyes remained scarily dead, so he allowed himself to be guided.

The cab driver put our luggage in the trunk. Levi gave him the name of the place and we were off. It really was one property over. The entire ride lasted about two minutes.

Even now, in the middle of the night, the sky was varying shades of gray rubbed down to a black horizon. A thin frothing line of white danced along the shore, the ever-present roar of the Pacific mirroring the scream stuck in my throat. The landscape was wild and raw and beautifully savage, every pristine lungful of air crisp with underlying notes of cedar and pine, but it was marred by shadows.

Once the cab was gone, Levi directed me to a small row of cabins in front of a larger condo building. Each cabin was isolated from its neighbors by a thick row of trees. His instructions were so precise that even blind, I'd bet he could describe them down to the last detail from memory.

I saved the luggage for the second trip, taking Levi and the briefcase to our corner cabin first. Between his tentative stride and my post-craving exhaustion, every step was a fight to hang on to him.

"I've got you," I said.

"Why don't you worry a bit more about yourself?" he snapped.

His anger and resentment flailed my raw nerves. I dropped my hold and walked back to the luggage, leaving him there. By the time I'd returned, he'd barely made any progress, his arms outstretched before him.

"Your current trajectory should land you in the ocean and out of my hair soon enough."

He dropped his arms. "Can you help me inside?"

My hands were full of bags, so I had him hang on to the back of my jacket and we lurched our way to the cabin.

The inside was small and cozy with red cedar window frames and ceiling beams. A dining table was all that separated the kitchen with its white appliances and butcher block countertops from the living room, with a sofa and two chairs grouped around a fireplace with a flat screen TV mounted above it. There were two bedrooms with a bathroom in between.

I dropped the bags and led Levi to the sofa.

He collapsed onto it, slumped miserably in one corner.

"Can I get you something to eat?"

He shook his head, so I flicked on the switch for the fireplace, desperate for its warmth to unthaw me. My skin was dotted in goosebumps and an all-around malaise was soaked deep into my bones.

Levi sat on one side, I stood on the other defrosting, and between us was this giant white elephant of what he'd seen me do. Part of me selfishly hoped his blindness would last until we parted ways so I wouldn't see his disgust again.

The feeling finally returned to my extremities, and since it was better to be useful than sit here brooding, I picked the briefcase lock.

"The only things inside are the vial with the smudge and a thumb drive." I gently tapped the vial, and the smudge burbled and flowed like a tiny lava lamp. "It's really a third-party smudge if we're going to be technical. You know, already torn away and out there floating free, versus magic that's inherently part of a person but has not yet been torn out, like what happened with Birthmark..." My voice was getting high and pitchy. "Fuck." I shoved the vial back into the padded foam encasing it in the briefcase.

Stay professional. I steadied myself and examined the thumb drive but there weren't any markings.

"Ash?"

"Yeah?"

"Thank you." Levi looked at me with a clear gaze.

"You're welcome. All better?"

"Yes." He paused. "Your bedside manner is shit."

"You suck as a patient." Our dynamic returned to its regularly scheduled programming.

He stood up to rummage around in the kitchen but his movements were clumsy. "Are you hungry?"

I shook my head. "I might take a..." I squinted out through the balcony sliding doors facing the beach. "Is that a hot tub?"

"Yeah." He removed a loaf of bread and some peanut butter from the fridge.

"Is it on?" I crossed my fingers.

"Should be."

I shucked off my boots and jeans and stripped off my sweater, leaving me in my sweaty T-shirt, bra, and boy shorts, then I shuffled outside, hopping from one foot to the other with a little yelp at the cold. I pulled off the cover and the hot tub hummed to life, bubbles floating to the surface.

Inching my way into the water, I rested my feet on the molded plastic seat next to mine and tucked my knees in to my chest. Hot tubs were the one luxury I'd kill to have on a regular basis. Baths weren't hot enough or deep enough to let me soak the way I wanted.

Nefesh had been stripped of their magic for this bullshit cash grab by persons unknown and they'd used individuals with powers like mine to further their aims. I sent up silent thanks that I hadn't completed the process with Birthmark Man and he still had his magic.

I turned my newfound understanding of smudges and my abilities around and around in my brain until the knowledge was, if not comfortable, then processed. If all my powers were unlocked and accessible now, who was driving this train? Was it some predator/hunter instinct of mine or was it *me*? Ultimately, how much control did I have over it?

Priya had been kidding about me being an A.I., but I didn't want to be a vessel, a machine, or a predatory virus. Or, worst of all, some magic-addled junkie ripping away people's powers for some reason hard-wired into me. I wanted to be Ashira Cohen with free will.

There was a gentle splash and Levi settled himself in the seat across from me. My first glance was to assure myself that though he looked tired, his color had returned and his movements were no longer lethargic. My second took in his soccer player's build: leanly muscled, with beautiful broad shoulders, and a light dusting of hair on his bare olive skin.

Were his legs—? Nope. Not looking.

Okay, maybe looking, but I couldn't see anything under the water. I sighed and stretched out. This exquisite heat was soothing me body and soul. Body, anyway.

"Make yourself at home," he said wryly.

"Too late. I'm never leaving. Expense it to the House." I pushed away the floating chlorine dispenser.

The weight of all the things no one wanted to discuss pressed down on us.

"How did you find this place?" I said.

"We're investing in some environmental tech with a company based in Tofino. Seemed prudent to have a place here."

"Oh."

We listened to the lapping waves, breathing in the faint tangs of chlorine and salt spray and my muscles unlocked.

"You dropped your glamour," I said, trying for a safe entry point into a debrief and realizing that after that shit-show there wasn't one. "When you saw me... when you saw."

"I know. Not yours though. And I don't think that guy noticed."

"No, he was a bit preoccupied," I said.

"If he did?" Levi shrugged. "We'll deal with it should the time come."

I pulled my eyes away from his chest to stare up at the stars that never shone this brightly in Vancouver. "For the record, I don't think you're a monster." I paused. "That's where you say, 'I don't think you're a monster either, Ash.'"

Please say it.

"I think the two of us are more alike than I even imagined," he said.

I shifted on to one of the raised seats, the breeze rapidly

cooling my heated skin. Not that Levi's opinion mattered, but this person who thought so little of me could at least draw the line somewhere, because saying I was a monster like him was awful.

Birthmark Man had looked shattered from that ant illusion. I hadn't known I could create smudges, but Levi had honed his monster self into a mighty weapon.

Or perhaps I wanted someone to say I was okay. That having this particular ability didn't automatically make me a horrible person and that there had to be some good reason for it.

I massaged my foot. "Jeez, Levi, that's depressing."

"Isn't it just?"

Well, fuck you too.

"For better or worse, we have to work together until these third-party smudges are destroyed," I said. "So we better find a way to peacefully co-exist, even though we're nothing alike. We're oil and water."

His gaze was too penetrating. "No, we're not. We've reminded each other of ourselves from the first day we met, and the reflection is a little too close for comfort."

We could argue this all night, he wouldn't see the truth.

"There are more out there like me." I shifted sideways, resting a hip against one of the massage jets.

"I figured. Did you know you could do that?"

"That I could create smudges? You got me," I said frostily. "I'm the one running around town doing this. I'm also working with Mr. Sharp and his people."

"Here's a wild idea. Try and see this from my perspective. Nothing about your magic fits the rules. I don't subscribe to this hairbrained theory about recessive genes turning on."

"It's a perfectly good theory, but how did you hear about it?" I jammed my thumb into the arch of my foot to get at an achy spot.

"Assume I know everything that goes on in my House. Obviously, you didn't create the smudges that are out there, but I'm still waiting for a plausible explanation about when your magic first showed up."

"Me too, but right now that gene theory is the only thing I've got, so stop making me feel like a criminal. *You're* having trouble with all this? Try living it. *Fuck*." I'd taken my anger out on my poor foot and squeezed my little toe too hard.

"Apology massage?" Levi said after a couple of moments.

I held out my foot. "Tickle me and I'll puke on you."

"Noted." He massaged my arch with strong fingers and the charged air de-escalated into a wary truce.

How much truth did I owe him about my magic? It was so much easier to see things clearly when it wasn't my truth at stake.

"I swear I didn't know about the smudges. But being able to take magic?" I exhaled. "Sharing. Not a thing I do much of."

"Another thing we have in common," he said.

I swear if he said that one more time I was gonna kick him in the nads.

"I suspected I could do it the night we trained," I said.

"Hence the freak out."

Not the only freak out anymore or even the worst one, but I wasn't ready to tell Levi how good taking Birthmark Man's magic had felt. Now that the cramps and distress had faded, I was kind of hoping that I'd overblown the entire thing.

He pressed some magic spot on my foot and I moaned.

"Foot massages. You've finally revealed your weak spot." He mimed twirling a mustache. "I've waited years for this."

I snorted. "You'd have to catch me to use it against me."

"I could catch you." His voice was low and his stroking fingers sent delicious shivers inside me.

I made a dismissive noise. And pressed my thighs together. "That's a terrible line. You're embarrassing yourself."

He raised a brow imperiously. "I am Levi Montefiore. I do not require lines. Women fall at my feet."

"More like your ego sucks up so much oxygen that they pass out."

"Can't let me have one win, can you?"

"We have a working pattern. Why break it?" I gnawed on my bottom lip. "I can't stop thinking about Meryem. What they might be doing to her. Hopefully that thumb drive will have answers."

"We'll see, but in the meantime, there are more of those vials out there and they can't be allowed to exist. Multiple smudges wreaking havoc? It'll be catastrophic." He released my foot.

"That drive is our only lead right now to finding the kids, the vials, and whoever is behind this. You have any other ideas?"

"No." He sank under the water for long enough that I kicked him to resurface. He slid up, water streaming over his pecs, and flicked his hair out of his eyes with a surety of movement, the moonlight catching on the tiny silver scar where I'd stabbed him with the fork over the doughnut. The one chink in his projection of strength.

I swallowed, oddly mesmerized by those elegant fingers and the play of muscle against the one long vein on his tanned forearm when he dropped his hand.

"Do you get manicures?" I blurted out.

His WTF look was answer enough.

"Why illusion magic?" I said, grasping at a change of topic. "I always thought it was because you're such a control freak that you had to bend the world to your will, but it doesn't fit my idea of you that you'd think it's monstrous."

"I'm not your puzzle to solve."

"Sweet summer child, everyone is my puzzle to solve. Besides you're the one who raised the whole onster-may thing."

Levi caught hold of my other foot. The one on my injured leg.

I tensed for a second before sitting back and motioning for him to continue. Foot massages in hot tubs were the life goal I didn't know I'd been missing.

"Drop it, Ash."

"Come on. You know all about my fucked-up life."

He massaged my toes and I tried not to squirm.

Levi regarded me steadily. "Actually, I don't. Your dad took off. Sucks but you kind of went over the top with the whole car thing, don't you think?"

I winced. "You don't pull punches, do you?"

Gawd, he really was Watson.

"Not with you. So?"

Pulling my foot away, I closed my eyes and sank up to my chin. I wasn't handing Levi my issues on a silver platter.

"Your dad was a Charmer. Did he have you charmed or something and that's why you went apeshit when he left?"

My eyes snapped open. "No. God. You knew about my dad's magic? How big is that file on me?"

"My father has no magic and it eats him up." Levi sounded downright smug about that fact. "He's also shady as shit, and had to subcontract certain jobs over his illustrious career in data security to people with the innate ability to charm others into business deals that benefited my father." He smiled tightly at me.

I sat up straight. "You're kidding."

"Would that I were."

"My dad worked for yours? Why didn't you say anything?"

"Adam was gone by the time we met and I didn't even know until several years ago. What was the point?"

"The...?" I stood up. "Fuck."

"Sit down."

I stared stubbornly out to sea.

"Ashira."

"Dad taught me there were two kinds of people in this world, cons and marks. And marks were the worst thing you could possibly be. I had that pounded into my head. But when he left us without a word, that's what I was. A stupid mark, because I'd believed him when he..." My voice cracked. "When he called me his little jewel and said how much he loved me. So sue me, I went a little apeshit." I did the quotes. "I swore that no one was ever going to play me again. Except then I found out that someone had tattooed a ward on my head and suppressed magic that hey, happens to be monstrous, and I'm realizing I've been played so many ways that I don't even know what the game is. Or if you're part of it." I stared at him dead-on.

"I'm not." His expression iced over, his lips flattened in a severe line and his eyes deepened to the flinty blue of the coldest winter's night.

"Whatever. Now you know. Mazel tov. All your worst opinions of me are confirmed."

I tried to climb out of the hot tub but Levi grabbed my arm. "What the hell are you talking about? I don't think badly of you."

I jerked away. "You think I'm lying about my magic."

"No, I don't understand why your magic wasn't present at birth, but I don't think you're lying. Anymore," he amended.

"And that I go around doing whatever I want."

"You do." At my snort, he held up a hand. "If I'm being honest, I admire that about you. Hell, I wish I could live that way. You're doing exactly what you want to, despite all the obstacles you had to overcome: being female, being Mundane. You're smart, you're tough, and you have no hesitation dishing shit out to me constantly. You know how rare that is? With very few exceptions, everyone either wants to kiss my ass or knock it down a peg."

Gaping, I sat down so hard in the seat beside him that I slipped sideways, splashing water into Levi's face. I grabbed his shoulders for balance, then frowned.

Levi flinched away from me.

"Levi." I flung out an arm to block him from getting up. "Let me see. Please?"

"Don't you have enough ammunition for one night?" he said softly.

"No."

"Great," he muttered.

"No, dummy. I mean…" Argh. I took a breath and tried again. "Do you know why I said you were Watson? Because he's the moral center and for all your many faults, you care deeply about your House and your people."

Levi placed his hand on my forehead like he was taking my temperature. "Methinks there was a compliment somewhere in that insult."

I smacked his hand away. "I'm trying to be nice here, but you make it impossible. Watson isn't weak, and this isn't about ammunition because scars aren't weakness. They're strength. They prove you survived. You know my scars. Let me see yours."

Grudgingly, he turned his back to me revealing the patchwork of thin white lines.

I gently touched one. "Do they hurt?"

Levi caught my hand and placed it in my lap. "Not anymore."

"I've seen you in a tank top. How come I didn't see them before? Whoa. Do you constantly illusion them away? That seems like an exhausting way to live."

"Since I don't walk around naked, no, I don't."

"You should try that next time you butt heads with the mayor. Might liven things up."

My brain was whirring. Nefesh magic was like Freud's Id. And what were two of the most primal drives? Love and security. We all worked with illusion, even if it was as small as putting on a smile for the world when we felt blue, showing confidence when we felt weak, or convincing ourselves that things weren't as bad as they seemed. But for that desire to become a powerful magic?

"You didn't have the perfect childhood everyone assumes you did," I said.

"Appearances matter," he parroted back to me in Lillian's voice.

"Can I get you some wine for your pity party?"

A startled laugh burst out of him. "Well played, Holmes."

"You do not have rights to that name," I said. "Only Pri gets to call me Holmes."

He booped me on my nose. "Ah, but I predate her. You get Leviticus, I get this."

"Try it and I'll gut you. I rue the day my grandparents sent me to that stupid camp."

He leaned back against the seat. "Moriarty and Holmes. Admit it, that was the best day of your life."

Levi's ink black wet hair was raked away from his face and his eyes were lit up with smug amusement. The day we first met may not have been my best one, but being here in the hot tub with him had elevated today out of being one of my worst.

Priya wasn't the only person in my corner, and my new ally smelled really good: of fresh air, a hint of sandalwood, and that delicious oaky aged amber scotch and chocolate magic.

A squirmy sensation that hadn't visited in a long time

shivered through me. Even using my vibrator was more work than it was worth lately.

"You can't call me that," I said. "We aren't Moriarty and Holmes."

"Why not?"

"Because despite a staggering amount of fanfic, Holmes and Moriarty never did this."

Then I kissed him.

Chapter 14

That kiss was spun sugar, soft and sweet, and the world fell away in a honeyed haze, his lips tasting faintly of peanut butter. I slid my hands onto his chest, Levi's thumb caressing my cheek. Each tease of our lips left me that much more breathless.

Then Levi crowded me up against my seat, his face close, and grinned.

"Best day of your life," he said, and crashed his lips down.

This kiss was dirty. Messy.

Reckless.

Shockwaves rocketed across my body, and I closed my eyes against the delicious onslaught, my breath shuddering out of me. Butterflies fluttered inside my chest. Half of them were doing lazy swoops but the other half were beating against my bones like the drums of war. Pure exhilaration.

While the cabin next door couldn't see us, anyone walking on the beach could have.

I moaned.

Levi cupped the back of my head, his tongue tangling with mine, and deepened the kiss.

Need slammed into me like a fist, hot flames of lust licking me from within. Our hands mapped each other's bodies, exploring every ridge and dip.

My head tilted back slightly to expose a spot on my throat that he sucked on, making me shiver with delight.

Levi tugged my shirt over my head. "This is weird."

"Phrasing, dude."

He blushed, which was adorably unlike him. "Not these. These are…" He sucked my tit into his mouth, bra and all and I melted into him. "Magnificent," he breathed. He removed my bra, fondling, licking, and nipping. His stubble rasped against my skin.

I tangled my fingers through his thick hair, trying to reconcile the sight of his dark head against my bare skin. "Okay, yeah, it's weird. Yay, weird."

His chuckle turned to a groan as I pinched his nipple.

That was nice, but I wanted more kisses. Here and now. I pulled him up, his intoxicating scent enveloping me. My world was the roaring of the waves, the stars that blazed even through my closed lids, and Levi's lips on mine.

He ghosted his fingers up my leg, flitting with the edge of my boy shorts and I arched against him, clutching his shoulders.

"Are you okay with this?" His voice rumbled through me.

"Put it this way. Stop and die."

"I didn't hear please. Etiquette is important."

"Evil bastard. *Please*," I said.

Talented boy that he was, he kissed me again as he lifted me up and pulled off my underwear in one fell swoop.

I sucked on his lip and Levi growled. His lashes fluttered open to reveal blue eyes that were glazed with a drugged out bliss. A crazy possessive urge to have him only ever look at me that way swelled up.

What was I doing? This is just sex, Ash.

It had to be.

I ran my hands over his body, pulling him closer.

The kiss grew rough, almost brutal, and then his clever fingers rubbed my clit and I braced one hand on the top of the hot tub to keep from drowning as my body went boneless. Heat curled off my skin. I rocked my hips, the water lapping against me, driving my frenzy higher and hotter in time with Levi's stroking. Aching for him, I wrapped a leg around his waist, wanting his scent and his touch to imprint on me.

"Are you imagining Santino?" he said, holding my hips with one hand to make me ride his fingers.

"Who?"

His eyes blazed in something that wasn't triumph, not entirely, then he licked and sucked his way down my neck, so careful of my bruises.

I rubbed his hard cock through his boxer shorts.

His breath hitched and he upped the tempo of his fingers, catching my small cries with his mouth.

Water lapped over the top of the hot tub and my orgasm crested inside me until it burst in a hot glitter bomb and I cried out into the hollow of his neck.

He placed his hand on the small of my back, cradling me to him. Tenderly. Like we were real lovers.

We both tensed at the same time.

No no no no no. Just sex.

I reached for the waist of his boxers but he stopped me.

"I don't have a condom," he said.

I wriggled against him, very pleased with the soft "Ashira" that fell from his lips like a plea. He rolled the "r" the Italian way and the sound of my name like that sent a liquid jolt of desire straight to my clit.

"I can think of at least six things that don't require one," I said. "Seven if you're very good."

Levi detached himself and pecked me on the lips. "I'm going in."

Huh? He got me off better than anyone ever had but I wasn't allowed to do the same? What guy would choose to stay hard when he had a perfectly willing woman to play with? Had I plummeted to a new low of stupidity by kissing him?

At the very least, I'd broken my cardinal rule. Never show weakness.

"Good idea," I said coolly. "My fingers are prunes."

I locked the sliding door behind us when we got inside.

"Ash…"

"Yeah?" Hold out your hand. Take me to bed. Prove I hadn't made a terrible judgment call.

"Nothing."

I lifted my wet hair off my neck and squeezed it out. "If you were going to ask me not to ever mention this, don't worry. I wouldn't dream of it."

His expression went tight, then he gave a curt nod. "Good. So long as we understand each other."

"Perfectly." With as much dignity as I could muster for someone who'd had the most mind-blowing orgasm of her life then been brushed off, I went into one of the bedrooms, and shut the door.

I promptly collapsed on the bed and screamed into my pillow. What a colossal fucking mistake.

But damn if I didn't want to make it again.

IT WAS A VERY LONG NIGHT. I masturbated as enthusiastically as possible, but the harder I chased my orgasm, the farther away it got, until it was fishtailing out, kicking up gravel, and giving me the finger as it disappeared laughing into the night.

I wanted Levi, on me, around me, and inside me. Most especially inside me. Instead, I lay there listening for any rustling sound that Levi was deeply regretting his decision and working up the nerve to come crawling, begging, but heard nothing. By the time daylight rolled around, I was tired and grumpy.

I got dressed and stumbled out in search of coffee.

Levi was talking to Miles on speakerphone, while standing in front of the bathroom mirror. The room was still steamy from his shower and smelled like citrus shampoo and Levi. He'd shaved, and I swallowed hard, remembering the scrape of his jawline against my breasts. Levi whisked his tie around his neck, the silky material sliding with a soft brush.

"I'll be there by nine." He ended the call and knotted his tie.

I curled my fingers into my palms, resisting the urge to grab and unknot it. To unbutton him, run my fingers through his meticulously slicked down hair, and dishevel him like I had last night.

The wooden plank squeaked under my foot and Levi glanced over. His cool, assessing stare showed no trace of that lust-soaked fog from the hot tub, but a curious expression flickered over his face before he turned back to the mirror to straighten the tie.

"About the hot tub," he said. "It was ill-advised. I apologize." Levi was locked down tight, all House Head and back in firm control. He'd even wiped away all remnants of his Italian accent. Too bad. I'd liked that other wilder side of him, even if this version was better for my well-being.

"It was a rollercoaster of a night. Shit happened," I said. We'd blurred some lines that probably should not have been blurred, but saying it was ill-advised and apologizing made me feel like I should be ashamed of what we'd done. Of what *I'd* done by kissing him to begin with. "All good."

He gave a stiff nod.

That stellar kickoff to my day was followed by a text from Talia, then a phone call when I didn't immediately reply, which I dismissed.

While I waited for the espresso maker to deliver my latte, I destroyed the smudge in the vial. It was much easier to do when it was contained, though no less icky.

Levi and I were exceedingly careful of each other's space, speaking only the barest of phrases like "pass the sugar" and "drizzly out there."

Scintillating conversation.

After yet another inane bit of small talk, I snapped and dropped my half-eaten toast on my plate, my appetite gone. "Is the tightness of your tie knot helping pull the stick up your ass? Might want to loosen it a bit, Leviticus. The human body is allowed to have some give to it."

"There were two more heart attacks. News got out and the press have decided that there's a magic virus killing Nefesh."

"Damn. I'm sorry. I take back the ass crack. I mean... Ugh."

Levi's lips quirked. "Regardless, I need to get home and hold a press conference. Find out where they got that idea."

"At least they don't know about the smudges. I'll get Priya working on the thumb drive. Maybe we can find out how many were let loose." I'd killed one and if Noemi's chemo hadn't killed the second one, then it had jumped into someone else, but there could be more.

"Thank you."

The silence stretched out several beats too long to be comfortable. Luckily, there was a knock on the door. A limo driver had come to take us to the airport.

There was very little traffic on the drive back. The trees lining both sides of the curving road were a mix of bare branches and thick firs, while the pale sun cast weak rays.

Cold enough for winter and not quite spring, March was a depressing month.

Once on the plane, I slid my earbuds in and cranked up my "one hit wonders" playlist. No point spending the flight in awkward silence.

Levi busied himself on his laptop.

Partway through the trip, he tapped my leg.

I turned off the music. "Yes?"

"Were you into Sherlock Holmes before your dad left?"

"He loved them, so he got me into the stories when I was stuck in bed with chickenpox. I was ten? Itchy and whining. He went to the library and brought me home *A Study in Scarlet*. Why?"

"You took an interest you and your father shared, an interest that had to do with solving mysteries and revealing the truth and made it your code of ethics."

"Sure."

"And your shield."

I slid the earbuds out. "Excuse me?"

"You convinced yourself that if you armed yourself with knowledge and a healthy skepticism then you'd never be a mark again."

"Are we playing dime store psychoanalysis?" I said. "Is it my turn?"

"Knock yourself out."

I raked a slow, cool gaze over him. "Nah. It's no fun if you're expecting it."

I returned to my music, staring out the window. Other than the fact that he could have been more diplomatic with the shield comment, I agreed with his assessment.

Levi had been thinking about me. Wanting to figure me out. Why? Should I be flattered or unsettled? I'd be lying if I said there wasn't some kind of bond between us, I just couldn't say with any type of certainty what it was. After years of sniping and one-upmanship, hell, after last night I didn't trust Levi and I'm sure he reciprocated the feeling.

On the other hand, something had shifted between us and it wasn't our hook-up. Being Lillian and Santino undercover together had been fun. We'd had each other's backs. I'd never had a partner to watch my six while I was out in the field and I gotta say, it was a nice change. Not something I'd want to do on a regular basis, mind you, but occasionally, with the right person? Maybe?

"Should we set up a training schedule?" I said.

"Can I get back to you? With this press conference and everything…"

"Sure." Brush-off received. I'd stopped myself from taking Birthmark Man's magic, so I had some measure of self-control, and I could destroy smudges and manifest weapons, but this Nefesh status was all still new, not to mention that while I'd taken a couple self-defense classes, I wasn't a proficient fighter. If Levi wasn't willing to train me, then I'd look elsewhere.

Levi got dropped off first at HQ to do damage control. "Good work last night."

"Yeah, you too." I swear I hadn't meant it like *that* but of course that's how it came out sounding. I busied myself with my phone, texting Charlotte Rose to check if she'd heard from Meryem and not looking up until the door had shut.

She hadn't. I assured her I was doing everything I could to stop her worrying and that I'd get her girlfriend back.

What fresh nightmares would today bring? An unknown number of smudges were loose, the press was breathing down Levi's neck about magic viruses, and people with blood magic were harvesting powers from Nefesh to sell to the highest bidder.

If these third-party smudges were hostless magic, what had happened to the people they were torn from? Did taking their magic kill them? I wished I had a mentor with the answers. And if ripping away magic didn't kill the hosts, where were the missing Nefesh? There were no reports of individuals showing up with bizarre tales of abduction and magic removal, so what had happened to them? Were they killed to hide the evidence?

How much danger was Meryem in?

The limo dropped me off in front of my apartment building. Had it really been less than twelve hours? Because I swear I'd aged a decade.

Priya sat on the sofa with her headphones on, hunched over her laptop and working on her corporate gig. Her eyes were bleary and red-rimmed and there was a mostly empty large bottle of diet Coke on the ground beside her. Another all-nighter.

Unlike the rest of Priya's pristine pink manicure, her thumbnails were bitten down and ragged, and she wore stretched out, tattered sweatpants with Dalhousie University Schulich School of Law embroidered on them. A hand-me-down from her brother.

I went into the kitchen, returning in a bit with some scrambled eggs and toast, since basic breakfast items were within my culinary skill set. I perched beside her and held up the plate.

She blinked back into awareness and slid one side of her headphones off. "Jump Around" played. My bestie liked her eighties and nineties rap.

"Eat something, idiot," I said.

Priya shut off the music, took the plate, and forked a bite of eggs. "You do not get to be mad at me because I'm still mad at you and my mad predates yours."

"You can Hulk rage at me all you want, but you're not taking care of yourself. Less talking, more eating."

She tore off a piece of toast and shoved it in her mouth. "I'm taking care of myself." It came out more garbled than that around her chewing but I got the gist.

"Really? How long were you sitting here by yourself doing this Quasimodo impersonation, Hunchy? You've wrecked your manicure from stress—"

She folded her fingers over her thumbs.

"And you're wearing your 'I give up' pants. Your battery is shot. You should have slept last night and then worked and recharged in some public space like the weirdo that you are."

I hovered over her until she'd eaten everything and let out a large yawn.

"You suck." She placed the empty plate on the coffee table.

"I know, and I'm really sorry about last night. I promise to interact with humanity more. I hadn't realized how closed off I'd gotten, or how much pressure that might be putting on you." I slid off the fuzzy scarf wound around my neck.

Priya stared at me.

Okay, apology not accepted? "I'll do better?"

"You have a hickey."

Eyes wide, I slapped a hand over my throat. I'd thrown on my clothes in the dark this morning.

"Other side." She smirked. "Apparently, you interacted with a human just fine last night."

"That's the bruises from before."

"Nuh-uh."

"You need to sleep," I said. "You're hallucinating."

"Ashiiirrraaaaa. Who did you get down and dirty with?"

I mumbled an answer.

Priya kicked me. "*You had hate sex with Levi*?!"

"Technically, there was no sex. It was all very…" Hot? Confusing? Wrong? Right? "Ill-advised."

She fell back against the cushions with a shriek. "Oh my God! He *is* as good as advertised."

"Not remotely what I said."

"You owe me a hundred bucks."

190

"Why?"

"Because two years ago I bet you that all this nemesis stuff between you was a cover up for your mutual 'gotta tap that bow chica wow wow.'" She held out a hand. "Pay up."

I dropped the thumb drive into it. "Consider this payment in full. A stolen drive that's password protected and may hold the key to finding Meryem and stopping further smudges from being created."

Levi had tried to access the drive on his laptop to no avail on the flight back.

"You *were* busy last night," Priya said.

"With work, Pink Menace." It might be fun to put her and Miles in the same room and see what happened.

"Huh?"

"Forget it. Look at the drive after you've napped."

"You give me a mystery drive to play with and then tell me to sleep? Pfft." Suddenly bright-eyed, she pulled the spare laptop that she kept for when she was dealing with potential viruses or things that could fry her motherboard out from under the couch where she'd left it, and inserted the drive. "Ooh. This is even better than that pashmina Mummy gave me for Diwali. It's not just password protected, this baby is encrypted."

"So, that's a 'no' to getting in to the files?"

"Ye of little faith. If the encryption scheme uses a password, I still might be able to crack it. But not if the password is really strong or if it's hashed properly."

I shook my head blankly.

"You know, with bcrypt or PBKDF2."

"Obviously."

"In that case, we'll be out of luck. Though I can do some research and see if there are any known flaws in their encryption scheme. If, however, the encryption has poor key storage, or lacks entropy, you know like keys that aren't random enough, or they use some bullshit homegrown crypto, then

I'll get in." Priya put her headphones back on, House of Pain once more audible, and shooed me away.

Priya loved her puzzles as much as I did. Guess she had other ways to recharge beside being around people.

Confident the drive was in good hands, I left her to it.

"Oh yeah. Ash?" Pri didn't bother looking up or taking off her headphones so she was essentially screaming at me. "I found a night nurse who'd been on your recovery ward. Sandra Chen. She asked to be transferred to a different ward while you were there. I left her details on your dresser."

Not Dr. Zhang. I did a happy dance out the door and left Sandra a message explaining who I was and asking her to contact me.

Which thread required immediate follow up? There was the mystery Van Gogh to interrogate. I wrinkled my nose, not wanting to get too close and risk ending up warded again. It wasn't like I could put him off any longer, but I had to get all this charged energy out of my system and get my head on straight to deal with him.

I changed into leggings, runners, and a turtleneck to hide the hickey and the bruises, which I'd liberally coated in arnica cream once more. Hesitantly, I approached Arkady's door on our shared landing. Fighting was part of my tool kit now. Better learn to do it properly.

Plus, Priya would be happy that I was spending time with him.

He flung the door open before I could knock, wearing low hanging board shorts with a T-shirt slung over his shoulder, and his hair in a high ponytail. There could be a daily inspirational calendar that was just photos of his abs. "Creepy lurker much?"

He blew on his black nail polish.

"I'm in need of punching things," I said.

"You've come to the right man. Enter." With a flourish, he invited me in.

The only thing in his living room was a giant TV screen showing the weather forecast for the next week and a punching bag hanging from the ceiling.

"Love what you've done with the place."

"I've got the basics. Hang on." He unmuted the television as Levi appeared on screen, with Miles quietly menacing off to his right.

Levi stood behind a podium mounted with a bank of microphones, wearing a sincere yet somber expression. "I want to assure the members of the press, the public, and most specifically my Nefesh community, that there is no magic virus."

"Levi!" A reporter in front waved his hand to get Levi's attention. "Can you be more specific about what's been causing the heart attacks since none of the victims were candidates?"

Yeah, Bob. Person or persons with imaginary blood magic are ripping powers out of innocent people, some of which got loose and are trying to stay alive. Don't feed them.

"I'm unable to comment further at this time," Levi said. "Again, you have my assurances that the House is doing everything possible to investigate—"

"Unless you're behind it?" A female reporter with a hungry glint spoke up. "Sources say you have plans to circumnavigate the laws governing Nefesh and take magic regulation into your own hands. Is this part of that plan?"

"Don't believe everything you hear, honey," Arkady said to the TV. "Right?"

"Right," I agreed.

"What motive could I possibly have for targeting my own people?" Levi looked at the woman like she was shit on the bottom of his shoe.

She shrank back into the press of journalists.

"Mark my words," he said. "Whoever is behind this? I am coming for you, and I won't stop until you've been destroyed and my people are safe." He smiled a wolfish smile. Waaay too many teeth. "Thank you."

The TV cut to Jackson Wu, an outspoken man of Chinese heritage and the provincial leader of the Untainted Party. He'd left a caucus meeting to tell a throng of reporters that his Party planned to introduce a bill for tighter control and overview of the Nefesh population.

"This failure of Mr. Montefiore to contain the menace at large is exactly why we will be proposing to disassemble all Houses in this country and remove the special status that this population has enjoyed," Jackson said.

My mother was the Senior Policy Advisor. Her fingerprints were all over this. It wouldn't surprise me if they'd been the ones to leak the virus rumor in the first place to leverage this situation.

I slammed a punch into the bag, sending it swinging.

"We will no longer sit idly by," Jackson said. "Today this virus is killing Nefesh. Tomorrow? Who knows? It's just a matter of time before one of them goes off like a ticking time bomb and innocents are hurt."

Arkady muted the TV. "I hate him. But damn, before? Levi was good."

"He has his moments."

"Are you kidding me?" Arkady launched into a two-minute fanboy spiel listing the magnificence that was Levi Montefiore.

"He's a competent House Head," I conceded.

Whatever had happened between Levi and myself didn't matter. Last night was firmly in the past, no hard feelings. The only thing I cared about right now was helping him destroy the smudges and getting Meryem and any other kids back home.

I punched the bag again.

Arkady winced. "Well, that is the worst form I've ever seen. Are you deliberately trying to dislocate your arm?

Because with that kind of strength you're going to end up in traction. Didn't you practice your powers, low level that they are?"

"Uh…" While I was trying to come up with a plausible lie, Arkady clicked his tongue and demonstrated how to punch.

"Make a tight fist," he said. "You look like you're about to blow on your lucky dice."

"So encouraging."

"Aw, pickle. You want me to be nice or you want me to turn you into a fighting machine in the fastest amount of time possible?"

"Fighting machine."

Arkady was a surprisingly good teacher. He fixed my form so that I turned into the punch with my whole body, got me to consistently land blows that didn't hurt my hand, and all he demanded in return was every single detail about my cases and personal life.

I told him my cases were off-limits and gave him the bare bones details about myself, including a little white lie about only having super strength.

"Quit holding your breath." He adjusted my fists so I held them more tightly by my face. "You're leaving yourself wide open. Keep your guard up."

"Generally not a problem," I said.

Arkady gasped. "Did you just make a joke about your anti-social tendencies?"

"Misanthropic, not anti-social."

"Nah. That makes it sound like we're the problem, when it's clearly you."

A laugh sputtered out of me. "You have absolutely zero filter."

"Right? So between me saying everything I think and you being super suspicious, we're like one normal human." He did the quotes.

"Is that supposed to go in the plus column?"

He shrugged. "Fuck if I know. Punch."

I shook my arms, bounced from foot to foot and executed a jab-hook combo, sharply exhaling as I did.

Arkady watched me with a critical eye. "I read some of those Sherlock Holmes stories. They're pretty good."

"What do you usually read?"

"Modern crime fiction. Like Elmore Leonard."

"Those are good, too. Though I've only read *Get Shorty* and *Raylan*. The TV version was better."

"That's because Timothy Olyphant is a hot piece of gunslinger in *Justified*." He demonstrated a change to the combo.

"True."

Hitting things properly was empowering. "Could we turn this into a regular thing?" I said. "Would you teach me to fight? Not just boxing moves, but wrestling stuff, too. How to pin someone down and keep them there. I could pay you."

He crossed his arms. "Do I look like I need money?"

"Well, you don't have furniture..."

"I have the basics."

"So, you'll do it for the sparkling pleasure of my company?"

"As if. I'll do it for food. One training session for one dinner."

"I can't really cook," I said.

"Can you order in?"

In the background, the TV switched from toothpaste commercials to another news report.

"Well, yes, but—" My eyes flicked over the headline and then I lunged for the remote and slammed the unmute button.

On the screen was a sketch of Lillian and Santino.

"...considered dangerous with possibly level five magic,"

the anchorwoman said. "Police are looking for these two prime suspects involved in an attack on a security guard at a private event. If you see them, do not approach. Call your local Nefesh police department."

The sketch was wrong. Lillian didn't have her ostentatious necklace. Instead she wore a Star of David. Why? *Think*, Ash. Birthmark Man must have told his employers that Lillian could create smudges and now they were after her. But what was the deal with the Star of David? It had to mean something. A message? A code of some sort?

As if things couldn't get odder, Thug Money came on, giving a sound bite debunking the rumor that a Dr. Doolittle was involved in the attack. "Given the condition of the guard," he said, "this was some kind of Tough Guy magic. Chances are the man you're after has excessive strength."

Oh, Thug Money, you sexist ass. I could kiss you for that accidental misdirect, but the fact that someone was circulating this sketch? I rubbed my hands over my face.

Bewildered, Arkady looked between the screen and me. "You okay?"

"I'm fine." The automatic response just slipped out.

"Okay." Arkady's eyes crinkled with a faint hint of concern but he didn't push, and his matter-of-fact acceptance of however I chose to play this made me change my answer.

"Actually, no. Not even a little bit."

"Anything I can do to help?"

"No. But thanks. For everything."

"Any time, pickle."

Chapter 15

I leadfooted it to House HQ, shivering all the way because I'd run out without a jacket and my car's heater hadn't magically fixed itself. Jostling my way through the lobby, I hit the elevator button thirty-seven times but it took its sweet time crawling down from the fourth floor.

"Nancy Drew. Making extra cash these days?" Staff Sergeant Novak poked his head out of the police department doors, miming a blow job. "Heard you've been *catting* around with the big boss."

"And I heard that if you make one more misogynist comment, I'll bury you so deep in sexual harassment claims that the only thing you'll have for company are dinosaur bones. Clear?"

He made a snarky face and huffed off.

Finally, the damn door opened, and I hopped from foot to foot waiting for the other passengers to clear out. When I got to Levi's office, I was thwarted by his snooty receptionist who took one look at my less-than-put-together attire and decided our Fearless Leader wasn't in.

"This is extremely important and Levi would be very upset if he missed me," I said.

"I doubt that." She smirked, picking an imaginary piece of lint off of the cute military jacket she'd paired with a pencil skirt.

Had that asshole guard Evan circulated my photo or something?

I leaned onto her desk. "You want to risk it?"

She held her ground. "He's not in."

"Okay, then. Another time." I walked a half dozen steps, then pivoted sharply and sprinted to Levi's door, throwing it open without knocking.

Levi and Miles looked up from their meeting. Levi's tie was unknotted, slung loosely open around his neck, his hair tousled like he'd been raking his fingers through it.

My hand tightened on the doorknob.

The receptionist's heels clicked in rapid distress as she ran up behind me. "Levi, I'm so sorry. She just barged in."

"She does that," Miles said.

The receptionist wrung her hands together. "Should I call security?"

"You mean Miles, who's standing right here? Up your critical thinking skills, lady." I snapped my fingers at Miles. "Yo, new bestie. Escort me out."

"Do I have to?" Miles whined.

"Dude, you're a mountain. Have some dignity," I said.

"At least say 'please,' you heathen," he grumbled.

Levi shifted, faintly blushing. His discomfit was deeply satisfying.

"*Pleaaaase* escort me out." I leaned into the word hard, earning a scowl from Levi.

The receptionist was getting redder and redder that I hadn't been turfed unceremoniously yet, the flush hitting her hairline like mercury soaring up in a thermometer. I stepped aside in case her head popped off.

"Move it, Miles," I said. "It's urgent."

Still grumbling, Miles got to his feet.

I dragged him to the elevator, refusing to speak until we were alone inside. "I need some me time with the Van Gogh."

I explained about the sketch and the Star of David and how there had to be a connection. "Pink Menace—" Miles grimaced at my use of his nickname for her. "Is working on the drive but that could take too long. This guy was babbling about betrayals. The smudges, me, all of this is connected and he knows something."

"He has a name. Yitzak Meiron. Seventy-two years old. Level five Van Gogh and retired former owner of Meiron Body Designs. Had a pretty devoted clientele." Miles led me through the security doors into the isolation ward where Yitzak was being held. Apparently, he'd attacked the two cops who'd escorted him to the jail.

Miles stopped at a small office. "There are monitored security cameras, and if you stay behind the white line, you won't be affected by the magic nulling on the cell." Before I could proceed around the corner to the hallway where Yitzak's cell was, Miles clapped a hand on my shoulder. "You may well solve this, which would take a load off Levi, but stop fucking with him."

"Did he say that I was?"

He tapped my turtleneck. "Used that trick a few times myself. And he didn't need to. I've been friends with him long enough to know when he's being weird about something."

"If something did happen, last I checked we were both of legal age and capable of saying no."

"He's in the middle of a shitstorm. He doesn't have time for your games."

"What games?"

"The endless game between the two of you. For once, back off."

"Fuck you, Miles. It's not like I'm chasing him. He hired

me, remember?" I stomped off to Yitzak's cell which was a large glowing cage within a larger room.

The old man sat on a small cot, eating mashed potatoes and ground beef from a plastic tray with a plastic spoon.

"If you don't talk, you'll rot in here." I pulled up a stool that was shoved in one corner, careful to keep it behind the white line painted about ten feet from the cell bars.

"Better in here than out there," he said.

"Why's that?"

He held up a spoonful of potato. "The Michelin-starred food."

I got as comfortable as I could on that stool. "Yitzak, Yitzak, Yitzak. You're a man of mystery. Why the Star of David? You could have chosen any design as a ward."

"I like triangles."

"That's nice. I like men who aren't duplicitous bastards. Is the Star of David a code of some sort?"

Yitzak stilled for a second, then he shrugged.

"What does it mean? Who uses it?"

He took a bite of potato, making a big deal of chewing loudly.

"Who made you ward me in the hospital?"

Yitzak laughed, meticulously separating his potatoes from his meat. "Wouldn't you like to know?"

One thing confirmed, at least. This had happened right after my surgery when I was thirteen.

Fifteen magicless years. What a waste. Then I remembered the craving for Birthmark Man's magic and reconsidered.

"This isn't a joke," I said. "Nefesh are dying and you could stop it."

"People die every day."

I tapped a finger against my lip. How was I going to make him crack? He was sitting there eating as if he didn't have a care in the world. Oh. That was it. I stood up. "I'm going to get the House to release you."

A flicker of fear crossed his face. "You can't do that. I'm guilty of assault."

"But I'm the plaintiff and I'll recant my statement. Levi can probably get the cops to knock down the other assault to a fine and community service or something. It'll be a very public release. Big apology from the House and their thanks for all your help. See, the press believe there's a magic virus out there killing Nefesh so they're camping outside the building trying to get comments. We'll make sure they know you've been a real help. With everything."

His spoon clattered to the tray. He bowed his head, his breathing shallow. Then, as if he'd come to a decision, he met my eyes. "I'm not a rat and I would never help you."

"What's your problem with me? I bathe. I pay taxes. I don't kick puppies." I stepped up to the cage, a flatness coming over me as my magic went null. "What awful thing did I do to you that you put that goddamned ward on my head?"

"How dare you take his name in vain?"

"His—God? Is that why the Star of David? You're religious? What does that have to do with me?"

He returned to his food, dismissing me.

Levi and I were in a weird place that could have really bad repercussions for working together, Miles was pissed off at me for toying with Levi, which I hadn't, and now this Van Gogh who had fucked with my life all those years ago, was blowing me off?

"Talk already, you piece of shit!"

"You're the worthless one. 'And the dogs shall eat Jezebel in the territory of Jezreel, and none shall bury her.'" Spittle flew from his mouth, the finger he pointed at me shaking with indignant fury.

"Am I the dog or the whore in this scenario, because

either way, not cool, dude." Was he some kind of god-warrior lunatic? "We'll see if you change your tune once you're released." I left the room.

Miles was gone, but one of the security guards on monitor duty in the isolation ward phoned him and relayed my message.

"He's coming back." The guard tossed his empty coffee cup at the trash and missed, so he got up to dispose of it.

The monitor displaying Yitzak's cell flickered.

"Did you—" I peered closer at the screen. Yitzak's cell was no longer glowing. The magic wards were down.

The guard hit an alarm and sirens wailed. There was a grinding noise like a steel gate coming down.

I sprinted around the corner, limboing under the gate that was sealing Yitzak's corridor in.

"Come back!" the guard yelled.

I crept to the door of the jail room and peeked inside. The magic nulling on the cell was still disengaged and a slender man stood inside it.

"… and we are very disappointed." He spoke with a heavy German accent.

Yitzak crowded into the far corner, cowering. "I didn't say anything, I swear."

"I would like to trust you, but it's not only my decision." The German pulled out a knife.

"No." Yitzak threw his hands up to cover his face. "I'll never talk. I promise. Please."

"Freeze!" I yelled.

The German didn't even glance back. With one swift motion, he slashed Yitzak's throat and disappeared.

I ran to the cell but it was still locked.

Blood gurgled out of Yitzak's throat and he reached out for me.

I screamed for help but it was too late. His eyes glazed over and he went still.

The alarms wailed for another five minutes and when they suddenly cut out, my ears continued to ring.

Miles and Levi ran into the room. I tore my gaze away from the crimson puddle.

"Whoever that was waltzed past all our security, magic and human, disabled the magic nulling on the cell, and got inside despite it being locked." Miles' voice was tight and he glowered with a barely leashed anger.

If Miles was a hot rage, Levi was scary cold.

"Fix this," Levi said. "I don't care what it takes to secure this building, think of every possible vulnerability and plug it."

"I will."

"Wait a sec." Both men turned to me. "Who knew that Yitzak had been charged with the assault?"

"A number of cops. Why?" Miles said.

"How did the killer know Yitzak was down here in isolation and not in the regular holding area unless he was tipped off?"

Levi and Miles exchanged a grim look.

"Who do you trust on the force?" Levi said. "Put together a task force of a half dozen of those men and get me a meeting. Also get your people digging for financial problems, anything that could indicate a crooked cop."

I added a little shooing motion to Miles' dismissal, which was petty but I was still angry about our earlier conversation.

Miles narrowed his eyes at me and jogged out.

Levi stared down at Yitzak, a thoughtful look on his face. "Come with me."

Back up to his office we went. Levi gave his receptionist, who it turned out was actually his Executive Assistant, a bullshit task to run so we were alone.

"The House is warded with my blood," he said. "Paid a Weaver a lot of good money for it."

"What's the point when anyone can walk into the building?"

"Think of a time when you wanted to kill me and then try and enter my office."

I eyed the doorway doubtfully. "With a set up like that? No, thank you. What would happen? Smote by lightning? Eviscerated by fire?"

"Like I'd let that happen to you." I felt somewhat pleased until he added, "I've already paid you a quarter of your fee. Not getting that back if you burn up. No, you'd be rooted in place and the ward would null your magic. It senses intent and guards against hostile emotion."

"Clever."

"You'd be surprised how many buildings have it."

"The killer knew about it. Did someone get hold of your blood to disable it?"

"No." Levi squatted down on the carpet outside his office door. He pulled out a pocketknife and cut his finger, squeezing a couple of drops onto the floor. A glowing white ring ran the length of the office wall. "My office has an extra ward on it. Still intact, as you can see."

Wiping off the blade, he handed it to me.

I didn't take it. "I didn't do anything wrong."

"We're going to work on you being super suspicious of everything I say. I'm testing a theory. Plugging a hole. Help me out."

I shivered, the memory of Birthmark Man's magic swamping me with a dark craving. This wouldn't be the same.

Would it?

But if I refused, Levi would get suspicious. "I don't need the knife."

I touched it and Levi's magic which anchored the ward danced to its surface.

"Can you break it?"

"No problem." I rubbed the back of my neck. It was just a ward, not a person. No one would get hurt.

"Any time now," Levi said.

"It's a delicate operation," I muttered. I called up a drop of my blood and hooked my magic into the glowing ring. The second it locked down, a rush of pure bliss surged through me. I twirled my finger in the air, wrapping the ward's magic around it to pull it out like taffy and make it mine.

It was an amber gold thread, a visual reflection of how Levi's magic smelled.

"Scotch and chocolate," I breathed.

Levi caught my chin in his hands, stared into my eyes, and swore. "Shut it down. Now."

I blinked slowly at him. "Yeah. Okay." I fell deeper into the sweet sensation, leaning so far forward that my hair brushed the ward.

"Ash," he barked and knocked me sideways, severing the connection.

The thread snapped and disappeared.

Hissing, I caught him around the throat.

If he'd shown fear, I might have given in to some hunter instinct and taken his inherent magic as well, but all he did was raise his eyebrows at me.

"Whoops." I laughed weakly and pried my trembling hands off him.

Levi put his arm around my waist and led me into his office and the comfy sofa. He poured me a finger of scotch. I could still smell his magic, so this was like he'd poured his essence into a glass. Except once that weird thought was in my head, I couldn't unthink it, and sat there blushing and staring at the tumbler until Levi frowned and pressed the drink into my hand.

"L'chaim." I shot the entire thing back. *And now I've swallowed him.* Oh my God, brain, stop! I peered into the empty glass like I was scrying to predict into the future. Anything to avoid looking at him.

My one lifeline in this horror show of embarrassment was that ward magic wasn't the same as magic that was alive in a person. Shutting down my connection to it hadn't caused the same level of withdrawal as with Birthmark Man. I'd gotten off with tight, hot skin.

Levi didn't press me. In fact, we didn't talk for a long time.

"The killer wasn't someone with blood magic," I said. "We can't teleport."

"There must have been an accomplice. Miles will review the security footage."

"Even if you caught the ward being taken down, they wouldn't be sloppy enough to show their faces."

"Probably not. Thoughts on why the killer went after Yitzak?"

I stared into the bottom of the glass and a single drop of scotch that was the same color as the ward magic. "When Yitzak first attacked me, he was trying to put the ward back on because he didn't want someone to know about my magic. He was terrified. The German killer must have been one of those people." I placed the glass on the table. "The German said that killing Yitzak wasn't just his decision. You saw the sketch of Lillian and Santino?"

Levi nodded.

"I think that whoever is selling smudge magic is part of some religious group, and the Star of David is used as some kind of emblem or code. Me, the smudges, this group, it's all tied together."

"Are the others with blood magic working with them or being kept against their will?" Levi said. "Either way, if Yitzak knew about your magic, why didn't he hand you over instead of warding you? You were a kid. There wouldn't have been much you could have done about it."

"A more compelling magic kept him from it."

"Speaking of compelling, how are you going to keep yourself from taking people's magic if it's like a drug?" Levi didn't sound judgmental, merely curious.

There was no point denying what he'd seen. "Willpower?"

"There has to be another way," he said. "If there's been even two people every hundred years with this blood magic stripping others of their powers because it was too addictive, someone would have heard something. The fact that blood magic has stayed off the radar all this time means that there's a way for you to not crave it."

"That would be good. Listen, I'm sorry someone invaded your House. I should never have brought Yitzak here."

"Not your fault. There was nowhere else you could have taken him."

"True." I sighed. "When I solve a case, I cast a wide net looking for possible suspects. That net gets smaller and smaller as I verify alibis, knock out red herrings, and account for evidence. But what do we have here? Magic on the rampage because of powers that aren't supposed to exist, a dead body courtesy of a shadowy organization, and at the heart of it, a Mundane who found out she wasn't so Mundane after all. This isn't a net, it's a spiderweb."

Levi's fingers twitched like he was going to reach for me and his expression softened in the way it did right before someone was going to say something pitying. Really had to watch my verbal diarrhea around him.

"Did I mention that Yitzak called me a whore?" I stood up. "Talk about false advertising."

"He did what?"

"Okay, not a literal whore. But he called me Jezebel. She's some famous biblical harlot, right?" I Googled her on my phone. "No. That can't be... No."

Reality turned to quicksand. Even though my life these

days was a crazy mystery and I had no idea what position on this gameboard I played or even a clear picture of my opponents, the rules, or the point, I still believed I'd find my way through. It might take a while to untangle, but my instincts were sound and I was smart. But reading what I just had? If the one truth I could always count on was a lie, how could I ever trust my instincts again? How could I move forward if I had no barometer of what to believe or who to trust?

Levi caught my elbow. "Ash."

"She said no lies. No games. It was the rule. And I believed her. Oh, God."

"Who?" he said.

"My mother."

Chapter 16

The Vancouver headquarters of the Untainted Party were located on the twenty-third floor of a bland downtown office tower, whose only distinguishing feature was that it was the only real estate in the city more expensive than House Pacifica's. They had offices in the provincial legislature building in Victoria, British Columbia's capital, but when Parliament wasn't in session, like now, or they had meetings or fundraisers here, it was important to have a base in Vancouver, the largest city in the province and the financial center.

The business suits fogged up the elevator with their disapproval when I got on. I was still in my turtleneck and leggings, my dark wavy hair in a messy, sweaty ponytail.

I seethed my way up to the Party's floor, ignoring a haughty thirty-something who was headed up to the investment banking firm one floor up. Entitled and possibly sociopathic, I "accidentally" elbowed him with more force than necessary getting out of the crowded elevator.

A few people on my mother's floor greeted me, but I barely responded, stalking directly for Sinaya, Talia's no-nonsense Filipina-Canadian secretary who'd assisted her for years.

"Tell Talia I want to see her, please."

"Can you wait ten minutes? She's on deadline reviewing a policy amendment."

"That wasn't a request."

Sinaya blinked at me, since I'd never been anything other than unfailingly polite. "Is something wrong?"

I gripped the edge of her desk. "Sinaya."

She picked up the phone and informed Talia that I was here. "Go ahead," she said, her brow furrowed in concern.

I nodded my thanks and entered the lion's den.

Talia's office was tasteful and efficient. One wall contained a bookcase filled with law books and political history relevant to her position as Senior Policy Advisor. Her antique desk was bare of anything other than her chrome laptop and a pen, while the chairs set out for visitor use, while aesthetically pleasing, weren't comfortable enough to encourage lingering.

My mother took off the reading glasses perched on the end of her nose and set them on the desk. "You've been avoiding my calls."

"Is that what you're starting with? Because I thought we could go with how you ruined my life."

"Didn't we cover this in therapy after the accident? Sit down." She motioned to a chair. "You know I hate having to look up."

I composed myself, as one did, by stuffing all my fury and resentment into a tight fist that pulsed in the center of my chest. Emotion wouldn't get me anywhere with her.

"Bubbe and Zaide were extremely religious," I said. "Kosher kitchen, segregated seating at synagogue, an all-girls' orthodox school for you, the whole nine yards."

"I was there," she said dryly.

"As a burgeoning feminist, you didn't agree with the sexism and outright misogyny implicit in Judaism, and so, in grade eleven, you did your religious studies project on the

Bride of Yahweh as a big fuck-you. Since Judaism had not yet become a monotheistic religion in that section of the Old Testament, the Bride was mentioned multiple times. She was even worshipped by many, including King Solomon, before the Yahwehists stamped out all mention of her."

Talia leaned back in her twelve-hundred-dollar Herman Miller chair. "Am I on trial?"

"I'm establishing context. The Bride had a very loyal handmaiden who did everything she could to keep her goddess' name and spirit alive. But the patriarchal Jews were having none of it and, in the end, she was thrown off a balcony, eaten by dogs, and her name and reputation dragged through the mud by Yahwehists. Poor Jezebel. They pulled off a pretty good smear campaign if she's still dealing with all that painted whore crap."

The Internet was a gold mine.

"And you were named for the Bride," she said. "The goddess Asherah. What's your point?"

"No point. A question. How did you convince the Van Gogh? How did you even find him?" I slammed my fist on her desk. "Did you think you were keeping me safe?"

There was a funny look on her face. One I'd never seen before on her which is why it took me a second to place it. Fear.

My heart sank. I was right. "No games, no lies. What a joke."

She came around the desk and crouched in front of me, wrinkling her pantsuit. "Honey, I think you need professional help."

"That would be convenient. Lock me up so you don't have to answer for what you did. It's bad enough what I missed out on, but people are dying, Talia, and it shouldn't matter that they're Nefesh. Just... tell me everything."

Why you did it. What I am.

She moved over to the window. "Is this because you've been spending time with Montefiore? Has he been filling your head with crazy ideas?"

"Are you spying on me?"

"Don't be ridiculous. A lot of people saw you with him at the aquarium." She fiddled with the cord of the blinds.

"Is that why you've been phoning me? Or was it because you know the ward was broken?" I crossed my arms. "Levi and I aren't hanging out and this has nothing to do with him. Stay on topic. The accident was when this all went down. You stayed by my bedside practically every second. Did the magic show up when I was unconscious? What did you know? What were you so afraid of that you made the Van Gogh do it?"

"Of course, I stayed by your bedside. You'd been in a horrible crash, you were in a coma, and I was scared I'd lose you. However, I don't know what magic you're talking about or anything about a Van Gogh."

"*My* magic. The trauma of the accident switched on a recessive gene."

"That's impossible." Talia glanced at the closed office door. "And don't repeat nonsense like that. You're a Mundane." She raised a hand against my protest. "We're done with this. No, enough. You don't have magic, Ashira. This is a delusion."

I blinked rapidly enough against the wetness in my eyes that she probably didn't catch it and hauled myself heavily out of the chair. "I won't bother you further."

"Wait." Talia sat down again and put her glasses back on. "I know you've always had this fascination with Levi—"

"The way the Hatfields were fascinated with the McCoys."

"But you have to stay away from him. There's something bad going on and the House may be involved."

I slammed my hands on her desk. "There's no virus and

no evil agenda and you damn well know it. This legislation of yours is draconian and completely unnecessary. If you put restrictive measures in place, you'll turn us into a police state where Nefesh are concerned."

Where I'm concerned.

"If there's no virus," she said calmly, "then the magic has turned on its hosts and is killing them. Unstable magic is a threat to the general population, and we'll do whatever it takes to keep our people safe. It's a dangerous situation."

Did she know about the smudges? "Meaning?"

"Stay away from him."

"What would I get in return?" I snapped my fingers. "How about one straight answer?"

"Ashira Ganit Cohen, I am your mother and I'm telling you to sever any and all contact with Levi."

I did a double take. Talia had never pulled that shit. Not even when I was fifteen and it might have been vaguely appropriate.

Two spots of red colored her cheeks and she clutched her pen in a death grip.

There was a knock at the door and one of Talia's staff poked her head in.

"Oh, excuse me. Sinaya wasn't at her desk. I didn't mean to interrupt, but Talia, when you have a minute, I need to speak to you." The young woman smiled at me and I smiled back automatically because she looked vaguely familiar.

I didn't recall meeting her, though with her hair pulled back in a low pony tail and her generic conservative suit, she could have been one of a dozen Untainted Party employees. The ink stains on her fingers indicated she'd recently tangled with the faulty photocopier on this side of the building where the upper echelon Party members and their assistants worked.

"No problem. I was heading out," I said.

She moved aside for me to pass and I caught a whiff of

her perfume. Chanel No. 5. I pulled up short, imagining her hair down, smoky eyes instead of her natural makeup, and a hot pink slip dress.

The woman's smile wavered and she touched her mouth. "Are there crumbs on my face? I just had a cookie."

"You're fine. Goodbye, Talia." I walked out of the office and out of my mother's life.

~

NO ONE EVER LOOKED AT me and thought, "Damn, I bet that chick can belt Aerosmith," but they'd be wrong. I sang the chorus of "Dream On" while throwing devil horns and headbanging, my loose waves flying around my face.

"Whoooo, baby!" Priya catcalled.

When I hit the high part, striking my best rock star pose and the mic held directly above my upturned face, the bar burst into cheers.

I killed that ballad and swaggered back to my table.

Blondie's was poorly lit, the bathroom floors got sticky after 10PM, and smart patrons stuck to French fries and beer. But it had karaoke and was my favorite drinking hole in the city.

Ruthie, a yoga pant wearing soccer mom who came to karaoke night once a month religiously with her sister, took the mike for her gravelly-voiced rendition of "Blank Slate."

"Nicely done, Holmes." Priya handed me a shot of Kick in the Balls, clinking her glass to mine.

I slammed the drink back, shuddering as the combination of Cuervo Gold, Jack Daniel's, and Yukon Jack burned its way down my throat, and stacked the shot glass on top of my other three, starting the next row of my pyramid. "Let's form a cover band. Aerosmith to Zamphir. Zeppelin? Z.Z. Top? Bah. There are no Z bands I like. Aerosmith to Young M.C. You can feature on 'Bust a Move.'"

Priya twerked her pink denim mini-skirted butt in her chair. "Hell, yeah I can."

She hopped up and ran over to the karaoke sign-up table, returning with a satisfied smile.

"Tonight, my good Adler, we shall be exploring the pros and cons of getting blitzed. My treat, because that's what emergency credit cards are for."

"Yeah! Who cares if your heater's still busted?" Priya threw her hands up in the air.

I grinned at her. "You're the cutest drunky drunk ever."

"God, I so am."

Jodie, our prehistoric server who'd perfected the art of dumping food on the table while texting, distributed our fries. I'd veered into poutine territory by ordering gravy, though after an unfortunate incident here involving cheese curds, I saved actual poutine for the Belgian Fry place on Commercial Drive near our apartment.

"Two more Kicks in the Balls, Jodie," I said.

She spared a glance away from her screen. "Don't tempt me."

"Have I ever told you that you're my model of misanthropy?"

"You've got to be able to do better than her," Jodie said to Priya.

"Yeah," she said, "but she's trained and I'm kind of lazy."

Jodie nodded like that was entirely reasonable and went to get our drinks.

We applauded Ruthie, and whooped when Jimmy, a dapper eighty-year-old in a fedora slanted low over his head, took the tiny stage to sing Sinatra's "My Way." Then we dug into our salty fried deliciousness. For fries that were crispy enough to snap when you broke them on the outside but soft and steamy on the inside with the right pow of salt content, Blondie's was unparalleled.

Pri and I had a ritual. No talking until we were halfway

216

through our massive platters of fries, because while they were superb when hot, cold was a whole other story. No wasting precious time with chatter.

At halftime, I popped the button on my new leather pants with a grunt, fanning out my fitted tank top. I'd wound a skinny metallic scarf around my neck like a choker to hide the bruises and hickey.

Priya dumped more ketchup on her plate. "What do you think Talia'll do now that she knows your magic is back?"

"Beats me. Depends if she thinks I'm a threat to her precious position."

"What if she really isn't involved? This was the second time she denied it."

"Then who?" I ticked items off my fingers. "One, the tattoo happened in the hospital when, by her own admission, she stayed by my bedside. Two, she'd have had a front row seat to my magic showing up. Three, Yitzak called me a Jezebel, handmaiden of the goddess that Talia happened to name me after. She did it."

I ticked off another finger.

"Four?" Priya said.

I shook my head, repeatedly ticking off that same finger. "Look how it bounces."

She pushed a glass of water at me. "None of that explains why he helped her. Who compelled him?"

"If she found him, how hard would it be to find someone to force him against his will? Another reason for him to hate me." I wiped off my face with a paper napkin. "I just wish I knew why she did it. She was still in law school then. Not a member of the Party yet."

"Unless she was planning ahead," Priya said. "Talia is a strategist."

"Mmm. True."

Kenneth, our karaoke host with the most, called Priya's name.

"Darn. The food soaked up my booze." She grabbed her untouched shot and slammed it back. When she stood up, she swayed on her high-heeled boots. "There's the buzz. Whooooo!"

She ran up to the front like she'd been picked as a contestant on *The Price is Right*, high-fiving everyone.

Not content to stay on the stage, Priya strutted through the audience, ruffling hair, shaking her ass, and wagging her finger, all while dropping a word-perfect rendition of "Bust a Move." Her face was lit up as she got everyone to sing back up for her.

There may have been an abundance of crap in my life but if that was the price to pay for having Priya, I'd happily pay it a hundred times over.

An hour later, I bundled her into a cab.

"Come home with me." She tugged on my arm.

I fluttered my lashes at her. "Baby, I've waited forever for those words."

"Where are you going?"

"A very short stop. I'm going to swing by Levi's."

"If it's short then save yourself the trouble and use your vibrator."

The cab driver turned around, blatantly eavesdropping.

I crouched down by the back seat so I could speak privately to her. "It's not a booty call. There's something else I learned at Talia's office today and as my client I think I owe him the courtesy of telling him."

She blew a raspberry at me. "Text him like a normal person."

"I'm not confident about my phone's security." Talia had absolutely been spying on me because one chat at the aquarium did not constitute "hanging out" with Levi. Until Priya went through my cell and checked for any tracking apps, I wasn't taking chances.

"I'll be home soon," I said.

"Fine," she grumbled and shut the taxi door.

I patted the top twice and waved her off. While I was no longer hammered, I was still way past tipsy. I could justify this visit to Levi's with security concerns, but it was brilliant-idea-o'clock and if I kissed him, I could have him because that's how it worked in the dark.

Maybe, in the dark, Levi *was* my Moriarty. The one who could thrill me and lead me on the chase of my life. It wasn't just his magic I craved.

My taxi dropped me off in front of his waterfront property on Point Grey Road, one of the most coveted streets to live on in the city. Levi lived in a Mediterranean-style villa painted a warm, mellow gold. I buzzed the intercom at the high fence.

"Yes?" Levi said.

"It's Ash. I need to talk to you."

"Can this wait until tomorrow?"

"I found out something about Talia that you need to know."

"Oh. Uh, okay." He buzzed me in and I walked up the short cobblestone driveway. The curtains were drawn on the ground floor windows so I couldn't see in.

I knocked on his front door.

Levi answered wearing tailored slacks and a casual button-down shirt that clung to his biceps. I could have him stripped down in under thirty seconds. "Come in."

On the wall behind him was an incredible painting of a boy seeming to come directly out of the frame, as if it was a trapdoor. More illusions. Dean Martin played through invisible speakers and the air was fragrant with garlic and tomato sauce.

I tried to snoop as Levi led me down a short hallway to his study, but I couldn't see any other part.

The study was pretty basic with a utilitarian filing cabinet and generic office furniture. Compared to the personality in his office at work, this was merely an overflow outlet that he didn't spend a lot of time in. Well, that would have been my assessment were it not for the large tank against one wall filled with a rainbow of tropical fish. A subdued blueish light filtered through the water. There were vivid orange fish with black V-stripes, skinny yellow guys with a thin red stripe and, the only fish I recognized, metallic blue and red neon tetras that swam languidly over multicolored pebbles.

Levi's desk chair was angled to face his home aquarium and I pictured him unwinding here at the end of a stressful day and letting the fluid swimming of the fish wash his troubles away. He didn't necessarily work in here much, but he dreamed in here. I'd lost myself in enough floating jellyfish tanks over the years to recognize the lure of an undersea escape.

I moved aside a green file to perch on the edge of a chair and keep the tank in view.

Levi hoisted himself onto his desk. "What's up?"

Are we playing games with each other?

I cleared my throat. "It's about Talia."

He rubbed his chin and I tried not to remember how soft his skin was under his stubbled jawline. "The Party told the press about the virus," he said. "It's an excuse to finally get us under their thumb."

"While they're confirming your involvement with the third-party smudges." I nodded. "Remember that woman in hot pink who was fairly insistent about the House being behind the smudges at the auction? She works for my mother. I met her today."

"How did they find out about the smudges? Or the auction? It wasn't public knowledge outside the criminal fringe." Levi absently reached for a container of fish food on his desk, then crossed to the aquarium. He shook flakes into the water, the fish darting to the surface to nip the food. "Talia's tight with them, is she?"

"No, but she's chummy with Daniel Hughes, the criminal defense lawyer." The man who'd mentioned he had information he thought Talia would be interested in, the night of the gala.

Levi shook the fish food another couple of times, his movements more forceful. When he turned from the tank, his look was inscrutable. "Why are you telling me? Talia is your mother. I'm just your…"

I waited with bated breath to see how he'd finish that sentence.

"You don't owe me this confidence," he said.

"I don't owe Talia anything either." I was about to tell him about what she'd done, when someone cleared their throat softly behind me.

"Hi. Sorry for interrupting. The timer went off for the pasta." A stunning redhead in a simple black dress stood at the door holding a glass of red wine.

I recognized her immediately. Dr. Caitlin Ryan, a Mundane, who'd recently gotten a lot of press pioneering some new procedure for early breast cancer detection.

"I didn't realize you were entertaining." Despite giving the wish my all, the ground did not open to swallow me whole.

"No worries," Caitlin said. "My work phoned at least four times before Levi poured the wine. I'll take the pasta off." She gave a little wave and left.

I should have stopped drinking two Kicks in the Balls ago. I swallowed against the metallic taste in my mouth. The names I'd called Levi over the years were legion but douchebag had never been one of them. "You neglected to mention your girlfriend."

"My what?" He frowned.

"Dr. Ryan."

"I see lots of people but if you're implying I'm exclusive with someone, I'm not." He got all frosty. "If I was seeing someone, I wouldn't cheat."

"Maybe you don't consider it cheating when only one of us got off."

"Cheating is cheating."

My relief was hollow. I hadn't wanted him to be that guy. That's all it was. "I'll take your word for it. But if that's the kind of woman you usually date, you're way outside your comfort zone hanging around with me. I'm nothing like her."

"Stop selling yourself short."

I laughed bitterly. "I wasn't." I stood up. "I'll see myself out. And note to self, don't bug you outside office hours."

"Wait." He jumped off the desk. "We made this date weeks ago."

"You're my client. You don't owe me an explanation." My heart was hammering and I eyed the distance to the door, calculating my chances of escape before I exploded in a ball of humiliation, an emotion I was becoming too familiar with when Levi was concerned.

He ran his thumb in slow strokes over my palm and damn if that tiny gesture wasn't erotic enough to make me shiver. "I had my fingers inside you last night. You called my name when you came. I'm a bit more than your client."

"You were also ill-advised, right?" I pulled away. "I'd had a shock. You were there and did an admirable job of getting my mind off things. Thank you for your service."

"Ma vaffanculo. So anyone would have done?"

"Well, they'd have to be pretty. I do have standards." I relished the tick of his jaw.

Neither of us moved, but fuck, how I wished he would. I'd lied so hard and I wanted him to call me out for it. No one else would have done, not last night and not now. I'd never experienced half the chemistry with anyone as I'd had with Levi and now that that genie was out of the bottle, I didn't know how to put him back. I wanted Levi to shove me up against the wall, his lips on mine and overwhelm me. I wanted him hard and hot inside me, pounding into me until I was boneless from pleasure.

Levi's breathing had slowed, a slight flush on his olive skin. His eyes were glued to the rise and fall of my boobs in my spectacular push-up bra under my tank top.

My body sizzled, desire radiating between us.

"Levi," Caitlin called out. "Where's the parmesan?"

My needy ache was doused with cold water. I gathered the torn remnants of my pride around me. "That's my cue. Move."

He stepped aside. "I'll see you at work."

Not if I see you first.

Chapter 17

Tuesday morning, I was woken up by two freezing cold feet pressed to my legs. Even through my fleecy pjs, those things were glacial.

"Kill me," Priya moaned. Her face was puffy, her hair a tangled mess.

I cracked my eyes open and ice picks burrowed into my brain. "I'll pay you five bucks to make coffee."

"I'll see your five and raise you twenty," she said.

Not enough. We lay there in mutual hangover misery. I barely mustered the energy to leave another message for Sandra Chen, the nurse who'd been on my ward, who might have been Talia's accomplice.

"Hey, Pri. Was Sandra Nefesh?"

"Yeah, a Shocker. Low level. Why?"

"Really?" I leaned up on my elbows and then quickly lay back down, because the world had lurched sideways. "Some Shockers' talents lay in manipulating brain waves. They're bio-electric, not going around throwing lightning bolts. What if that was the magic that the Van Gogh couldn't resist? Even at a low level, that magic would pack a punch if she physically manipulated him until he agreed to ward me."

"It's something to consider."

I read the three texts that Charlotte Rose had sent during the night. The last one read "She's dead, isn't she?"

I texted back "NO!" hoping like hell I wasn't lying.

"Where are you at with the encryption?" I said.

"Good news. It wasn't a cryptographically secure hash algorithm so I ran a rainbow table. It might be finished." Priya elbowed me. "Go get my laptop."

"Why me?"

"I'm the brains, you're the grunt. Fetch."

Gingerly, I sat up. Not only was I nauseous but my skin felt coated in stale grease. I stuffed my feet into my fake fur slippers and shuffled to the living room.

"Make coffee," Priya called out.

"Calm your tits," I muttered and brought the laptop back to bed. "Is your rainbow thing done? Did it work?"

Priya grabbed it and typed some rapid-fast command. "Damn, I'm good. Voilà."

She clicked on the icon of the drive. There was a single excel spreadsheet in it.

"Not exactly the detailed villain agenda I'd hoped for." I crowded in to read the opened doc over her shoulder. "The ones with 'M' beside them are Mundanes and 'N' means they're Nefesh. Column A is dates. It goes back three months." I scanned the dates. "They stopped taking Mundanes a month ago. Charlotte Rose was right and Mundanes were being experimented on. These auction people must have started out really attempting to make magic stick and when proven that it didn't, went for the con anyway."

Priya expanded one of the columns. "Check it out. A bunch of the Nefesh have a serial number, type of magic, and level. It's their cataloguing system."

I counted them. "Sixteen potential vials with the ability to make more. Except two of them have been crossed out."

"The vials were lost or destroyed?"

"Or the smudges got loose," I said. "If that's the case, this is our one piece of good news. I've already killed one, so we're only looking for one, provided it wasn't already killed during a chemo treatment."

"There are no air elementals listed," Priya said. "Maybe they didn't take Meryem."

"Or they didn't get to her yet. I'm not sure how fast they can collect the magic. It would depend on how many people with blood magic—"

"Jezebels," Priya said.

"What?"

"There had to be a reason Yitzak called you that. Talia named you after Asherah. So why call you Jezebel?"

"Misogyny?"

"That too, but he hid your magic from a group that obviously is interested in that power, seeing as they're using it to create these smudges. So there are more than one of you with that ability. You're a magic type and types have names. Van Goghs, Blowhards, Sirens, Blockheads. You're a Jezebel."

"The other names have connotations to their magic. Jezebel and blood, not so much." I mulled it over. "Unless... What if we're looking at it the wrong way? Magic came into being by ten men who were such devout believers in Yahweh that they tried to achieve this high level of communion with him. They failed but they still got magic and blood magic is the one thing that can strip theirs away. Undermine it, the way that Jezebel undermined the Jewish patriarchy with her continued insistence on the worship of Asherah."

"She was a danger to them." Priya elbowed me. "How cool would it be if all Jezebels are women and you're part of some secret kickass female society?"

"I could live with that. If we're correct, we have an unknown number of Jezebels being forced, I hope, to strip magic to be sold to the highest bidder. How fast and how often can they do this? Meryem was taken. I'm sure of it, but how much time does she have left? Where are they holding her? There's no convenient address."

"Yeah, actually. There is. Sort of. 7VMX+96. Check it out." Priya took the laptop away from me and brought up Google Maps, dropping a pin on the Vancouver Public Library. Then she opened the info box. Underneath the address was written "8VHM+WP Vancouver, British Columbia."

"What's that?"

"A plus code. Plus codes give addresses to everywhere, even locations that don't have roads. In case someone needs a delivery or emergency services, they can be found. There are two parts to them. First is the shortcode which is six or seven letters or numbers, and then the city because you can have the same shortcode in different cities. 7VMX+96 is a shortcode but there's no city. Just a heart emoji."

I flung an arm around her. "You're a genius. The heart is the city. The lab is in Hedon." I jumped up, calling back to her as I ran to my bedroom. "Can you check my phone for spyware while I get dressed?"

"Sure."

I hopped into the shower, washing in record time before tugging on my last pair of clean black jeans and a black sweater. The bruises and hickey had faded to tolerable levels, but I applied the arnica cream one more time and tied the metallic scarf over top to hide them.

Today was going to fucking rock. We had the bastards. I was going to find Meryem and bring her home. I fist pumped.

Priya entered my room with two coffees and the phone as I pulled my damp hair into a high ponytail. "No spyware or tracking apps on your phone," she said, "but it's easy enough to locate someone."

"I know." I slugged back half of my beverage while

texting Miles that there was potentially only one smudge loose out there.

Priya watched me layer on black eyeliner and red lipstick. "You're armoring up. Where are you going?"

"The Queen rules Hedon, but it's the black market and there are bound to be shifty people doing things they want kept off her radar. If you can't bring something in through the front door, then sneak in through the back. It's a magic space. All you'd need is an architect to build a way in."

"Coders build back doors all the time," Priya said. "Makes sense. You know where this back door is?"

"I believe I do." I grabbed my leather jacket and stuffed my feet in my motorcycle boots. "My M&M stash is in the back of my closet behind a fake right-side panel."

Priya jabbed me in the chest. "Take back your suicide mission candy confession."

"I bequeathed you Moriarty when I went to Hedon the first time, but you're getting upset about the chocolate?"

"Moriarty is a piece of shit and I already have the keys. This is your hidden stash that I've never managed to find."

"Relax. You're not getting rid of me that easily. The M&Ms are thanks for all your help."

"In that case." She crawled into the closet, emerging with the bag held aloft. "Oh yes, my preciouses, you shall be mine." She poured the peanut candy directly into her mouth.

"Way to keep your dignity, Adler."

She shot me the finger, her cheeks bulging with chocolate.

～

NOTHING about the golem's routine had changed, nor was there anyone else on site at the warehouse. Where did they keep this thing when they had the parties? Did they stash him in a closet? Cram him in a wheel well?

I positioned myself inside the warehouse, my fingers closed around the red throwing star that I'd manifested, the sharp bite amping me into a high wire alertness.

When the golem entered, his roughly drawn eyes widened comically in recognition.

"Hey, big boy. Remember me?" I fired the weapon into his left eye.

The golem ran at me, not deterred at all.

My heart pulsed in my throat in time to his thudding footsteps. I made another throwing star and blinded his other eye.

He sped up.

I fixed an image in my mind and called on my magic. A second later I held a pike with a curved blade on the end.

Closer and closer he came, while I ignored every smart instinct to run. I swung, catching the golem mid-section.

He doubled over with a soft grunt and tore free, his clothing torn and a chunk of clay missing from his center. He looked like a tree that had been partially eaten by a beaver. The golem grabbed the pike by the blade, but I held fast, the two of us caught in a tug-of-war.

My shoulder blades burned from hanging on and my heels slid on the dusty floor.

The golem ripped the pike away, tossing it in a corner with a clatter.

We danced around each other, the golem taking swipes, until I grabbed the pike again.

Believe in yourself, Ash. Don't overthink.

I charged him, my blood magic coating me in a spiked armor. Say now, that was more like it. Holding the pike right below the blade, I slammed it into his middle.

The golem battered me with punches. My armor miti-gated most of the damage, but every blow reverberated through me and I was terrified he was going to puncture a lung. If I bled out, there was no do-over: no convenient healing magic and no partner to call for help. Even if I killed him first, according to all video game logic, he was only a level one minion, so what kind of shape would I be in to find the kids and take on whichever ultimate boss awaited me?

I leaned harder into the blade, gaining ground into slicing him in half inch by excruciating inch. Clay glooped over my armored hands. With a roar, I put everything I had into one last push.

His torso fell flopping to the ground, while I stood out of grabbing range, bent double, heaving, with sweat dripping off me. Once I'd caught my breath, I sliced off his hands and kicked them away, along with his jerking legs.

He blinked expressionlessly at me which was super creepy.

The Hebrew word "emet" or truth had been carved into his forehead. If I erased the letter "aleph" that would change the word to death and he'd die, but I needed him alive. For now.

I touched his torso, but didn't feel anything through my armor. This next step involved a fine sensitivity to his magic, so I willed the armor away. It took a few tries, but at last, it disappeared. I felt kind of naked without it.

This time when I touched him, the magic animating him pulsed through his skin against my fingers. It didn't feel like any magic I'd sensed before. It was thick and dull and flat. Exactly like mud, but mud with an awareness.

Holding his top half in front of me like a cross warding off a vampire, which hopefully did not exist, but who knew anything anymore, I slowly walked the perimeter of the warehouse, playing "Cold, cold, hot." Trust me, I felt a hundred kinds of ridiculous.

My hypothesis was twofold. First, that one empty warehouse plus one golem guard dog equaled one back door into Hedon. Not only was it easy to bring kids through when they were already on site for the parties, but why else have the golem guarding the place? Second, and this was the part that was more of a longshot, according to the Jewish mythology that I'd read up on, golems would faithfully perform the task they were commanded to do. I couldn't change his programming and there was no reasoning with this thing, but if he was tasked with protecting this portal, there was a chance he was keyed to it in some way.

His magic pulsing remained constant through the entire property, but when I entered the office, it rippled.

Back and forth, I inched my way across the room. When I hit the far-right corner, his magic flared.

"Good boy." Propping his torso against the desk, I crouched down. The cheap linoleum was worn shiny in a two-foot radius. I placed my hand in the center of it.

Magic.

The trouble was that my magic would strip *this* magic away and thus, might shut down the portal entirely. There were probably multiple people who needed access to this door, so how would they all activate it?

I eyed the golem, then stomped back and retrieved his hand. It was still warm. Ew. But when I placed the hand on the floor, nothing happened. I stood where the portal should have been and turned around slowly. One spot on the wall was noticeably grimy, like it had been touched multiple times.

If I activated this back door, likely, I'd be alerting someone or many someones to my presence. Blood magic and enhanced strength aside, fighting the golem had already drained me.

Pacing in a tight circle, I tried calling Levi and Miles but both of them had their phones off. No, I couldn't wait.

Meryem didn't have the luxury of time. I'd just have to be extremely careful.

I pressed the golem's hand against the spot and voilà. A glimmering blue door sprung up.

"Great knowing you and, uh, sorry about the disembowelment. No hard feelings?"

The golem gave me another of his blank stares.

"I knew you'd understand. Sweet dreams." I rubbed the aleph off his forehead and his crude lids fell shut for good.

Crossing my fingers, I stepped through the portal and into a bloodbath. Red splatters slicked the walls and floors like a demented Pollock painting while puddles of viscera glistened wetly.

I threw my arm over my nose, the charnel stench slithering down my throat, choking me. Bodies lay where they'd been slaughtered, carelessly crumpled on the ground between empty gurneys and banks of medical monitoring equipment.

Their heads had been piled into a neat pyramid.

The Queen.

I bolted back to the portal, but was grabbed and surrounded by a phalanx of people in black tactical gear with mesh obscuring their faces and the Queen's logo stitched on their upper arms.

Fear clawed through me, chilling me to my core, but it was replaced in an instant by a hot, thick anger. What had they done?

I stuffed my fury down. Antagonizing these people wouldn't get my desired outcome. "Take me to your leader."

Marching in step like a well-trained army, they ushered me down a long corridor to a small room filled with video monitors that were trained on the room I'd been in. Viewed through the screen, the massacre was reduced to nothing more than another TV show.

The Queen and White Rabbit Man were deep in discussion, but she broke off abruptly when her soldiers stopped with a heel click.

Her hair fell in luxurious dark red waves down her back and she wore another red dress. If I didn't want to kill her right now, I'd admire the hell out of her style and absolute authority. "I said I didn't want to be disturbed."

"Apologies, Highness," the soldier in front said. A woman, her voice muffled by the mesh.

They parted to reveal me, standing there like a Kinder Surprise.

She flicked a gaze over me. "I know a good hairdresser. You should call her."

"Where are the kids?" I insisted. "Tell me."

One of her elegantly sculpted eyebrows rose incredulously. "Demands, blanquita?"

My fingers twitched. I could rip the magic from all of them and force answers, but not only would that tip my hand, stripping magic involved blood contact, which was more an intimate and interactive gesture, and not suited to en masse removal. I'd never get close enough to the Queen to try.

Too bad.

"How did you get past us?" she said. "We've been standing here by the door."

"That's the front door," I said. "I came in through the back. Where are the prisoners?"

The Queen's face puckered in distaste. "Gone. They got them out during the attack. Five or six of them. That's all. When we verified that the people left behind had no knowledge of where they'd been moved, we, cómo se dice?" She snapped her fingers twice. "Sí. Tied up those loose ends."

Her voice remained steady, her body relaxed. There was no unusual gesturing or eye movement. She was telling the truth.

That didn't make it better. I shrugged free of the soldier. "Was there a dark-haired girl in the prisoners? Sixteen?"

"We didn't get a good look at any of them," White Rabbit Man said.

Meryem was still alive. I could still save her. I refused to believe otherwise. "Can I go?"

"How come my associate didn't see you at the auction?" the Queen said. "I went to all the trouble of getting you an invitation."

"Then he wasn't looking very hard. I saw you," I said to White Rabbit Man. "Third row from the front, left side. A friendly piece of advice. Maybe diversify your fashion choices. Try a pop of color."

His lips quirked. "Back at you, Jessica Jones."

"Black is very practical," I said.

He yawned theatrically.

"Hiding in plain sight?" The Queen's voice was gentle, her Spanish-accented English caressing. Only a fool would be lulled into underestimating her.

"Something like that."

She tipped up my chin with one red manicured nail, her light floral perfume weaving around me. "How did a Mundane such as yourself find this place?"

There was no harm in her knowing, so I shared what I'd found on the encrypted files, including the plus code and how it essentially provided an address to this place within Hedon. I explained about my suspicions of a back door, which led me to the warehouse and the golem. Though I lied and implied trickery, not magic, in opening the portal. Unlike Levi, she showed no surprise or disbelief when I mentioned the creature.

He was going to have to wise up, fast.

"Chica lista," the Queen said. Off my inquiring look, she tapped her head. "Smart."

"Highness?" White Rabbit Man glanced at the Queen, who nodded. "This way."

"You going to knock me out again?" I said.

"Only if you keep talking."

I followed him and the Queen back into the slaughter room. He touched the side of a cabinet and a dim light came on through the dark glass, revealing a kind of humidor with vials of smudges. Fourteen of them to be exact.

"These people died protecting this," he said.

"You could make a lot of money off of them." I kept my voice as neutral as possible, thinking furiously about how I could get them away from the Queen.

"I could," she said, "if acquiring magic wasn't a fantasy." She gestured at a headless body. "One of these pendejos was quite forthcoming about that. Also about the fact that two employees had stolen vials."

"The smudges that got loose." I was right about the crossed-out entries. I tapped the cabinet. "Are you going to sell them, knowing what will happen?"

She wrinkled her nose. "That type of chaos doesn't interest me."

What kind did?

"Well, you can't let these exist and if you try and destroy them, your people will die," I said. "Give them to me. Levi has a way to dispose of them safely."

"Does he? How convenient," she said. "I believe I'll hold onto them for now."

My cool "as you wish" was nothing like the giant "fuuu-uuuuuuuuuck" that I wanted to scream.

"Whoever is behind this has been working hard to shift blame onto the Queen," White Rabbit Man said. "We're going to put them out of business. Permanently."

"And the people that were taken?" I said. "They're helpless victims."

"They're yours," he said. "If we find them first, we'll contact you and hand them over."

He didn't ask for my phone number. I was becoming very popular.

"Thank you." I hadn't expected that from them. I gestured at the bodies. "Their employers will amp up operations now," I said. "The clock is ticking."

"Sí. And whoever is behind this?" The Queen sliced her hand across her throat.

While I didn't dare protest, I also didn't stifle my grim smile. These people had played their cards, now let the chips fall where they may.

Chapter 18

How much blood did I have on my hands?

If I hadn't gone to the Queen in the first place, would she have found out about this operation? Would those men still be alive? Would Meryem and any others have more time before their magic was stolen? Or would all this have played out with or without me and Meryem was already a loose end that had been tied up?

And what would the Queen do with all the smudges?

Overhead a seagull cawed, the sky and waves here at Jericho Beach a melancholic gray.

I dropped my head into my hands. I'd been so blithely certain that I'd come back with Meryem and I'd failed. A million "if onlys" trumpeted through my brain. If only we'd decrypted the drive faster, if only I hadn't freaked at the auction about my magic-stealing abilities and instead gotten answers from Birthmark Man. If only. If only.

I opened up my text chain with Charlotte Rose, but I couldn't bring myself to update her. I wanted to drown myself in a party-sized bag of ripple chips with a three-pound chocolate bar chaser. Instead, I mentally indexed any possible leads. The warehouse location was burned; there was nothing further to be found there. The Van Gogh was dead and the encrypted files hadn't yielded anything else to pursue. Talia was connected to the Van Gogh, but she wasn't connected to this, so that avenue was out.

If the German killer had been identified from the video footage, that would be worth following up, but that was it for viable leads. I punched the steering wheel.

My phone rang with an unfamiliar number. I almost sent it to voicemail, but answered at the last second. "Hello?"

"Is this Ashira Cohen?" The woman was tentative.

"It is. Who's this?"

"Sandra Chen. You left me a message?" The nurse from my post op ward.

"Yes. Thank you for calling me back. I wanted to speak to you about something that might have happened when I was a patient fifteen years ago."

There was silence and then she sighed. "I know what you want to talk about. It's why I hesitated phoning you back."

I dropped my head against the seat. Part of me had been holding out hope that Talia hadn't done this, but if the nurse was reluctant to speak about this? It didn't bode well. "I can come to you, if you'd feel more comfortable."

"No. I don't want to see you. I appreciate that this wasn't your fault, but it scared me and no one at the hospital took me seriously. My complaints were ignored and worse, I was chastised for saying nonsense because you were a Mundane." Her voice shook.

"My fault for what? What did I do to you?" Because if we're going to assign fault here and you coerced Yitzak, there's plenty to go around.

More silence.

I closed my eyes, my gut filling with lead. "I tried to take your magic, didn't I?"

"Yes."

"I'm sorry. For what it's worth, I was a Mundane. Until a few days ago, that's how I lived my life. It's complicated, but the short version is that someone warded my magic back then without telling me."

"I'm sure he did it for your own good," she said. *He?* She knew about the Van Gogh.

Sandra must have manipulated Yitzak with her bio-electric magic, forcing him to comply. Could I blame her for a gut reaction, doing something to keep me from harming her? Emotions warred in my head.

But that aside, Yitzak loathed Jezebels. Assuming that was a magic type, and he'd had no choice warding me and hiding my powers, then the logical conclusion was that he'd rather I'd have been found. Probably by whatever group the German killer belonged to and who Yitzak was so desperate to please.

Why? Because Jezebels stole magic and created smudges? Or was something else at play?

"He didn't have much of a choice, did he, thanks to you?" I said.

"What are you talking about?" Sandra said.

"You forced Yitzak to tattoo me."

"Who's Yitzak? I'm talking about Adam. Your father."

My phone clattered to the floor mat. A strange disassociation from my body, from the entire world, enveloped me. I was outside myself looking down at this pale frozen figure and only the tingling of my skin assured me I was still rooted here.

"Hello?" Sandra said.

I fumbled for my phone. "I'm here. Are you sure it was my father?"

"Dark hair? Charming? Very fond of lemon candies."

My stomach sank into my toes. "When was he there? What did you tell him? Where was my mother?"

"I'd convinced her to go home and shower. Take a break

for a couple of hours. He showed up in the middle of the night, after I'd had this episode with you. I was upset, especially because my supervisor didn't believe me."

"But he did?"

"Not at first. He claimed you were a Mundane, but then he saw for himself and said to leave everything to him."

There are two kinds of people in this world, little jewel. Dad had swung me high in the air, always smiling, magnetic, a compelling personality even without his magic.

Oh, fuck. Compelling. The ultimate charmer. People fell over themselves wanting to help Adam out. My father followed a Robin Hood principle of stealing from the rich and the shady. He'd never scammed an innocent person, and while he'd compelled Yitzak into betraying his principles, the Van Gogh was no innocent.

But I was.

My father had stolen my magic, redirected my life down some narrow path, and vanished once more. If he'd really done this for my well-being, he would have stuck around and helped me through it. No, whatever had gone down had benefited him and fucked me over.

All the idyllic childhood memories that I stored deep in my heart slipped ninety degrees out of alignment, leaving a dull throbbing ache.

"Then what happened?" I clutched the phone like a lifeline.

"I don't know. I left early, but no one else reported the same thing. Seems he took care of it."

"Yeah." I laughed bitterly. "He did."

"Do you have better control of your magic now?"

Well, I was sitting in my car in an empty beach parking lot with blood crawling over my skin, so I was gonna go with "no."

"Much better," I assured her. "One last thing. Did you ever tell my mother about this?"

"I never got the chance." Sandra paused. "Are we done? Did you get what you needed?"

I opened my mouth to answer her, but the truth was, I didn't know. Blood magic roiled over my body and there was a chopped-off golem's hand on the passenger seat. What did I need? A return to a world that made sense, maybe?

"We're done," I said.

I lost track of how long I sat there in this slowed-down bubble of time. The beach, my car, everything dropped away into a cold fog. I'd had a happy childhood with two parents I adored, but Dad and I had had a special bond. He was the one who watched endless cartoons with me, taught me to ride my bike, and took me for secret ice cream trips, throwing Mom a wink and an unrepentant grin when I returned home sticky.

It had taken me years to reconcile those memories with the man who had abandoned us without a word and the only way I'd managed was to believe that he had no choice. That one of his cons had gone wrong and he'd had to leave. It didn't ease my heartache, but the alternative was to accept that he hadn't wanted us anymore. That we'd served our purpose, same as any other mark, and now he'd moved on.

But now I had proof he'd come back. I should have been ecstatic, but rage sent my magic pulsing and spurting off my skin like a fucked-up fountain. He'd come like a thief in the night and taken away my magic.

I was halfway to Talia's office before I realized I'd left the parking lot. It was a miracle I didn't kill anyone.

People scurried out of my way without a greeting. And that was with my magic carefully shut down. Sinaya took one look at me and hit the intercom button to let Talia know I was here.

"Have you come to apologize?" My mother looked up from her laptop and did a double take. "What's in your hair?" She came around her desk and touched my dishevelled ponytail, frowning at her fingers when she pulled them away. "Is that clay? For fuck's sake, Ashira. If you're going to fall apart, then let's get you some help."

I stepped back, my hands up. "After Dad left, did you ever see him again?"

"No. Your sainted father never showed his face again." She snatched a tissue from the box and scrubbed the clay off her hand. "Good riddance as far as I'm concerned. The son-of-a-bitch couldn't even bother to return my call when I told him you were in the hospital."

"You told me you didn't have his new number."

"I didn't want you begging him to come back." Talia dropped the soiled tissue in the trash. "He'd left and made it pretty damn clear we weren't a priority. You were angry enough. I didn't want to see you trapped in some cycle of false hope."

"Then why call him after the accident?"

"He was still your father and I didn't know what was going to happen." Talia rubbed her eyes, exhaustion etched into every line of her body. "I assumed he'd give a damn. Obviously, I was wrong." She sat back down at her desk, spine straight, glasses on. Ready to take whatever the world threw at her.

Never show weakness. I hadn't only learned that lesson from Dad leaving.

"What's this all about?" she said. "What's done is done. Why bring up past history?"

It wasn't the past. It was the present and maybe even the future if I couldn't answer all the questions his presence that night raised. Even if I'd tried to take his magic, why was Dad's first reaction to bring in a Van Gogh to ward me up and suppress it? Why didn't he tell Talia? How did he know Yitzak? Was he aware of whatever organization Yitzak was betraying? Did Adam believe I was a threat to some scheme of his?

"I thought the worst thing Dad had done to me was to leave." I shrugged and sat down on the arm of a chair.

"But the worst thing was not coming back when you needed him?" She reached across the desk and squeezed my hand.

The gesture nearly undid me.

I half-rose up to hug her and seek the comfort she'd always been willing to give when I was a child. How had Talia and I gone so wrong? Even though Dad and I had been closer, I'd loved my mom, but I'd shut the door on needing her. I'd taken Dad's teachings about cons and marks and applied it to her as well, distancing us until we sat on opposite sides of this impossible gulf.

Despite all that and the fact that we sat here in her world that had no room for magic, I almost busted out my powers to prove this wasn't a fantasy born of drugs or mind-fuckery on Levi's part because I was lost and I wanted my mom, but I couldn't even force any words past my clogged throat.

I stood up. Talia had nothing to do with Yitzak or the tattoo. "I'm sorry for the things I accused you of before. It's been a really long week and I was wrong. I should go."

No lies. No games. I shouldn't have doubted her.

"Ashira…" Her eyes sought mine and hope surged through me that she had a way forward for us. "It's dangerous out there. Watch what you say."

Did she believe me about my magic? Was this a veiled warning? Or a heads up? Her expression held no clarification.

"And if you insist on fraternizing with Levi," she said. "Be careful."

"Trust me, I want to see him less than you want me to."

That seemed to satisfy her. Well, that made one of us.

I drove to House HQ on autopilot. One quick errand and then I could melt down.

I snapped my fingers at the snooty Executive Assistant. "Levi."

"He's not to be disturbed." She didn't bother looking up at me.

I slammed the golem hand on her desk. It was still wearing its glove so as far as she knew, this unhinged person had presented her with an overly large severed human hand. Heh. "Make sure he gets this."

She wheeled her chair back so fast that she hit the wall behind her and bounced forward. "Go right in."

"You sure?" I waved the hand in her face. "I don't want to be a bother."

"Go!" she shrieked.

I rapped twice on his door and entered.

Levi leaned back in his chair, reading a document, his feet up on his desk, and a pen in one hand. "Hmmm?"

His suit cost more than my rent and fitted him like it was sentient, calculating the best ways to enhance his aura of power, showcase his muscled thighs, and highlight his flexing biceps as he turned the page. His midnight black hair didn't have a strand out of place; nary a wrinkle marred his clothing. Nothing dared be disordered in his world. This man didn't fail, not in his job and not as a person.

My hair was half-falling out of its ponytail and streaked with bits of clay, my pits were sweat stained, and even though I was doing my best not to look, I was pretty certain there was a bloodstain on the toe of my boot. I unclenched my jaw. "Did you get a hit on the killer?"

Levi finally looked over, eyebrows raised. "New look?"

"Deluxe spa treatment. You got a name for the German who murdered Yitzak or not?"

"No. He's not in any database we have access to and there were no hits with facial recognition software."

Of course there weren't, because the universe was determined to ride my ass today.

"I'm assuming you're here because Priya decrypted the drive," he said. "Any leads on who's behind the auction?"

"Not yet. But the Queen has all the vials."

He sat up straight, his feet hitting the ground. "What's she going to do with them?"

"Hold onto them. So she says."

"Do you believe her? Because if not…" He snapped his pen. A regular cheapo pen, so no great loss. "I can't sneak into Hedon and steal them back."

"She wouldn't look kindly on that, no. But I believe her. For now." I lobbed the golem hand at Levi. "Catch."

Levi pulled it out of the glove, his own hand dwarfed by the golem's. "What's with the gag gift?"

"Golem. They exist. Happy early birthday."

He dropped the hand on his desk. "Ash."

I hightailed it for his door and didn't look back.

"Damn it. Wait."

He caught up with me by the elevators. "You can't just drop that bombshell and leave."

"And yet that's exactly what I'm doing." I stabbed the elevator button, my jabs growing more frenetic, my need for a place to melt the fuck down expanding inside me like a balloon filling with helium.

The doors opened to reveal a crowded car.

"Out," Levi said.

Everyone scrambled to abandon ship.

How fucking rich. I stalked inside.

When we were between floors, Levi hit the stop button. He planted himself directly in front of me, his arms crossed. "Finish your status report."

"You're not as all-knowing as you think you are."

"Spare me the insults."

"But Leviticus, that's our schtick. And for the record, that was the status report. Big House Head, so powerful and in control. You don't know shit about what's going on. None of us do."

"Why are you mad at me?"

Because you're here and he's not. Because I'm mad at myself but it's easier to take it out on you. I took a breath. "I found the lab, but I was too late and the kidnapped Nefesh had been moved. I promised Charlotte Rose and I failed her. I failed Meryem. All I've got are loose ends."

The memory of a pile of heads, each with an identical blank stare boring a hole in my soul momentarily blacked out everything else. I wrapped my arms around myself and stuffed my hands into my armpits, but I couldn't stop shaking.

I willed everything down. Falling apart around Levi was a bad habit and it ended now. I wasn't a damsel in distress. I'd get through this.

"I'm guessing the lab was in Hedon if the Queen was there. How bad was it?" he said.

My eyes drifted down to the bloodstain on my boot and just as quickly bounced off it. "Don't ask. Even I don't hate you enough to put that image in your head."

"Grazie," he said sarcastically. "Where did you leave things with her?"

"She's not coming after me. I'm her new favorite enigma, remember? In fact, she's doing what she can from her end. If she finds the kids first, she'll hand them over. Status report complete," I said, proud of how cool and composed I sounded.

Levi's eyes searched mine. "There's more."

"Meryem is still out there having god-knows-what done to her. That's not enough?" His unrelenting stare got under my skin. "We're not friends, Levi. Save your heart-to-hearts for Miles. I've told you everything you need to know." I restarted the elevator.

"You haven't failed anyone," Levi said, his hands jammed

loosely into his pockets. "In fact, you've done more than anyone could have asked. All of this, the magic, the smudge —it blindsided you and with every setback, you keep going."

Blindsided was a good word. It was like those games of Pin the Tail on the Donkey where they tied a scarf around your eyes and turned you round and round. I was spinning in the dark and the weight of it all was too much to bear.

"We're not friends," I said softly, resting my head on Levi's shoulder. Allowing myself this comfort for a few precious seconds.

"Perish the thought." He kissed the top of my head and sputtered. "I swallowed golem," he said in a strangled voice.

I laughed, my cold bubble finally bursting.

The elevator pinged, the doors sliding open to the lobby.

Miles stood on the other side, a dozen highly trained men and women in House uniforms arrayed behind him. "The smudge just went public."

Chapter 19

"Darwinism is a lie." I stomped my foot in lieu of throwing someone.

Hey, humanity. A piece of free advice: when there was a thirty-something dudebro with black shadows slithering over his skin, how about *not* lining up to take selfies with him? This gene pool needed some damn lifeguards.

He stood in the middle of Robson Square, a multi-level, pedestrian-only area a few blocks away from House Pacifica that backed onto the Vancouver Art Gallery, or as we locals called it, the VAG.

Hard "g."

It featured a tiny ice rink that turned into an outdoor dance venue in summertime and was a busy hub of activity during Jazz Fest, special events like when we'd hosted the Olympics, or today when the gawkers were out in full force. Didn't these people have jobs?

To their credit, both the Nefesh and Mundane cops had pushed most of the crowd back, herding them behind cordons on the upper plaza. The press stood to one side reporting that they were live with a virus victim at Robson Square while a small group of chanting protesters held signs like "Stop the Nefesh peril" and the ever pithy "Lock them up."

Miles issued orders to his people and they jumped into the fray clearing out the rather aggressive selfie-wanting crowd.

Dudebro, who should have been put down like a dog for wearing yellow board shorts, a blue shirt with red bowtie, and a backwards baseball cap, had his arms around two girls making cutesy faces and throwing peace signs.

"Screw it," I said. "Let the smudge have them."

"I'm seriously tempted," Levi said. "They see his facial snake, right?"

The smudge slithered from one of Dudebro's cheeks to the other.

"Please use that term on a regular basis," I said.

I grabbed one of the peace sign girls after Miles broke up the party. "Why are you taking selfies with him?"

"We're proving to those haters that there's no virus," she said. "He's a level five and his magic is showing itself to the world. I wish I had that. It's awesome." She skipped off to catch up with her friend.

Miles jogged over. "Get back to HQ. I can't protect you and deal with all this."

"I'm not leaving," Levi said.

"Those assholes will tear you apart." Miles kept an eye on the protesters. "They're hyped."

"Fuck them. I'm not running away. Can you kill it or is it too strong?" Levi asked me.

"I've got this. But there are too many cameras. I don't want to come out this way." It would be a disaster. The Queen, the Untainted Party, the shadowy organization that Yitzak's killer belonged to—the longer we put off any of them learning about me, the better.

"There's nothing can do about the press," Miles said.

"But we can do something about Ash," Levi said. "I won't let you be exposed."

"That's really kind of you, but I don't know how you plan on getting rid of that smudge without me." I shook my head. "This isn't a good place for you to suffer any... setbacks."

"She's right," Miles said. "Everyone is going to be watching you."

"Which is precisely why I can't stand here with my thumb up my ass. Should the worst happen, we implement Plan B," Levi said.

"Plan B is more dangerous than the initial problem. No way."

"Not your call, Miles."

"Not my—?" Miles puffed his chest out, then exhaled slowly and gave Levi a tight nod. "Yes, Sir."

Yikes. Mommy and Daddy were fighting. More importantly, what was Plan B? Levi being blind wasn't great and obviously Miles wanted to protect him from that, but the smudge problem was enough to warrant dealing with the consequences.

The Chief Constable came over to have a word, looking haggard. "Do we need to empty the plaza entirely? Is whatever that is about to go nuclear and take out half of Vancouver?"

"Keep everyone back and no one will be in any danger," Levi said. "We've got this and will neutralize it."

"See that you do, because this?" He gestured to the protesters. "Is a powder keg and one innocent victim could be the spark that ignites the communities for good." He strode back to the officers.

"So, no pressure," I said.

"Do you want the Lillian glamour?" Levi said.

"No. Make it seem I'm you." I tilted my head at the protestors. "It'll shut them up and remind everyone of your strengths." I kept a close eye on Dudebro, currently protesting the loss of his adoring public. "No matter what's between us personally," I said. "I believe in you as House Head. You want to do right by your people, and that's the leader Nefesh need. So if I can keep some crap off your plate like a city going full riot, then let me. And if that's not reason enough, do it because it'll put the spotlight on you and keep it off me."

"The first reason was pretty good," he said, softly.

The smudge made a particularly aggressive slither along the right side of Dudebro.

"The smudge has never made itself visible before," I said. "I've been the only one to reveal it, so why the change? You think it found a permanent host? Were we wrong about it not taking root in a person?" I really hoped not, especially with all those vials in the Queen's possession. I bounced on my toes, psyching myself up. "I'm starting to see the appeal of magic that follows rules."

"Hallelujah, she sees reason," Levi said.

The wind shifted, and I gagged hard. Even from this distance, the smudge's toxicity was nausea-inducing.

"What?" Levi said.

"You don't smell that?"

He and Miles shook their heads. Lucky me.

I cracked my knuckles. "That thing is history."

Levi placed a hand on my shoulder. "There are innocents here. Don't get carried away. No… setbacks, okay?"

"Destroying smudges isn't problematic for me. I'll keep everything in check."

Miles clipped a tiny mic to my collar and handed me an earpiece. "It's tuned to a closed frequency. Only me and my security team can hear you. You need anything, ask."

I slid in the earpiece. "Got it."

"Ready?" Levi asked.

"As I'll ever be."

He pressed a quick kiss to my mouth. "Kick ass, Ashira Cohen."

When he released me, a tiny tingle of magic rippled through me.

"Fuck, that's weird," Miles said.

I looked down at myself and saw the suit Levi had been wearing. Levi was now my twin.

"You could have left out the clay in my hair," I said.

"My illusions are faithful reproductions. I am a maestro and my art includes all details."

"Asshole." I ran across the plaza toward Dudebro.

The crowd went nuts when they saw me-as-Levi. Half of them burst into hysterical swoons over his safety, the other half jeered that they hoped he died.

What a bunch of ingrates. I had a new appreciation for the BS Levi had to deal with every day, having only seen the shiny adoration for him, and not the ugly flip side of people actively wanting him to fail.

One very pouty, very gelled guy in his early twenties who was dressed in a fitted paisley patterned shirt and white rolled up jeans refused to be evacuated behind the cordons, threatening to slap a lawsuit on two of Miles' guards if they so much as touched him. "I need this selfie for my scavenger hunt. This'll win it."

I stormed over to him, grabbed him by the collar, and lifted him off the ground, starting at the sight of Levi's hands instead of mine holding the guy. Levi had really talented fingers. I flexed them, my thighs clenching in response.

The man I was holding turned an odd shade of purple. Right.

I lowered my voice into an approximation of Levi's. People heard what they expected to. It was close enough. "Move, or I'll throw you across the damn plaza."

I lifted him a bit higher to prove I meant business.

He nodded frantically, but as soon as he touched the ground again, he held up his phone. "Could I—"

I lunged at him and he bolted, holding tight to his dumbass porkpie hat.

"Levi Montefiore. My man." Dudebro high-fived me, but his smile was tinged with a sly malice.

I dug my nails into my palms, the smudge's reek of rotting flesh and feces making my eyes water. "What's your name?"

"Rick."

"Good to meet you, Rick. What's your magic?"

"Level five psychic." Rick fired double finger guns at me. "Kapow."

At that level, he'd be assaulted with voices and need extremely strong drugs to help shield himself. "What meds are you on?"

Rick rattled off a list that would fell a moose. They should have slurred his speech and slowed his movements, so either he'd built up some crazy unusual tolerance, or the smudge had given him a new alertness. He thumped his chest. "No more voices and I ride the buzz. You feel me?"

I felt several I.Q. points lower. Did that count? "All the feels."

"Huh?" The smudge swam through his eyes and down his cheek. I really wished it would quit doing that.

Rick cupped his balls and waggled his tongue, giving the crowd ample gross frat boy photo ops. He let out a loud whoop.

"Don't get too attached to that good mood," I said.

"Why not?"

His meds could easily have thrown his magic immune system off-whack, leaving the smudge free to move on in and stay awhile. This wasn't a marriage made in heaven, more like a squatter's paradise. Humans couldn't handle an infusion of magic not inherently theirs. One way or another, this smudge would kill Rick, and then it would be loose and rampaging again.

There was only one possible ending to this story.

"This might tickle." I clapped Rick on both shoulders, sending my blood magic into him. Gritting my teeth, I ignored the beckoning song of his inherent magic and sought out the third-party smudge. Not hard, since it had invaded him like a pernicious weed.

Since it was a foreign body in his system, I was able to lock onto it without making Rick bleed, but I almost ran screaming because this smudge was living death.

My previous experience of these types of smudges were as a cohesive unit, but this one was fractured, hugely unstable, and going haywire bouncing around inside him. It was the magic equivalent of roadkill after a week, trying very hard to look like what it once was, but not fooling anybody.

No wonder it had gone public like this: it couldn't have hidden its presence, even if it wanted to.

The wriggling maggots were no longer merely a sensation; they were a million tiny tangible entities now feral in their attempt to survive. These abominations wound up my arms in a parade of seething squiggles that were rot and a primal shriek, buffeting me in their dark arms.

The smudge turned Rick's eyes black and he swung at me.

I ducked his punch, catching his fist and flipping him to the ground.

Believing it to be Levi going all badass, the crowd went nuts. Damn it, I'd probably single-handedly tripled the number of House Cats.

I straddled Rick and dragged the smudge slithering frantically under his skin out of him one agonizing inch at a time. My head was thrown back in a roar and my tendons strained. Blood tears streamed down my face.

Rick went limp; his eyes rolled back showing the whites.

Once it was three-quarters of the way out, I forked my red magic branches through it, making it cohesive once more. The smudge bucked violently but I overpowered it.

White clusters bloomed and fed, and the smudge was destroyed.

I checked Rick's pulse. "He's unconscious but breathing," I said into the mic. "Pulse is a bit elevated. Get a paramedic."

I pushed to my feet, chest heaving.

The plaza fell silent for two seconds. Then it went wild. Pure pandemonium.

All the cops and Miles' team could barely restrain people from rushing me-as-Levi.

Heh. This wouldn't stop any time soon. Levi was going to hate everyone wanting a piece of him. There was just one more thing to do. I flung my arms up in victory, smirking at the flurry of cameras that went off. If I was lucky, this photo would haunt His Lordship for the rest of his life.

I glanced over at Levi, still my doppelganger. He was doing that rapid blinking thing again. Before I could take more than three steps toward him so he could drop the illusion, a microphone was shoved in my face.

"I'm Leah Nichols, here with Levi Montefiore." A black female reporter in a smart green suit stood next to me. "That was amazing."

I nodded directly into the camera like of course it was.

Miles was partially blocking Levi, their heads bent close, having an intense discussion.

"Was that the magic virus?" Leah said.

I glanced at the men. Miles twirled his finger in a "wrap it up" motion.

Easy for him to say. I'd watched Leah before. The woman was a shark. There was no catch and release. She ripped every inch of information from her target, discarding its used carcass when she was done.

Hell of a reporter.

I smiled at her and launched into my best Levi voice. "Leah. We both know better than to believe in magic viruses."

She smiled back. "Then where did it come from? What was it?"

"The heart attacks, this shadow mass, stemmed from… a sick game the Nefesh involved were playing. I'm pleased to report that House Pacifica infiltrated and cracked this ring and has now stopped this highly dangerous and illegal activity. There is absolutely no danger to the public. None."

Leah met my eyes and I tensed, then she leaned forward. "Let us reiterate, there is no danger to the public."

Whoa. She'd bought it. Miles made a more insistent motion to finish up.

"How did you do it?" she said.

That was a very good question since Levi's illusion magic was a matter of public record and what I'd done didn't fit.

"I can't give away all my secrets now, can I?" I winked at her.

Miles put his arm around Levi, who leaned heavily on him.

I touched my earpiece and lied like a pro. "Excuse me, Leah, I have urgent House business to attend to."

She couldn't really protest that, so she wrapped up her segment.

I bolted to Levi's side. "Sorry. Sorry. I didn't want to make her suspicious."

"It was the fight." His eyes bore that scary dead look and he sounded hollow and distant. "Took a lot out of me to match the illusion to you grappling with the smudge."

"Over there." Miles nodded toward a bench away from everyone.

We got Levi installed on the bench. House security

256

immediately formed a ring, their backs to us, both affording privacy and keeping us from public view.

Levi dropped the illusion, bent over with his elbows braced on his thighs.

"How bad is—what the fuck is that?" I shied away from the EpiPen looking thing with the disturbingly long needle that Miles brandished.

"Plan B," he said grimly and jammed it into the base of Levi's skull. "Hold him."

It took all my strength to keep Levi still in a hug, his body bucking against me. His heartbeat stampeded to a dangerous level, pounding hard enough to snap out of his ribcage.

He clamped his hands onto my biceps, but I wasn't sure he knew it was me.

"Ride it out, you stubborn motherfucker," Miles said, as Levi's entire body was wracked by violent tremors.

His heartbeat stuttered… stopped…

"Miles!" I yelped.

A milky film rolled over Levi's eyes, then he gave one last shudder and sighed.

"I'm good." His voice was raspy and his eyes were clear.

"This time," Miles said.

"That's all I needed." Levi gave him a cocky grin. I couldn't blame Miles for flexing his fingers like he wanted to punch his boss, because I felt the same way. That little stunt had shaken me down to my core.

Levi straightened his clothing and ran a hand over his hair. "Lose the security. People need to see me."

Shaking his head, Miles marched off, calling away his crew.

Levi sat there, to all appearances utterly composed. His only acknowledgement of what he'd experienced was to ask me to get him some water.

When I returned with a cold bottle a few minutes later, I handed it to him with a high five. "We did it."

"You did it," he replied.

I threw my shoulders back. "Hell yeah, I did. But with a firm assist from Montefiore. You done good today, kid."

"Gee, thanks. What did you say to the reporter?"

I gave him the run down. "One step closer to solving this case. Now to find the lab."

"About that." His entire demeanor changed. Any high-fiving camaraderie leached away in favor of a bland professional face. "I'm going to put my people on it. They're a good team. The loose smudges have been dealt with and your blood magic isn't necessary to rescue the kids."

Why? Is it ill-advised?

"I still have a brain and you hired me to also find whoever was behind their creation."

"Circumstances have changed. Your story about an illegal game isn't going to hold up. I have to let my team in on this now."

"I handled that interview the best I could. I was put on the spot."

"I appreciate that." He kept that same calm tone like he was patiently explaining things to a stubborn child. "But the smudge is now very public knowledge. The more brainpower on this, the faster we find Meryem, right?"

I looked out over the crowd. The protestors had dispersed and most of the others remaining animatedly rehashed the takedown. I should have been celebrating this victory, not fighting to keep my composure. "Are you firing me?"

"There are going to be questions and it's safer this way. I'm keeping the spotlight off you. Like you wanted."

"Don't twist my words." I shook my head. "You know what? Fire me all you want. Charlotte Rose is my client and I'm not letting her down."

Levi stood up to loom over me. "If I get even a hint that you're still moving forward on this, I'll arrest you for obstruction of justice and personally ensure your P.I. days are over. I'm not kidding."

This was the House Head speaking. Not Levi Montefiore, the guy I'd grown up with. Not the man who'd kissed me half an hour ago. And definitely not someone who I'd almost called my friend.

"Message received. Sir." I marched off, head held high without punching him in his fat face.

That was today's real win.

Chapter 20

I ducked into the VAG, beelining straight for the bathroom. A thin line of blood streaked down my cheeks, but nothing was broken and I didn't have any new bruises.

How dare he take this case away from me? I'd saved his ass and that was how he repaid me? His point about more brainpower was valid, but that didn't mean he had to fire me with some lame-ass excuse about keeping me safe. That had never been a concern of his and even if he had developed some misguided chivalry, it wasn't necessary.

And to threaten my P.I. license?

Hell with him. He could put every Nefesh he employed on it and I'd still be the one who found Meryem. I didn't give a damn about coming out a hero, I just didn't trust anyone else to care as much.

Adam, Levi, I was done getting screwed over by the men in my life. Not that Levi was in my life. Not anymore. The one good thing that had come out of this.

I came home armed with three boxes of pizza and a six-pack of a local pale ale and banged on Arkady's door.

"Enter."

I swung the door open, flinching at a loud thwack as his

muscular calf connected with his punching bag, and held up the pizza. "First payment, if you're not busy."

"What flavor?" A too-small pair of pink sweatpants hung low off his hips exposing a dusting of hair between his waistband and his "Sounds gay. Count me in." T-shirt. His black nail polish was starting to flake off and his hair was pulled back in a ridiculous blue scrunchie that didn't detract from his hotness one iota.

"One veg, two Italian sausage and arugula."

"Veg?" He said it like I'd offered him a steaming dose of syphilis. He dropped into his fighter stance, his fists transforming into stone as he brought them up to his chin.

"I didn't know if you ate meat."

Arkady executed a fancy combo, his stone fists practically punching through the bag. "Pickle, please."

"Gay people can be vegetarians."

"Not if they're doing it right." His next punch knocked the bag off the hook. It thudded to the floor, plaster raining down into his hair. Arkady dusted himself off before picking up the bag with his stone hands. "Okay. Scram. I'll be there in twenty. I gotta finish training and you're too weak to take in the full display of my manly prowess."

"Yeah, well I gotta take a shower and you're too weak to take in the full display of my womanly prowess."

Arkady snorted. "Meh."

"You're a pain in the ass, Choi."

He grabbed a towel off the back of his sofa, flexing his tatted-up biceps, his body gleaming with sweat. "That's not what the boys say. Scurry along now."

Fighting a grin, I opened my apartment door. "Hey, Pri? I brought pizza and Arkady is coming—oof."

A pink blur rushed me in an attack hug.

I held the pizza and beer up out of harm's way. "Did you eat my entire stash? Is this one of your touchy feely sugar rushes?"

"You could have been killed, dumbass."

"Not really. The golem was scary but—"

"*Golem*?!" she screeched.

"Nope. No golem. What are you talking about?"

"That thing at Robson Square that you destroyed."

"That was Levi."

Priya smacked me. "We are not playing that game. You can take magic. That wasn't Levi. That was you under some illusion to look like him."

"Brains and beauty." I put the pizza in the oven on warm and the beer in the freezer, the cool air easing the sweat on my forehead. No one else knew what I could do. I was safe.

"Are you okay?" she said.

"I'm fine. Other than the fact that I found out my father was the one to ward me, I got to the lab too late and they'd moved the victims, and Levi fired me because my skills were no longer needed."

"Yikes. We might need another beer run. You want to talk about any of it?"

"Not particularly. Tonight I want to hang out with my friends and pretend I am a normal human being with a normal job and absolutely no vendettas."

Priya clapped her hands. "Did you say 'friends' plural?"

"That's what you picked up on? Yes, I admit, Arkady may have a certain likeability factor. He's been given probationary status."

"Ashira made a friend," she sang. "And now you're having your first playdate."

"Pri." I clasped her shoulders. "You can't mention what you know to anyone."

"D'uh. Your secret is safe with me."

"It's not about that. I couldn't live with myself if anything happened to you because of me."

"It won't." She pushed me out the door. "Go bathe, stinky."

By the time I got back to the living room in my black pjs with "Unlikeable" written in white across the chest, Arkady and Pri were halfway through one of the sausage pizzas.

Stomach rumbling, I curled into one edge of the couch and pulled the other meat pizza closer. I couldn't stuff the first piece in fast enough. Luckily the cheese had cooled down from "burn my mouth" territory. This was proper pizza: thin crust, baked in a wood oven, with sausage that was rich and meaty, juicy San Marzano tomatoes for the sauce, and arugula that had a spicy bite. There were definite benefits to living in the Little Italy area of Vancouver, stellar coffee and pizza being among the tops.

The TV was tuned to the local news which was a constant replay of earlier.

This was the first time I saw what everyone else had. The illusion really was flawless. It looked like Levi lifting the selfie guy off the ground and scaring him off.

"That man is incredible," Arkady said between swigs of pale ale.

"Yeah, Levi is something else." Priya slid me a beer.

I cracked it open, but didn't drink, my attention riveted to the TV. Onscreen Levi spoke to Rick. The cameras had been too far away to catch what was being said, but I remembered every word of it.

Rick swung at Levi and Arkady shook his head and pointed at Dudebro. "Sloppy. Telegraphing a mile away."

As remarkable as it was to watch the illusion mirror my actions with Levi flipping Rick to the ground and straddling him, the true artistry of Levi's magic became apparent when I was fighting the smudge.

While Levi onscreen was grappling to pull the smudge out, there was no sign whatsoever of blood magic. Not even a single blood tear. It simply looked like Levi fought to pull it free, put his hands into the smudge and tore it to pieces. He'd hidden all signs of the magic that I'd used to destroy it, and he'd done it in real time, fooling a live crowd and cameras. He'd gone above and beyond to keep his word and keep me out of the spotlight.

It was almost heartbreaking that no one would ever know.

Equally if not more confusing was why he'd fired me afterward. We'd been a good team.

I almost snorted beer through my nose at the victory pose I'd struck.

Arkady frowned. "That was a tad over-the-top."

Priya nudged my leg, grinning.

The interview came off fairly believably, if Arkady's nodding was anything to go by. I'd played Levi both suitably imperious and coy. I did a bang-on impersonation of him, if I did say so myself.

"To Levi." Arkady saluted the TV.

"To Levi." Priya clinked her can to mine.

"Yeah. What a guy."

We hung out until almost midnight, falling down a YouTube rabbit hole, first watching Justin Timberlake and Jimmy Fallon take us through the history of rap, and then with Arkady introducing us to the joys of K-Pop with BTS and BLACKPINK.

It distracted me from everything waiting to weigh me down.

Things were a tad less bleak when I woke up Wednesday morning, since my feverish dreams of labs and smudges had given me a lead to pursue. I got dressed in my best navy trousers and a smart blazer, twisted my hair into a chignon, and applied a light and natural makeup look. Satisfied with my "young professional" vibe, I grabbed my heels and slid them on at the front door, careful not to wake Pri.

With Moriarty deigning to start after a couple of sputtered protests, I drove over to Olympic Village, the waterfront area that had housed the athletes during the 2010 games. Those buildings had been transformed into expensive condos with hip restaurants and cafés lining the ground floors, all centered around a plaza with a pair of giant bird statues that were over fifteen feet tall. They were supposedly inspired by the Hitchcock film, so you know, not creepy or anything.

I threw them a chin nod as I walked between them on my way to the trendy new Italian café, complete with a "CEO of Coffee." Pretentious much?

The pastry case was stuffed with freshly made goodies in various shades of buttery gold. I selected a half dozen sfogliatelle, similar to croissants with a variety of fillings, and got them tied up in a to-go box with a gold bow. Bribes weren't mandatory, but they never hurt.

I got to Vancouver Mundane Police Department HQ and asked to see Sergeant Tremblay.

A few moments later, Sergeant Margery Tremblay, an officer with the VPD for the past thirty-five years, emerged from the glass doors to the bullpen. Flawless makeup, even at 8AM in the morning, her silver hair in a pixie cut, she cocked her hip, one hand on her gun when she saw me.

I held out one of the lattes and the box. "I still say that if this cop thing doesn't work out, you have a bright future in Mary Kay cosmetics."

Margery took the coffee and sipped it. "It's cold."

"But the pastries are warm." I waved the box under her nose, the smell of flaky dough and butter making my mouth water.

She snatched the box away. "What do you want, kid?"

"You haven't been to karaoke night in two months. I was worried."

Margery barked a laugh. "Pull the other one. You know damn well Delphine and I were on that cruise. Besides, you only ever play dress-up when you're trying to impress me."

"Busted." I glanced around the lobby but everyone else

was coming and going without paying any attention to us. "I need a favor. Is there still a warrant out for those two Nefesh suspects? The older woman and younger man who attacked a security guard?"

"Far as I know." Margery was a liaison with the Nefesh police department.

"Can you find out who filed the complaint?"

"Complaints are confidential."

"I'm the woman," I said. "I was undercover on a job and came across information that some powerful people would rather I keep quiet."

"But you're Mundane."

"Exactly. There was no assault." I'd checked the House database before I came. I still wasn't entered into it so my story would hold up. "Canadian law dictates the person has a right to know the name of who complained in order to give their side of the story."

Margery finished her sfogliatella before she answered me. "Can you prove that was you?"

"If there are details of where the attack occurred listed in the complaint, I can tell you where I was and you can see if they match." I gave her the address of the auction in Tofino.

"All right." She stood up and brushed crumbs off her jacket, taking the pastry box with her. "Wait here."

I remained in the lobby, watching cops come and go, tapping my foot impatiently. My relationship with Mundane police had never been as antagonistic as with the Nefesh ones. They didn't love private investigators but none of them had the hard-on for me that Novak did. I'd skirted Nefesh jurisdiction once too often.

Finally Margery returned. "Sorry, kid. The complaint was filed anonymously."

"In an assault charge?"

"Yeah, it's highly unusual. There's no name of who was assaulted either."

"Trumped-up bullshit."

"Ash, be careful. There's pressure from on high to find these two and if they were willing to make your undercover persona seem that dangerous, they won't stop until they find you."

That was what I was counting on.

I dumped my empty latte cup in the recycling bin. I was so consumed with what my next move was, that I didn't see White Rabbit Man waiting next to Moriarty until I was practically on top of him. "Geez."

"Nice car. Four wheels and everything," he said.

I held up a warning finger. "No one disses Moriarty but me."

"My most heartfelt apologies. A more magnificent vehicle I have never seen."

I made a snarky face at him. "What do you want?"

"The Queen requests your presence."

"'Requests.'" I snorted. "That makes it sound like I can refuse."

He smiled. "You can try."

"Fine." I pulled out my car keys. "Get in."

"Why?"

"To drive over to Harbour Center."

He pulled a thin gold chain out from under his shirt. On it was a gold replica of the coin with the "H" that Miles had given me. "All-access pass."

Before I could double check that I had enough time on my parking meter, we'd shifted.

My ears popped hard, the world snapping back into focus. I shuddered. "That was horrible."

"You build up a tolerance. This way."

As always, it was night in Hedon. The magic wasn't as unsettling as on my first visit and I'd been too distracted at the lab to notice one way or the other. I was only mildly queasy instead of wanting to puke my guts out, and could plausibly blame it on the jump, which was good, since White Rabbit Man couldn't know that I had magic.

"You know, I never asked your name," I said.

"I never intend to give it." He led me through a narrow pathway between unkempt hedges into a courtyard strung with fairy lights where a bunch of empty picnic tables were scattered around a lone parked taco truck. Throw in some bearded hipsters drinking from mason jars and, if it hadn't been for the magic pulsing against my skin like waves lapping at the shore, I wouldn't have believed we were in Hedon.

The Queen had her back to me, studying the short menu tacked to the food truck. Today's outfit consisted of red pants, a red blouse, and red leather stiletto boots. I so needed a signature color.

Part of me wanted to be her when I grew up. Without the beheadings.

White Rabbit Man motioned for me to continue on to her alone.

I stopped next to her, reading the offerings chalked on the menu.

"What do you want?" A light breeze teased the ends of her dark red hair and she held it back with one hand. She'd been in the sun since I'd last seen her, her skin a richer, deeper bronze.

"What would you suggest?"

"The carne asada." She held up two fingers to the guy manning the truck, then sat down at one of the picnic tables. "It seems my debt to Levi Montefiore keeps growing. First, he alerts me to these people using my name on their business dealings, then he gets my nephew out of harm's way."

"Who's your nephew?"

"Scavenger hunt selfie." She sighed. "Muy guapo, but dumb as dirt."

"I'm sure Levi isn't keeping track."

"I'm sure as well, blanquita, since we both know that wasn't him yesterday. Ah, gracias, Andrés."

The chef set down our plates. Each one had three small corn tortillas topped with grilled steak, avocado, pico de gallo, and a hard, crumbly cheese, as well as a side of rice and beans. He also left us glasses of water.

I squirted the lime over the first taco and bit in. A flavor party exploded in my mouth. The avocado and cheese lent a creamy smoothness to the sharpness of the lime and the fresh spiciness of the pico de gallo. These were the best tacos I'd ever eaten, plus chewing bought me time answering the Queen.

She allowed me two tacos and half of my rice and beans before she cleared her throat.

"That was Levi," I said. Stellar comeback.

"Comemierda. Illusion magic doesn't do that. No matter what some people try to pass off on TV." She speared a piece of steak.

I wiped off my hands. "I'm not sure what you want me to say. I'm Mundane and not privy to anything Levi may or may not have done yesterday."

The Queen didn't push it and we ate the rest of the meal in silence.

"Thanks for the food."

"My pleasure, chica. Though, it's a shame."

The lights in the food truck went out.

Unease fluttered through me. "What's a shame?"

"That someone like yourself, who keeps popping up in such interesting ways, doesn't know more about who I should thank for my nephew. Because if I did owe someone, I'd want to repay them. Perhaps allow them five minutes with an old friend."

A chair shot out from the shadows. Mr. Sharp was

bound to it, his eyes wide with terror above his gag and his hands cuffed with the magic-suppressors.

"Did he say where the lab is?" I said.

"I didn't ask."

"You promised to help."

"I don't like being lied to." She spread her hands with a smile. "Of course, everyone is entitled to their secrets, especially with a stranger, but I'd like to think we've become friends. I help my friends. That one?" She tilted her head at her prisoner. "He is not my friend. Are you?"

White Rabbit Man stepped into the light behind him holding a long sword.

I choked down my mouthful of taco. What the fuck should I do? Mr. Sharp was high up enough in his organization to know where the lab was and right now he was my only option at finding the kids. Not just mine, Levi's as well, because for all his "brainpower," I doubted his team had any more leads than I did.

The ideal outcome would be for the Queen to get answers and then let me deliver Mr. Sharp to Levi to be dealt with through official legal channels.

Light glinted off White Rabbit Man's sword. That wasn't going to happen.

But if the Queen learned that I had blood magic and especially that I could take people's powers, what would she *request* of me? I'd done it again, thought I'd been too clever by half, but I was out of my league. She was the Queen and I was a nothing little pawn on this chessboard.

White Rabbit Man raised his sword, awaiting my decision. Did he care who he ultimately used it on? I sunk my neck into my shoulders as terror clawed through me. Did I value my own skin over Meryem's?

You bet I did.

"It was me yesterday." I screwed up my face, hearing a heavy door clang shut on a future free of the Queen.

"You lied about being Mundane."

"Only sort of. About a week ago, I discovered that someone warded my magic for my entire life. Suppressed it. I believed I was Mundane, but when I met you, yes, I knew otherwise." I spoke to my feet not her face.

"More and more interesting. What's your magic?"

"Blood. I can take magic and…" I exhaled shakily.

She put her arm around me, all grandmotherly concern. The fierce fifty-something was Mafia grandma if anything. "Rip it off like a Band-Aid."

"Destroy it."

The Queen squeezed my shoulders. "That wasn't so hard, now was it? So, Ashira Cohen, may I repay my debt to you?"

Said the devil. Her cinnamon and chili magic danced around me like a noose.

I wasn't stupid enough to believe this made us even. One way or another I was in her clutches. "Please do."

She snapped her fingers and White Rabbit Man lowered his sword, blending back into the shadows.

"Have fun," she said, and walked away.

I approached Mr. Sharp. "She's still going to kill you. It comes down to how you want to die. Sure, she's famous for that one clean stroke, snick. Off with your head."

He flinched.

"But she's my friend and she owes me. So it could easily be a slow carving." I ran my hand down his arm.

His green eyes spat hate at me.

I yanked down his gag. "Where's the lab?"

"That's for me to know and you to never find out." Still so properly posh, even on the verge of death.

"Those kids are being tortured, stripped of their magic."

"It's wasted on them. They were never going to reach the full potential of their powers. Why not let someone more adept benefit from it?"

"Like thieves? You're despicable. And a liar. Magic isn't transferable."

He shrugged. "You won't find them."

"Maybe not." I removed his wallet from his back pocket. "Edmund Bottom. No wonder you went with 'Sharp.' Well, know this. I will find everyone you care about and rip their magic from them the way that you people have done to these kids."

His brows came together and then understanding hit and he drained of all color. "And of Jezebel the Lord also said, 'The dogs shall eat Jezebel within the walls of Jezreel.'"

"What is it with you people and the dogs? Also, you're a bunch of hypocrites. We both know what the 'technology' actually stripping the magic out is."

Priya was right and Jezebel was a type of magic. This man had answers about me that I couldn't ask questions to because my time was limited and Meryem was my priority.

I swallowed my disappointment, flipped a blood dagger into my palm, and pressed the tip against his jugular. "Where's the lab?"

"And some of her blood spattered on the wall and on the horses, and they trampled on her. Then he went in and ate and drank. And he said, 'See now to this cursed woman and—'"

I punched him in the gut so hard his chair fell backwards.

Once he'd stopped coughing, he laughed. "They'll find you and they'll kill you."

Fucking enough. I broke the cuffs off him.

A strand of fairy lights tore loose and wrapped around my neck.

Grappling with this noose with one hand, I used my other one to slice him across his left pec with the dagger.

He gasped, his magic hold loosening enough for me to tear the strand off.

"Don't like it? Let me give you a taste of what your people are subjecting those kids to." Pressing down on his bloody cut, I rode his magic.

He was a Lightweight, a type of wind elemental that moved things with surgical precision, used for everything from earthquake rubbish removal to stealing safes. His magic felt like dozens of translucent feathers bobbing on a current and tasted like spun sugar.

Sharp convulsed in his chair.

I forced myself to slow down, but every part of me throbbed, craving all the magic at once. The world turned soft and dreamy and I sighed, flexing my bloody fingers against his skin.

My cheeks were flushed, my breath slow and full. Only dimly did I register the burst blood vessels in his eyes and his pained howls.

I swiped a bloody index finger over his brow. "Relax. Ride it with me."

I crooned at him until he sang along with me, and all the while, his magic danced inside him, hooked to mine.

Once I was sated, I teased his magic out, watching the smudge flow from his body through blissed-out eyes. My entire body tingled and I was more alive than I ever had been.

I'd stepped into my destiny.

My branches forked through his magic, blooming into the white clusters that devoured it. There was no maggoty sensation like with the third-party smudge, no foul smell, just a gentle release from my high once the magic was gone, like waking from a lovely dream with the taste of sugar crystals on my lips.

That's when I realized that Sharp wasn't singing.

He was screaming, a mostly nonsensical gibberish broken by sobs and a street address.

I dropped to my knees fumbling at his bindings. He

flopped free, his pupils dilated with terror. I looked at my hands as if I could bring his magic back and heal him, even though I knew, deeper than my bones, that it was impossible.

"I'm sorry," I croaked, bowing my head, but there was no absolution. I would have to live with this the rest of my life.

There was a soft rustling. I glanced back to find the Queen watching me.

"Muy interesante."

"I didn't mean..." Under her all-knowing stare, I bit off the rest of that lie. "Can you help him?"

"I will end his pain."

White Rabbit Man appeared and carried Sharp away.

I scrambled to my feet and vomited into a scraggly patch of bushes.

The Queen handed me a stick of peppermint gum. I nodded my thanks, allowing the minty flavor to take away the foul taste. If only the stain on my soul was as easily removed.

"Pobre cosita. You didn't realize how deep the shadows go. My advice? Save those kids. Celebrate that victory."

"It doesn't erase what I did."

"You made a choice that now allows you to make a different one. One that is easier to live with. That's all life is. A string of choices and in the end, we hope we come out ahead." She pressed her hand to my cheek. "Go."

In a blink, I was back in my world and back in the sunshine.

But there was no warmth at all.

Chapter 21

Did the ends justify the means? Did the pain of a single individual, especially one already condemned to death outweigh that of the many? When was "for the greater good" a moral imperative and when was it merely a justification for doing what you wanted?

I had never been one for violence, never tortured or physically intimidated anyone before my magic had shown up. That wasn't who I was, so how could I reconcile that fundamental part of me with this willingness—no, this eagerness—to perform such an extreme and inconceivable act?

If the trauma of the accident had flipped my recessive magic gene to "on" when I was thirteen, what was the primal urge inherent in my blood magic? Because the only answer I had was "rage." Was that the common trait to all Jezebels? A burning rage that elevated us beyond the everyday fire elemental, beyond the Hot Heads and the Van Goghs? A fury so inherent to us that it was part of our blood?

Jezebels took magic and it was a horrible, painful thing for the victim, but others sought to use us, so was our magic a defense mechanism? Was I a warrior? An assassin? Did I stand for good or for evil? Did I even have a choice?

I didn't have answers, but I had an address and the power to make sure no more of the missing experienced the horror of losing their magic.

Time to make a choice I didn't hate myself for.

I drove home to pick up a few key items, debating whether or not to tell Levi. My big fear was that his team was a giant unknown. Even if they were as well trained as Miles' security people, would more people all going in blind turn this into another bloodbath? I could slip in and out like a shadow, get the lay of the land and then call in the cavalry with solid intel. But if I was captured, or worse, then no one would come for those kids. Meryem would be doomed.

I pulled up in front of my apartment. Decisions had always been fairly black-and-white for me, but how to save these people was fraught with a dozen shades of gray. I closed my eyes, running the pros and cons of every option, listening to my gut. I'd trusted it before and I had to keep believing it would steer me true.

I left urgent messages for Miles and Levi detailing where the lab was and that I'd meet them there. Choice made, I sprinted up the stairs and into my apartment, noticing the dried blood on my fingers when I unlocked the door.

My stomach heaved and I ran to the bathroom sink, scrubbing my skin raw. If I'd had time, I would have done the same to my entire body. I threw on leggings and a tunic-length shirt, stuffing my hair under a knit cap. A trifecta of black clothing.

Pulling a metal trunk out from my closet, I gathered up a couple pairs of magic-suppressing cuffs, a pocket-sized Taser, a small high-powered flashlight, and my sonic weapon, stuffing them all into the pockets of my leather jacket. Any other weapons I'd manifest on site.

Arkady ran into me as I was clunking down the stairs in my motorcycle boots.

"Where are you off to?" he said.

"Work."

He blocked me. "I did four years in the army."

"Yeah. You went in right after high school."

"No Google searches for you, huh? You jumped straight to the full background check?"

"I like to know my neighbors. What's your point?"

"My point is I know that flat-eyed determined stare. You're off to do something dangerous. Let me help."

"You don't know what you're asking. And I'm not about to put you in danger."

Arkady put his hands together in a begging motion. "I'd kill for some danger. The most lethal thing in my life right now is my sparring partner's gym bag. Besides, you're strong but you're not as trained or competent at fighting as I am. And I'm very good at following orders."

I'd told Talia the truth about having magic and she didn't want to believe me. Levi had shut me out, and the Queen, well, I didn't want to dwell on that. That left Priya as the only person in my life I didn't have secrets from and to whom my magic was irrelevant. All she cared about was me, Ash.

She had my back. That was priceless.

Miles or Levi might not get this message for hours. This might come down to me alone and it would be good to have someone in my corner. Despite my best attempts, I liked Arkady. But could I trust him?

Did I dare because this wasn't about me, it was about Meryem and the others? What would give them the best shot?

"I'll give you the details on the way over."

"Sweet!" He flung an arm around my shoulders. "But we're totally going to have code names."

⁓

"THIS CAN'T BE RIGHT." I tugged on the glass front doors to Mindscape, an escape room in a fairly rural area outside Vancouver. A sign taped to the door proclaimed it permanently closed and thanked patrons for their business. All was dark and quiet inside.

We checked the back door. It was steel with reinforced strike plates on the door frame and jambs.

Arkady studied the lock. "No way through without some heavy duty tools. I bet the door has rebar through it sunk into the frame. They really don't want uninvited guests."

"So why leave the front doors as is?"

"It's a funnel. If you know the boobytraps and pitfalls, all good. Otherwise, you're fucked. There's something here worth protecting. Your call."

"There aren't any security cameras on either of the doors," I said, "so they're pretty confident that whatever they've got inside will take care of things." Could Arkady and I handle whatever awaited us?

I left more messages. Why was everyone's freaking phone turned off? I even contacted Levi's assistant who told me that they were in an emergency meeting. I stressed the urgency of Levi getting the voicemail I'd left him.

"I'm going in." I was haunted by the sound of Sharp's screams. If there was the slightest chance of preventing any more magic loss from innocent people, I had to take it. "Last chance to turn back."

Arkady raised his hand. "Dibs on picking the lock."

He made short work of the front door.

The only light into the reception area filtered in from the drizzly outside and it had the musty smell of a place that had been closed up for a while. There were four doors in the lobby. One led to the bathroom and the second to a staff room. Both were dead ends.

That left the escape rooms.

Arkady lowered the flashlight that he'd stopped by his apartment for. "If we get separated, our earpieces will keep us in range."

He'd equipped us with the same mic and earpiece gizmos as Miles had given me. I was going to get myself a couple pairs after this. No reason why only boys should have these toys.

"Alcatraz or Cannibal Row?" he asked, referring to the two escape room options.

The poster for Cannibal Row depicted a hooded participant in a bloodstained basement. Behind him was a crazed-looking man holding a severed foot in one hand and an ax in the other. The Alcatraz poster showed a long line of open jail cells with hardened prisoners closing in on a fleeing participant.

"They're both such appealing choices," I said. But I'd met my quota of severed limbs for the month. "Island Prison for a hundred, Alex."

Arkady held the door open for me. "Ladies first."

I swung my beam around the starting room for the Alcatraz game, which was an empty jail cell. There were numbers painted on the walls, a prison sink with a twisted tap, and a bunk with a scribbled notepad on the mattress. Arkady and I scoured the room for the hidden doorway to the next room.

He punched the walls with his stone fists but failed to make a dent.

I twisted one of the taps. "It's loose."

The door to the room slammed shut. There was a hiss and gas seeped in from the baseboards. We pulled our shirts up over our mouths and noses but the gas stung. My eyes were swelling and there was a bitter taste at the back of my throat.

"We got the upgraded package," I croaked.

Between the two of us, we pulled, pushed, and pried

every single thing in the room. The door we'd come through had disappeared. The gas swirled thicker and thicker, our flashlights growing weaker. It grew harder to think, harder to stand, and harder to breathe.

Dizzy, I crashed against the wall. My flashlight tumbled to the floor, illuminating the ceiling above the bunk. The seam between two of the tiles was slightly misaligned.

I grabbed Arkady and tugged him to the bunk, pointing up.

He jumped up and punched the ceiling, revealing a trap door that was easily accessible once you stood on the mattress. He hauled himself through it and I quickly followed, kicking the trapdoor shut behind us.

Coughing, we gulped down fresh air. All was dark and creepy as fuck, but when the first fluorescent light clicked on, casting a whitish-blue glow, I almost jumped out of my skin.

"Motion detector," Arkady said.

My eyes were so puffy that I could barely see the prison hallway we stood in. It was the one from the poster, a long metal corridor lined with closed cells. At the far end was a metal door.

"I hate haunted houses where actors jump out at you." I shone my flashlight into the nearest cell to assure myself it was empty. "I would never have come here."

Our footsteps squeaked as we inched forward, shoulder-to-shoulder.

No one attacked us or tried to gas us out. We reached the exit without incident and tested the knob. The door was unlocked, though we kept it closed.

"They wouldn't just arm the first level," Arkady said. "Something's going to happen when we open this."

"Guillotine? Poisoned arrows? Giant boulder falling on our heads?"

"No boulder or rocks," he said. "I'd sense them."

If the boobytrap was manual, there was no way to suss it out. But if it wasn't? I touched the door. Not even the faintest tingle of magic, so there was no ward.

"Here goes nothing." I opened the door.

A dozen eyes snapped open and golems swarmed us, the fluorescents from the hallway giving them an eerie glow.

"Whoa." Arkady's eyes lit up.

It was all well and good that I'd told Arkady about my previous run-in and the way to power them down, but we still had to get close enough to rub the "aleph" off of them and we were outnumbered.

Arkady brought his stone fists up, clearing a path through the room. Three of them dog-piled him, his grunts the only sign he was okay.

I manifested a pike with a curved blade. Going with the tried and true, I jabbed it at the closest golem.

He lunged for it, but I danced back into the corridor, and he followed like I was the pied piper of golems. Soon as he was in striking range, I swung the blade through his knees, lobbing one calf off.

The golem toppled over then stretched out his arms and dragged himself toward me. I slammed the blade down into the top of his head, slicing right through the Hebrew letters carved into his clay forehead. That worked. He shuddered and fell still.

Leaving the embedded pike where it was, I wiped a smear of golem off my cheek and called up two daggers. The other two golems clambered over the body of their fallen comrade.

Firing daggers into the letters didn't stop them.

Head down, I rushed one. He grabbed me around the waist and slammed me into the wall. Fire wracked through my left shoulder, but I held on to his forearm like he was an amusement park ride, sending my magic inside him and hooking into his.

His next Wrestlemania move landed me on my back, the wind knocked out of me. Oh, to be able to use my blood armor right now. My shoulder screamed in agony and my head wasn't feeling too hot either, but the rush of taking his magic, though far, far weaker than it had been with Mr. Sharp, amped me up enough to tear away the magic animating him and destroy it.

The golem's lifeless body fell on top of me. I shoved him off in time for my third attacker to grab me by the hair and lift me up.

"Son of a bitch!" My scalp was going to rip free. Luckily, he'd brought me eye level with him. I reached out and scraped that pesky "aleph" off, flicking the clay against the wall.

The golem toppled like a Douglas fir, but I got clear, remaining upright. Jumping the bodies, I ran back to Arkady. He'd killed two of them and was sitting on the third, systematically caving in its skull. He was covered in clay, a terrifyingly blank look on his face.

His next punch took it out for good, but Arkady didn't stop whaling on it.

"Arkady." I whistled sharply.

He looked at me, fist in mid-air, and blinked back to awareness. He slowly lowered his hand, his cheeks flushing, and got to his feet, avoiding eye contact.

"So I never shared the part where I have blood magic and can rip out people's magic leaving them a broken mess," I blurted out.

He was silent for a moment, and then his lips quirked in a grin. "What's a couple of exceedingly unnerving dysfunctions between friends?"

"Dysfunction is the new black."

We shared a bittersweet look of perfect understanding.

I kicked aside a golem corpse. "Where are all the lady golems? Obviously only men are creating these monsters."

Arkady kicked a path to the next door. "Let's see what other treats they have in store."

There weren't any.

"That's the trouble with evil villains," I said, when we'd cleared the remaining two escape room sets without incident. "They get too minion dependent. Bites them in the ass every time."

The final room had a "Congratulations" banner and a chalk scoreboard with past successful escapees. There was another bathroom and a red exit door, that I presumed led out the back of the building.

"We did *not* just do all that for nothing," I said.

"Ash." Arkady put his fingers to his lips, peering through the exit door that he'd cracked a fraction of an inch.

I clapped my hand over my gasp.

Four people in filthy, shapeless clothing were crammed into a cage probably liberated from the cannibal escape room. It was too short for them to stand up, so they either were on their knees or lay on their sides on the floor.

Another cage stood empty beside it.

In the center of the room was a chair. An older woman was chained to it, the dozens of thick coils binding her almost cartoonish in their excess. Every inch of her was battered and dried blood clotted her nostrils and caked her lashes.

One of her hands was bent at the wrist at an unnatural angle and I wasn't positive she was conscious. Or alive.

"Understood." Two men, one of whom was on the phone, stepped into the room through a gap between two thick sheets of black plastic taped from ceiling to floor. He finished his call and then jerked his chin at the cage. "Finish up. I'll load the bodies."

Bodies? I glanced at the empty cage.

He disappeared back behind the plastic.

The second man took out a set of keys, inserting one in the cage with the people.

My vision clouded in a red haze. I ran at him and slammed his head against the bars.

He slumped to the floor.

Arkady had already sprinted after the first man.

Relieving this man of his keys, I dragged him into the empty cage and locked him in. Then I opened the first cage door.

"You're safe," I said softly. "Come out."

The prisoners hunched deeper into themselves.

"Meryem? Are you here? Charlotte Rose sent me to find you." I bit the inside of my cheek to keep the tears at bay. "It's me. Ash. We met before."

Finally one of the figures turned toward me. It was Meryem, her dark eyes wide and haunted. A bruise bloomed along her jawline.

I curled my fingers into my palms, keeping my voice calm. "Sweetheart, did they… did they take your magic?"

She shook her head. "Charlotte Rose really sent you?"

"I swear. You're all safe. You can come out." I moved away from the cage so they wouldn't feel intimidated by my presence and moved to the woman, who had a faint pulse. I tried every key on the ring until I found the one that fit the fat padlock around her waist.

She was so weak that when the chains loosened, she fell forward into my arms.

A shock ran through me, as our skin, our magic, connected.

She peered at me through swollen eyes. "You."

"Are you a Jezebel?" I held her emaciated frame carefully. This woman was as much a victim as those kids.

"Yes."

"Are there any more of you here?"

She shook her head. "We looked for you. Couldn't find you."

"That's not important right now," I lied. "I need to get you out of here first."

Her answer was lost in a coughing fit that brought up specks of blood.

Arkady stepped through the plastic. "The other target is subdued."

I frantically beckoned him over. "Help her!"

The Jezebel whispered something that I didn't catch. I pressed my ear to her lips.

"Risen again," she whispered. "We have to stop them."

"Who?" I said.

She motioned feebly to the cages. "Chariot. Promise."

I'd meant who was "we" because that sounded suspiciously like an organized group of fellow Jezebels who'd have expectations and shit. But she gazed at me so impassioned that I didn't have the heart to clarify.

"I promise."

She squeezed my arm and fell still.

"Give her mouth-to-mouth," I demanded.

Arkady shook his head sadly. "She's gone, Ash. Look at her."

I closed her eyes, uncertain of what to feel. Grief? Anger? Anxiety?

The kids had shuffled out of the cage, holding hands.

"Ash?" Meryem stood at the front of their hesitant procession. She looked so lost.

I'd found the kids, but instead of the thrill of victory, I was pierced with sharp hooks of helplessness. Rescuing them didn't close this chapter, that would require a lot of healing from their emotional and physical fallout, and I wasn't equipped to handle that. But I couldn't just turn them loose, either.

One step at a time.

I pasted on a bright smile. "We're going to get you out of here now, okay?"

She nodded, sending a ripple of agreement down the line to the last person, a gangly male with a limp.

Life was a series of choices. Taking Sharp's magic had been one of my darkest ones, but it had led me here. If pressed to do it all again, I wasn't sure I'd do anything differently.

A door banged open, thudding boot heels growing closer.

Whimpering, the kids crowded together. I threw myself in front of them like a shield. Whoever this was would have to kill me to get to them.

Three people in anonymous tactical gear entered. None of them were familiar to me.

I grabbed my Taser from my jacket pocket with one hand and manifested a blood dagger in the other.

"Ash. Stand down. It's Levi's people," Arkady said.

How could he be sure? Unlike Miles' team or even the Queen's, there were no identifying marks.

One scanned the room, then said, "clear," into a mic clipped to his lapel.

Levi stepped through the plastic, accompanied by six paramedics and a kind-looking woman with an iPad. He had dark circles under his eyes and his shirt was wrinkled. Mildly so, but on Levi the effect was profound.

Meryem clutched the back of my shirt.

"It's okay, sweetheart. I'm not going anywhere." I stuffed the weapons in my leather jacket.

One of the paramedics carefully scooped the Jezebel up and removed her from the room, while another took the chair. A couple of Levi's people worked on moving the cages out of there so the kids wouldn't have to see them anymore —or the still-imprisoned man who'd been one of their jailors.

The woman approached me. "Ms. Cohen? I'm Sarah Blumfeld. I'm a social worker." She smiled gently at Meryem. "Would it be all right if these paramedics checked you all out? Your friend can stay here with you."

Meryem held me tighter, but she nodded.

The paramedics tended to these kids with patience, compassion, and tenderness. They even made a couple of them laugh. Thank God, they could still laugh.

Sarah explained to me all the resources that Levi was putting at these kids' disposal, including a safe place to live, meals, and treatment for as long as they needed it.

"How are they supposed to get over this?" She stabbed angrily at her iPad. "I want to kill someone."

"Get in line," I said.

Meryem tugged on my sleeve. "Can I use your phone to call Charlotte Rose?"

"I think that's probably fine, but let me check with Mr. Montefiore." I approached Levi who was chatting with Arkady.

The two of them stood together with the body language of two people who knew each other, angled inward. People who were close usually left a very small private distance between them, whereas if someone was standing away from a group with their arms folded, that person was most likely a stranger. Or pissed off.

Which *I* most definitely was.

"Meryem wants to call her girlfriend," I said in a tight voice. "Any reason she can't?"

"No." Levi studied me. "You still mad about me taking you off the case?"

"Among other things."

Arkady stepped back but I hauled him back in to our little circle. "Call off your spy, Levi. Good pick, though. I really believed he wanted to be my friend."

Levi's brows knit together and then he burst out laughing. "You think I sent Arkady to spy on you? Why? I already have the complete file."

I planted my hands on my hips. "So his living next door was a big fat coincidence?"

"Pretty much," Arkady said. "I didn't even know you two were friends."

"We're not," Levi and I said.

"What about all that mixed martial arts stuff?" I jabbed Arkady in the chest. "Your background check held."

Levi laughed again. "Welcome to the paranoid mind of Ashira Cohen."

Arkady glared at him. "Could you not? Pickle, I am in the league. It keeps my fighting skills up and it's a handy cover story since my work for Levi is so hush-hush. Not that there's been much work lately." He brightened. "This was fun. I like golems."

Golems. Arkady had earth magic and golems were clay, so why hadn't he sensed them? Or had he and lied about it? Oh, Arkady, if you're running a con, you picked the wrong person.

"Good. I foresee many more adventures together," I said.

"You may apologize now," Levi said to me.

I shot him the finger and went back to the kids.

Chapter 22

It took hours before we'd settled the Nefesh, the oldest of whom was barely nineteen, in their new home, and stocked them up with food and clean clothes. Sarah wasn't just any social worker, Levi had hired her to live on site and work exclusively with them, starting with tracking down any family that they wanted to reconnect with.

I typed her number into my contacts. "When did Levi hire you?"

"Monday morning."

"He did all this in two days?"

"When you refuse to take 'no' for an answer and have the money to remove potential roadblocks, you can achieve anything."

"Sure, but even rejigging budgets to free up House cash would take some time."

"This wasn't the House. Levi is paying out of his own pocket so these kids don't get caught up in red tape."

Fuck. I was going to have to apologize to him.

With Levi's, Sarah's, and Victoria's permission, Meryem had been allowed to stay at Charlotte Rose's place. Apparently, Victoria had kicked her husband out.

We'd barely pulled into their driveway, the front porch lights casting a cheery glow on the cool night, when Meryem scrambled out of the car, Charlotte Rose running across the lawn toward her. The girls crashed into each other crying and hugging.

Seriously adorable.

I walked over to Victoria. "You sure this is okay? There's a lot of trauma. It's not going to be easy."

"Nothing worthwhile ever is," Victoria said. "Sarah is going to come by tomorrow, set up therapy, private tutoring when Meryem's up to it, and make sure her uncle has no legal claim to her custody." She flicked a gaze over me from head-to-toe. "You want some tea before you hit the road?"

I glanced at my phone. "Geez. It's after midnight. No, I'm gonna go. Call me if you need anything. Hey, girls, I'm off. Uh, okay." I patted them on the tops of their heads as they squashed me in a giant hug.

This wasn't the worst.

C.R. looked up at me. "Oh, the babysitting money."

"Forget it, kid." I squeezed them back. "It's paid in full."

This case was closed and their joyful reactions made all the obstacles I'd faced worth it.

I drove Moriarty around for a while, changing radio stations as I tooled around the quiet city streets, but there wasn't even a whisper of the lab. How'd Levi manage that?

It had been less than a week since I'd learned about the ward. All I'd wanted was to know who had put the tattoo on me, so sure that answers equaled certainty, answers equaled closure, and though the truth could be hard to hear, it was always better to have it.

The joke was on me. Not only would I pay good money to not know what I was capable of, all the answers had done was lead to more questions. What made a Jezebel and why were there no records of us? Why did we have blood magic?

Who or what was Chariot and why was it on us to stop them? What was my father's connection?

The euphoria of taking Sharp's magic had masked the horror and lulled me into believing in destiny. Except I didn't. Life was what we made of it, I just wasn't sure what to make of mine. There was a team out there searching for me, expecting me to join them in this fight. Did free will come into it? What if I didn't believe in the cause?

What if I didn't want to be a weapon?

I cut the engine in front of Levi's house, my feet carrying me up to his intercom before my brain could register a logical protest, and leaned on the buzzer.

The gate swung open.

Levi stood at the front door in frayed jeans and a worn T-shirt, his feet bare.

My brain kind of stuttered, unsure of what to unpack first. The dusting of flour on his shirt? The fact that his home smelled like freshly baked cookies? Or the black rectangular frames he wore that drew attention to his thickly fringed eyes that were the dark blue of deep well water?

"I forgot you wore glasses."

He'd worn them one year at camp when he'd lost a contact lens during Capture the Flag. Teen Levi had looked like a geek, but adult Levi was obscenely hot. Not just sexy, but vulnerable. This was the man at the end of the day who loosened his tie, set aside his mantle of power, and was himself. The man who'd show his scars.

"It's late and I'm tired," he said. "Could you harass me about my weak eyes in the morning?"

"No. I mean, Sarah told me how you were personally paying for everything and you must have thrown around a ton of House power to keep today out of the news. So explain one thing to me, how could you be so protective of those kids and have treated me so callously? We'd defeated the smudge for fuck's sake and then you shut me out." I paused. "It hurt."

Levi sucked on his bottom lip and shifted his weight from one foot to the other. "There's something you need to see."

I stacked my boots neatly on the doormat, and hung my jacket on the knob of his coat closet.

He led me in the opposite direction from his study, turning the corner into a jaw-dropping space that was all bleached wood and brick, with floor-to-ceiling windows overlooking the beach.

Levi crossed over to a coffee table and picked up a creased piece of paper which he handed to me.

"'We know it wasn't you,'" I read. "And?"

"This appeared in my jacket pocket when you went to get me water at Robson Square."

"This is why you fired me? Why didn't you tell me?"

"I told you to back off for your own safety and you got all huffy."

"You didn't tell me why. You threatened to destroy my livelihood. Take away the thing I love most."

"Yes." He threw up his hands. "I stupidly assumed that throwing you in jail and ruining your business would be enough to get you to run the other way from this. Would you have backed off if you'd seen the note?"

"Of course not, but that wasn't your call to make."

He pushed me back a few steps so I wasn't glowering nose-to-nose with him. "You're Nefesh now. You're under my protection and I made a call. For your safety and the safety of my House. If your power becomes known, who knows what threats we'll both be facing?"

I balled the note up and dropped it on the coffee table. "*When* it gets out. You can't keep it a secret much longer. You'll have to formally register me. And if there is a threat, then I would have rather faced it with someone I could trust."

Levi reached for the note, but I blocked him. He waited me out until I stepped aside with a frustrated huff.

He picked up the paper and smoothed it out again, before putting it into his pocket, folded once more. "That's our fundamental problem, because I rightly didn't trust you to see the bigger picture and step aside, and you don't trust me period."

"So where does that leave us?"

He pushed his glasses up his nose in a weary gesture. "We keep circling back to that, don't we?"

A timer went off. Levi stalked off, me jogging at his heels.

I'd expected some showpiece, enough stainless steel and fancy tech to build a space station, but the kitchen was cozy with red appliances and glass tile that mirrored the sunny blue of his eyes when he was amused. Round spice tins were stuck to a long magnetic board with braids of garlic pinned to the window frame. It was a room made for cooking, not impressing.

It was all too easy to picture him and Dr. Ryan drinking wine and making pasta together, passing each other with intimate touches on their lower backs.

Trays of golden brown biscotti were spread over the quartz island countertop, cooling.

Levi put on an oven mitt shaped like a boxing glove and removed the final pan from the oven. "Go ahead. Make your snarky comment."

It was late and I was tired, too. "Who taught you to bake?"

He deposited the tray and snapped off the dial. "My nonna used to bring me into the kitchen with her when things got… tense around our home. My father would never deign to come in there. Baking became a way to destress."

"My father was the one who warded my magic before pulling a disappearing act. Again." I watched him carefully for any sign of pity but he merely flapped a spatula at me.

"Sit down. Might as well help me eat some of these."

Surprise edged out the tightness in my chest. I perched on one of the tall barstools pushed up to the island and helped myself. The biscotti was still warm. I nibbled on the edge, a delicate lemon flavor filling my mouth.

"These are really good."

He set another one in front of me. "No kidding."

We ate in almost companionable silence, Levi leaning on the counter across from me.

"I'm sorry for how I handled things," he said. "Everything had gotten so far out of my control, and this seemed like one element I could bend to my will."

"And I'm sorry I accused you of spying. Everything had gotten so far out of my control and this seemed like one more thing you'd bent to your will."

He threw a biscotti at me, which I caught.

"How'd you find the lab so fast?" Levi said.

"The Queen gave me a present." I dropped the biscotti, my appetite gone.

Levi caught my hands in his. "You know I can't think any less of you, right?"

I half-sobbed, half-laughed, and swatted him away. "She gave me five minutes with Mr. Sharp."

He searched my face. "You took his magic."

I crumbled the biscotti into crumbs. "He was going to die anyway, but I sure tenderized him for her. Wrecked him but good. It made your 'devoured by ants' trick look like a walk in the park."

"You're so competitive." Levi swept away the crumbs I'd made into the sink. Then he stilled. "The Queen knows about you."

"Yeah. But she wasn't the one that sent the note. She's a

lot more direct. And oddly, after it was all over, she gave me some advice that helped." I frowned. "Telling you helped, too. Weird. Maybe we could start a monster support group. Take turns bringing pastries. I can't tell my mom, not that I would, and while Priya knows the broad strokes, I won't share the specific gory details, because I don't want her to see me differently."

"And since you don't care what I think…"

"Not a whit," I replied.

"Even if your magic is monstrous, it's not your defining quality."

"That's my humor and intelligence."

"Let's not get crazy. You defied me to find those kids, risking everything you'd built for yourself. You care deeply. You may just be the awesomeness that humanity is desperately in need of."

I ate the second biscotti, my appetite restored in the face of his words. "How does it make any sense that the person I trust the least is the one who gets me the most?"

"We've always gotten each other. It's why we don't trust one another. And there's a part of you that gets off on that, same as I do."

"Why, Levi Montefiore, are you propositioning me?"

Levi took off his glasses and set them carefully on the counter. "Yes."

"What happened to 'ill-advised?'"

He shot me a wicked grin that lit me up. "Oh, it's definitely that, but I find that I don't care right now."

"I see. In that case…" I slid my shirt over my head and dropped it on the ground.

Levi lunged for me and with a coy look back, I raced into his living room, where he knocked me onto the sofa.

I fell with a laugh and a wince when my shoulder hit and Levi froze.

"Golem," I said.

"Oh, good. I was worried we wouldn't have the proper foreplay."

I laughed and hooked my ankle around his, bringing him down on top of me. "Surrender."

He positioned his body between my open legs. "I think that's my line."

I rocked the heel of my palm over his impressive erection. "You love it when I fight you. Meeting me was the best day of your life."

Levi pinned my hands above my head, speared me with a hot look that sizzled through me, and crushed his mouth to mine. The kiss was explosive, almost violent in its passion, and I reveled in it. He still held my hands in his iron grip, so I wrapped my legs around his waist, trying to worm closer. His lips were full and smooth and his stubble scratched my chin, sending tremors through me.

Levi broke the kiss to look at me, his eyes practically smoky in their desire. We stayed there like that a moment, then his hold on my hands loosened. Gently, tenderly, he brought his hands to my face and kissed me with incredible sweetness.

I tried to push him off me, because we didn't play that way.

He kissed me again, a long slow drug of a kiss. "Surrender," he whispered, trailing kisses down the hollow of my neck.

"Never," I sighed, leaning my head back.

Unclasping my bra, he flung it across the room. He took one of my nipples into his mouth and suckled it.

"I can be very persuasive when I want to." His voice rumbled against my skin, his sentence punctuated with the rasp of his teeth over one nipple.

I threaded my fingers through the black silk of his hair, arching back in delight.

"Is this your choice of weapon?" I ran my hands over his

hard body, marveling at the tight definition of muscle and how he gasped involuntarily when I touched his inner thighs.

"What if it was?" he asked, pulling me onto him so I straddled him, my knees gripping his hips.

"Then I'd be very careful it didn't go off prematurely," I murmured.

"It is rather tightly sprung," he conceded. Gliding his hands down, he hooked them beneath my knees, jerking me up his thighs.

My clit rubbed against his rigid cock, and a moan slipped out of me.

Levi claimed my mouth, catching my cry, his tongue tangling with mine.

I raked my fingernails down his back. "Lose this." I tugged his shirt off, brushing my breasts against his chest.

The musky odor of his arousal teased me and I rocked against him.

Levi lifted me off him, relieving me of the rest of my clothing. Setting me on the couch, he slid to the floor and pushed my knees apart.

I placed my hand on his chest. "Not that I'm complaining, but you wouldn't let me do this to you in the hot tub."

"Bella, we didn't have a condom, and if you went down on me, I would have given new meaning to 'thirty-second wonder.' No way I was giving you that kind of ammunition."

He'd called me "bella," the word all silky, pronounced by a true Italian. I almost giggled. However, being the cool, collected woman I was, I tossed my hair off my shoulders and spread my legs wider. "Proceed."

"Thank you for your most gracious permission." Levi licked into me and I swear I had a religious experience. He was all hot wet heat, fucking me with his tongue.

I gripped his shoulders, his scars thin ridges under my

fingertips. He wasn't hiding them from me. Levi was this unpredictable wild card: arrogant, caring, powerful, thoughtful, and a dangerous thrill.

"Get a condom," I panted.

Levi looked up at me, his chest rising and falling in ragged breaths and licked his lips. "Now who's the thirty-second wonder?"

"Shut up and fuck me, Leviticus," I said sweetly.

He slid his hand slowly up my inner thigh, tsking me. "Etiquette."

"You just like to hear me beg."

"That's a big part of the appeal, yeah." He crawled up my body, caressing me. "But we don't have to rush."

"An emotional tornado ripped through my life. I want to be taken hard and rough. Fuck this week out of my brain. Please," I added.

He grasped my chin and kissed me again. "With pleasure," he growled and sprinted off, returning a minute later with a condom in one hand, and holding his pants that slid off his hips with the other.

He shucked them off, kicking out of them entirely. "Turn around. On your knees. Hold the top of the couch."

There was a rustle and then the sofa depressed as he leaned his knee onto it and pressed his cock against me, holding my hip with one hand.

I rested my cheek on the back of the sofa.

"Touch yourself."

"Now who needs an etiquette lesson?" I said.

"You want to lead, I'll happily let you play teacher next time." He put my hand on my clit, rubbing it. "But right now, I'm in control." He bit the back of my neck and I shuddered.

"Yes. Tell me what to do." Don't make me choose. Not tonight.

"Keep stroking yourself." He slid inside me partway and

a soft gasp escaped my lips. I forced myself to keep still, savoring the anticipation of having all of him inside me, filling me up.

Levi raked his nails along my spine, then thrust inside me hard. He smacked my ass lightly. "I didn't say stop."

I squeezed my eyes shut, drowning in the hot, tight spiral gathering force.

"Wider." He jerked my legs farther apart, the angle of his thrusts changing, hitting me deeper. He pulled my hips toward him so hard that each meeting of our bodies sounded like a blow.

Sweat rolled down between my breasts.

Levi pressed against me. "Surrender," he whispered.

I shattered.

In one fluid motion, Levi pulled out, flipped me on my back, then lay over me, braced on his elbows. He unleashed himself on me, his ruthless fucking sending a million delicious aftershocks quaking under my skin.

I clasped the back of his neck and leaned up to meet his mouth, our kisses hot and messy.

He caressed my cheek with his knuckles, then, his face twisted in savage pleasure, he stiffened and came with a shout.

Our sweaty bodies slid together as he collapsed on his side, the two of us jammed close to fit on the sofa. Levi traced the curve of my hip.

Okay, I could do this. I could post coital like a mother-fucking boss.

Our eyes met and … "Nope. Too weird. I'm out."

I crawled over him, Levi sprawling onto his back totally unselfconsciously to watch me dress. A lock of hair had fallen into his eyes and I picked up the pace of dressing so I didn't do something mushy. Never show weakness. Slinging one leg into my jeans, I hopped back far enough that hopefully my face, my expression, was indecipherable.

"What happens next?" he said.

Find my team, get the vials back, figure out what I'm meant to do and what I stand for.

I pulled on my boots and flicked the lock off his forehead. "General awesomeness."

Levi reached for me, but twisted mid-motion to grab his pants instead. An odd pang speared my chest along with the thought maybe I should stick around to strategize over biscotti, but he was already zipping up and the moment was lost.

"So no actual plan," he said.

"Plans are a problem for tomorrow me." I grinned, and throwing a finger wave over my shoulder, headed into the night.

THANK YOU FOR READING BLOOD & ASH!

Brace yourself as things heat up in DEATH & DESIRE (THE JEZEBEL FILES #2).

Angel of Death.

Black market magic.

When you're Ashira Cohen, smart is the new kickass.

When Ash is hired to solve her first murder, it seems like a perfectly normal, open-and-shut case of family feuds and bad blood. Until Ash discovers an evil magical artifact and her lead suspect is of the winged, white-robed, celestial variety. As if that weren't bad enough, if she can't find the perpetrator quickly, fourteen vials of lethal, ghostly magic will be sold to the highest bidder.

Her quest to figure out her Jezebel powers and find the shadowy organization responsible for stripping teens of their magic isn't going any smoother, either. Can't a girl just pursue her dream career without getting caught up in a mysterious destiny? Or, for that matter, playing a dangerous

Sherlock-Moriarty game with the infuriatingly hot alpha male in charge of Vancouver's magical community?

But when Ash accidentally crosses the cunning and deadly Queen of Hearts, ruler of the magic black market, all those cases may go unresolved.

Permanently.

With the clock ticking, it'll take all of Ash's intelligence to survive with her moral center—and her head—intact.

The game is afoot and failure is not an option.

OR why not check out my other funny, sexy urban fantasy series?

Dive into THE UNLIKEABLE DEMON HUNTER.

An all-male brotherhood hunts demonic foes. But their biggest threat could be a foul-mouthed, romance-impaired heroine who's gonna show these boys a thing or two about how to really slay a monster…

Odds of survival: meh.

Odds of a good time before she bites it: much better.

Every time a reader leaves a review, an author gets … a glass of wine. (You thought I was going to say "wings," didn't you? We're authors, not angels, but *you'll* get heavenly karma for your good deed.) Please leave yours on your favorite book site, especially Amazon. It really makes a difference in terms of discoverability to rate and review the first book in a series.

Turn the page for an excerpt from *Death & Desire* ….

Excerpt from Death & Desire

I never expected *Touched by an Angel* to stray into bad touch territory.

"Tall, white robes, white wings. Was there a celestial light? Did anyone see a halo?" The questions I asked in pursuit of the truth.

"It's an Angel of Death. It kills people." Husani Tannous, a late-twenty-something Egyptian, adjusted his baseball cap to hide his receding hairline. "It doesn't get a halo."

Ironclad logic from a man who'd paired his masculinity issues with the semi-automatic at his feet. Like fine wine with cheese. Or gasoline with a match.

This living room was as much a battlefield as any muddy trench. There was even a dead body upstairs, and if the animosity down here got out of hand, more casualties to come. The fluttering in my stomach did double duty as nerves and a coiled excitement.

"I'm not trying to be facetious," I said, steepling my fingers and leaning back in a fancily embroidered chair. "But I do need the facts."

"The facts are that it murdered my brother!" He shook his fist. "And I will avenge him!"

His cousin, Chione, slowly stroked a finger over the handgun in her lap, all the while sucking butter off her toast.

I leaned in, fascinated by her particular brand of multi-tasking.

"Big talker, Husani. How will you find this angel? Are you going to fly up into the sky?" Chione said in Arabic-accented English.

"Don't be ridiculous. Flying magic doesn't exist." Rachel Dershowitz, early fifties and mother of the bride-to-be Shannon, was as bitter as the gin and tonic she gulped down. The gaudy rock on her finger had fewer facets than the sneer she shot Chione.

Chione's hand twitched on her gun and I stepped between the two women. "Did Omar have any enemies? Any reason why anyone would come after him?"

"Omar is a good boy. No enemies. This is a hate crime. Those sons of dogs killed our firstborns before and they're doing it again!" Thank you, Masika Tannous, the grandmother and matriarch of the clan visiting from Cairo. While the little old lady was knitting a sweater like many a sweet grandma, she wielded her needles with a savage ferocity that scared me more than the Uzi of questionable origin propped against her side.

Between Masika, Husani, and Chione, this mercenary family packed more firepower than the Canadian Armed Forces, but like I'd always said, Mundanes didn't require magic to be dangerous.

The physical weapons from the Tannouses were countered by serpents made of light magic that writhed above the table, ready to pounce on their victim and squeeze the life out of them.

I wanted to smack sense into all of them, but it was hard

enough doing my job, never mind exuding enough badass vibes to keep these two families in line.

"You brought death into my home. Jews shouldn't mix with Egyptians," said Ivan Dershowitz. The fleshy home-owner on my left sat next to his wife and daughter on a high-backed chair with spindly legs that strained under his weight. His light magic bobbed like a cobra.

The two families hurled racist epithets back and forth, this season's bridal registry must-have.

The delicate-featured Shannon let out a hysterical wail that probably used up her caloric intake for the week. However, she was the only one acting appropriately in my opinion, given her groom-to-be had been murdered. The heavens agreed with my assessment as a shaft of sunlight cut through the clouds on this March morning to confer a kind of benediction upon her.

What can I say? When I was right, I was right.

I whistled sharply. "Assuming we take the story of Passover literally, Malach, that Angel of Death, killed *all* the firstborn sons to free the Jews from an oppressive slavery. While it is Passover this week, we have only the one death, though I'm monitoring that." I turned to Masika. "I'm deeply sorry about the loss of your grandson Omar, but one murder isn't exactly mass smiting, not to mention, the Jews are sitting right here in their own home." Low class, but hardly enslaved. "We need to keep an open mind. Perhaps it's an Angel of Death and perhaps someone is using a good story, preying on centuries of superstition and hatred to hide what's really at play."

You point out one hard truth and suddenly the place was all twitchy gun fingers, snaky beams of light, and a knitting needle jabbed at you like a curse.

My command to shut it down was ignored. Fantastic.

The person standing in the center of the room cleared

his throat, and everyone immediately fell back into their corners, muttering angrily.

In his forties, he had white hair and a white suit that veered sharply towards the 1970s. Between his wardrobe choices and the fact that he was the right hand man of the Queen of Hearts, my moniker of White Rabbit Man was hardly a stretch.

One day, I'd call him that out loud.

Given his overall vibe, he shouldn't have commanded any respect, but the motherfucker of a sword in his hand helped.

Big deal. I could decapitate a few dozen people and get that response, too.

"If someone could show me upstairs so I could examine the scene?" Collecting the shreds of my patience, I met the cold beady eyes of the showpiece of this ostentatious living room: a massive crystal chandelier in the shape of a bird with its wings outstretched, soaring overhead.

Even the decor wanted out.

"Mr. Dershowitz," I said.

"Rebbe," he corrected.

Yeah, right. Ivan had earned that nickname not for his religious leanings but because, during his high-profile incarceration for assault and battery, he'd beaten a fellow inmate into a coma with a copy of Genesis. Can I get a hallelujah?

I gritted my teeth. "Rebbe—"

Ignoring me, he sent his serpent slithering to the ground where it circled the room. The urge to pull my feet up was strong. "This marriage was a mistake," he said.

No, the real mistake was coming to this shitshow. Although it wasn't as though I'd had a choice to refuse this "request."

"We can stand here and argue the existence of angels," White Rabbit Man said, "or you can allow Ashira, the private investigator vouched for by the Queen, access to

Omar's room so she can determine precisely what happened."

After another couple minutes of mutually insulting each other's matriarchal lineage coupled with some anatomical suggestions that I never intended to Google, Rachel called for a maid. Husani and the help escorted White Rabbit Man and me through the mansion down a long hallway filled with bookshelves that contained zero books but an extensive and disturbing collection of china bird figurines.

Birds! They're just like us. They nest, they whistle, they rub their genitals against tufts of grass in a lusty manner.

"Was beheading too fast a way to torture me?" I muttered at White Rabbit Man.

The tiny quirk of his lips was the only thing on his impassive face that betrayed his amusement.

"We can take it from here," I said to the people following us, when we reached the stairs to the second floor.

My escorts didn't move.

"The Queen thanks you for your service. I'll be sure to mention to her how you allowed me to do the job that she so kindly recommended me for."

Still nothing.

"We'll call should we require your assistance," White Rabbit Man said.

Sure, that got them going.

I stomped up the stairs, stopping in the doorway of the guest bedroom to gather my first impressions.

Become a Wilde One

If you enjoyed this book and want to be first in the know about bonus content, reveals, and exclusive giveaways, become a Wilde One by joining my newsletter: http://www. deborahwilde.com/subscribe

You'll immediately receive short stories set in my Nava Katz and Jezebel Files worlds and available only to my newsletter subscribers. There are mild spoilers so they're best enjoyed in the recommended reading order.

If you just want to know about my new releases, please follow me on BookBub: https://www.bookbub.com/authors/deborah-wilde

Acknowledgments

All the thanks to my beloved daughter Kiki, for always being willing to spitball plot and mythology ideas with me. How clever I was to train you in character and three-act structure growing up! Lol You are my joy and my delight, kid.

To my editor, Alex Yuschik, we are now officially into crazy amounts of books together and I wouldn't have it any other way. Thank you for being so brilliant that I get excited for your notes because they will always push me and make my stories better.

And to all my amazing readers, my beloved Wilde Ones, I win, because I have all of you. Thank you for being so passionate about my characters and for keeping me sane while I talk to them. You are all truly the best!

About the Author

I'm Deborah (pronounced deb-O-rah) and I write sexy, funny, urban fantasy.

I decided at an early age to live life like it was a movie, as befitted a three-syllable girl. Mine features exotic locales, an eclectic soundtrack, and a glittering cast—except for those two guys left on the cutting room floor. Secret supernatural societies may be involved.

They say you should write what you know, which is why I shamelessly plagiarize my life to write about witty, smart women who kick ass, stand toe-to-toe against infuriating alphas, and execute any bad decisions in indomitable style.

"It takes a bad girl to fight evil. Go Wilde."

www.deborahwilde.com

Printed in Great Britain
by Amazon